ORON AMULAR

BOOK III: POWER UNIMAGINABLE

MICHAEL J HARVEY

malcolm down

PUBLISHING

23 22 21 20   7 6 5 4 3 2 1

First published 2020 by Malcolm Down Publishing Ltd.
www.malcolmdown.co.uk

British Library Cataloguing in Publication Data
A catalogue record for this book is available from the British Library.

ISBN 978-1-912863-50-1

Cover design by Esther Kotecha
Art direction by Sarah Grace

Printed in the UK

ACKNOWLEDGEMENTS

The love and support of many people has helped to bring *Oron Amular* into being. I owe a great debt of gratitude to those whose belief and encouragement sustained me in both the writing and the hunt for publication. I wish to thank my parents, Ian and Lucie, for raising me in a home of love and faith, and for setting my feet on this path. I reserve special thanks for Kelly Jamieson, for being so vocal a fan, right from the start, and for your friendship since. Phil Dobbs, it wasn't quite your thing, but you always encouraged me along the way and never stopping asking about it. Pat Eisner and Matt Taylor also deserve my appreciation, for being among the first to read it, and for much practical support and helpful input. No one has done more to make this novel possible than my beloved wife, Lucy, my *Soleithébar*. Thank you for letting me have all those hours; thank you for believing in me; thank you for walking this road with me as the best of companions. Most of all, though, I wish to thank God, from whom comes every good and perfect gift (James 1:17). You gave me this imagination, these ideas, and this talent, and I honour You with every word written.

CONTENTS

SUMMARY OF BOOK I:
THE CALL OF THE MOUNTAIN

In *The Call of the Mountain*, Book I of the *Oron Amular* trilogy, our adventure begins. Seeming chance has brought together the King of Maristonia and a mysterious wayfarer. In the city of Mariston, they join forces to answer the summons of Kulothiel, the Mage-Lord, to a Tournament at the forgotten Mountain of Oron Amular. Lords, knights and champions from many lands have been invited to compete at this ancestral home of High Magic. The prize on offer, *Power Unimaginable*, is proving irresistible to all those thirsting for adventure and power. King Curillian is no different, though his motives might be nobler than some. Yet for all his strength and reputation, he does not know how to find the Mountain. The wandering conjuror Roujeark offers his services as a guide, for he has business of his own at Oron Amular and has received a summons of a different kind. Together they set out and, braving many dangers by road and sea, they embark upon the quest of Oron Amular. Yet they have not gone far before troubling news disrupts their plans. Circumstances force Curillian to take new counsel among the Wood-elves who live on his borders. Beneath the eaves of the ancient forest of Tol Ankil, he hears confirmation of the news that has troubled him. Despite the misgivings of Lancoir, his Captain of Guards, he pledges to rescue the elf princess Carea who has fallen into the hands of the evil mountain-dwelling harracks. His quest is no longer quite so simple, but is there also opportunity to be found in this dangerous diversion?

SUMMARY OF BOOK II:
RITE OF PASSAGE

In *Rite of Passage*, Book II of the *Oron Amular* trilogy, Curillian and his companions venture into the mountain-realm of an ancient enemy to attempt a rescue of the elf princess Carea. Battling both the elements and the enemy they soon find themselves in dire straits, which only the newly discovered powers of Roujeark and unlooked-for help will enable them to escape from. Having completed their mission, they bring Carea back to her home and her people. Their reward is permission to cross ancient Kalimar in search of Oron Amular, the Mountain of High Magic. With Roujeark as guide and the elves grudgingly letting them pass, they must traverse a storied landscape and find the hidden Mountain where the Tournament awaits them.

Map of
Astrom

Icy Seas

Retorn Ocean

Troizon Ocean

Urunmar

Oron Cavardul

The Haunted Pass

Gulf of Urunmar

Ciricen

Guard Hills

Rohandur

Hendar

Malanar

Kalator

River Goralar

River Goralath

Beachbone Bay

Kalimar

Oron Amular

Paeyrir

Hamid

Dorzand

Black Mts

Aranar

White Hills

Ithrill

Silver City

Arkania Forest

Nimrell Bay

Tel Astia

Maristonia

Silver Bay

Carthak

Mariston

Manston Bay

Sapheil Ocean

Mandossa

South Folo

Marble Bay

Lurallan

Urundair

Sapheil Ocean

© Michael J Harvey

N
W   E
S

Map of
**Oron
Amular**

© Michael J Harvey

I

Oron Amular

INSIDE The Mountain the darkness was complete. For the first few steps they had been aided by the faint moonlight outside, long enough to see that they were in a tunnel, but very soon they must have turned a corner, for even that small light was lost, plunging them into utter blackness. Roujeark's eyes strained uselessly against the darkness, but he couldn't even see his hand in front of his face. He could hear, though. Hear the sounds of others blundering blindly up ahead, of feet scuffling and armour clinking, of curses muttered under various breaths and the nervous calls of one to another. Yet even those sounds seemed to fade after a while, as if the various parties were being separated and devoured by the terrible darkness, one by one.

Roujeark reached out his hand to feel for the tunnel wall, but it was further away than he thought. Straining for it, he nearly fell over before coming to rest against it. To his surprise, the rock wasn't rough, but smooth to touch. Feeling with fingers and feet, he found that both the wall and the floor were smooth as polished gems and flat as paving slabs. No blemishes or snags could he find. But he had only gone a few doubtful steps when he bumped into something. It was one of his companions. Clutching the arm, Roujeark felt the armist quivering.

'Who is that?' he whispered, hearing his words vanish in the swallowing darkness.

'Aleinus,' came the barely audible reply. In fact, they were all there, stopped dead in the middle of the tunnel. Groping darkness was before them and behind them, above them and below them. The very air was thick with potency, harsh to taste and seeming to tingle on the tongue and fingertips. In the face of this invisible barrier the lion-hearted armists faltered, unnerved and uncertain. Here, normal boldness was of no avail. Even Curillian was at a loss. When Roujeark discovered the king by touch, he found him still and tense, staring into the impenetrable darkness. Long moments passed in silence, with only the sound of shallow breathing hanging in the air. Slowly, Roujeark stepped forward. The air seemed to be full of whispering spirits, murmuring long-forgotten secrets and creeds. He was terrified, but the feel of this place, heavy, forbidding, mysterious, was slightly less daunting for him than for his companions. He felt some sort of affinity with it.

He stepped forward into the watchful air, having to drag himself against unseen resistance. Even with so little a step he had moved out of sight of his companions, but after a heartbeat or two the king moved up behind him. Curillian was completely out of his comfort zone, but his courage was conquering his fear. Lancoir defaulted to sticking as close to his king as possible, and each armist followed suit, all afraid of being left behind in the gloom. Roujeark had them link hands and stretch out so they could fill the tunnel, touching it on either side. Yet it was wider than any of them had imagined, a vast corridor fit for princes. The wide space quite belied the sluggish movement of the airs and cheated noises, which seemed not to behave as normal. But stretched out, and hands joined, they felt slightly more at ease, and proceeded cautiously forward.

Reluctantly, the blanket darkness gave way before them. Now and again they felt the tickle of some wind filtering down from an unseen vent above their heads, and occasionally they caught muffled sounds from ahead. With a veritable army ahead of them, they might have expected to hear more, but the sounds just weren't carrying. Nerves tautened like harp-strings and hairs stood on end as each member of the company began imagining what end had already befallen their competitors. Their powers of reason and deduction seemed to have been left behind outside, like their courage, so they found themselves at the mercy of their senses, quite convinced by the distortions that were being reported to them by eyes, ears and noses. The cool night from outside had been replaced by a stuffy heat, such that beads of sweat started to form on their brows and hands, and they twitched and crackled as if toyed with by delinquent sparks in the air.

They followed the tunnel, feeling it bend and twist in slow, deliberate curves. The darkness seemed to lessen an iota, or so their hopeful eyes claimed, but still nothing definite could they see. Their feet were more certain in reporting a gradient and, following that long smooth slope, they came to a place where the tunnel walls gave out on either side. The air suddenly felt very different. Still queer and laden with intent, it now scurried about and carried sound more easily. They began to hear other groups about them. Suddenly sounds seemed to be all round them, boots scuffing and scabbards banging, leather creaking and mail clinking, heavy breathing and sniffing. The place was teeming with life. Voices began to call to each other, some in fear and some in suspicion. Then an almighty clatter split the air as two metal objects collided. The armists drew close and stuck together in a tight group, but even so, they bumped and jostled with unseen neighbours.

Roujeark felt the tension ratcheting up inside him as he groped blindly in the intolerable darkness. He felt enclosed and exposed at the same time. With every passing second he feared a collision, or a sly knife sliding out of the jet black air. Panic was building up within him, ready to burst out in a shrill scream, when all of a sudden a silver flame burst into life. Poof! Up above them, it seemed to hover in mid-air. Then another joined it, and another. Poof! Poof! Poof! In the blinking of a suddenly seeing eye, there was a ring of silver fires up above them. In their velveteen light, the inhabitants of the hall might have seen one another, except they were all straining their eyes upward. Glimpses they caught of ancient grandeur, carvings, friezes and sculpted vaulting, all dancing in a firelit ceiling high above. The fires seemed to burn out of sconces set on some sort of raised gallery.

Just as the contestants were adjusting to take in this vague information, a blinding light filled the roof like sheet lightning. A moment later there came a multi-layered boom like rolling fireworks, then cascades of iridescent sparks were falling among them. Those who had the presence of mind raised their shields to ward off the hazard, but still many eyes were dazzled and not a few burns caused. Yet the sparks had not been without purpose, for their passing had ignited wall-torches all around the place, and now there was enough light to see by. Not enough as could be wished, but enough to fit everything else together. The contestants were now able to take one another in, resuming their uneasy acquaintance after what seemed like an eternity. Together they found themselves in a vast and glamorous cavern, like the anteroom of a strange old palace. It was a perfect circle, flat and smooth and painted in a colour that one moment seemed terracotta and then mahogany the next. There were portraits and engravings everywhere, depicting strange scenes of wizards and magic.

Above these murals, which were uncannily lifelike, there swept a lip of bronze, crowning and encircling the walls. Beyond that lip there seemed to be a circular walkway, lost out of sight. The only thing marking the head of the chamber was a little indent in the bronze lip, where a small balcony jutted out. So awed by their surroundings were they that it was some time before the contestants noticed the figure standing there, still as stone. The murmuring amongst the company died down as one by one the contestants became aware of the statue-like person above them. Their eyes were drawn irresistibly towards him, and then were locked, unable to look away. The figure was clad in a dark green robe. His long hair was white, and silver was the wispy beard that fell to beneath the rim of the wall. He looked old beyond reckoning, but he stood erect, unbent by whatever years lay upon him. His gaunt face was proud and grim, a study in fascination, yet unknowable. Long clever hands rested on the bronze lip in front of him, and a curious staff leaned beside him. Beneath his unwavering gaze, each and every person in the chamber felt like a child, tiny and inordinately young. After what felt like an eternity, the words came.

'Hail, contestants from afar, the Keeper of the Mountain welcomes you to the Tournament of Oron Amular.'

The words seemed to emanate out of the rock itself, impregnated by the slow march of all the years this chamber had witnessed. They didn't even see his lips move. Quiet but booming, unguessable but certain, each person heard the words as if from within his own head.

'They who were summoned here by invite are welcome, and their retinues with them, but woe to him or her that cometh here unbidden. Guest and intruder alike, both have passed within the doors, and they are now shut. They shall not reopen until the Tournament has run its course. The signal moon waxes in the night sky above, and she shall have passed away ere this business is done.

'Eight doors there are...' Immediately as he said this, eight portions of the spherical wall, in which no join or crack had before been evident, swung noiselessly inward. '...Eight doors, eight routes beyond, and eight leaders to tread the way. Each way leads into the Tournament, and though the aspect of each may vary, each will lead inexorably to the same destination. Which of you can know what you will find upon the way? But verily, at the end awaits the prize which you all seek…Power Unimaginable…'

The last two words echoed and reverberated around the chamber, rumbling on and on, and as they did so the silver fires went out as suddenly as they had been ignited. The wall-torches too were extinguished, and the timeless speaker vanished. The only light that was left was a faint glow around each of the eight newly-revealed doorways. As if by some hidden signal, the eight parties gravitated towards their own entrance. The elves of Ithrill went to one, the elves of Kalimar to another; the dwarves of Carthak had their own, as too did the armists of Maristonia; one each was set apart for the men of Hendar, of Ciricen, of Aranar, and of Lurallan. None of them saw the additional opening prepared for the interlopers, they who had seen no invite and followed no flag. None saw them go, but the screams that marked their expulsion from the chamber, like the hunting cries of vampire-demons, transfixed with horror those that heard them.

That terror was only deepened by the menace of the doorways, the eerie light around them and the complete lack of light in the blackness beyond. What lay without? Would they step into a void and tumble into oblivion, or would other horrors be waiting? Some tried to get out of the chamber, back the way they had come, but to their consternation they could find no trace of the broad sloping passage that had brought them hither. While the others were gripped by panic, Roujeark took it upon himself to lead. He stepped under the glowing arch and then into the blackness beyond. His companions were hesitant to follow him into so dark a place, so a sudden idea came to him. He conjured a small flame in the palm of his hand. Turning, he raised it to his companions, shedding a little light on their fearful faces. It looked for all the world like he was holding a small oil lamp. In its small light, they could all see that what lay beyond was just a tunnel, a tunnel like any other. Now revealed, its terror diminished somewhat.

Roujeark could not keep the flame in his palm indefinitely, but just as it was starting to waver, bringing all the guards' fears back, he came across a long disused torch in a wall brazier. Once the torch was alight and burning brightly, the young conjuror handed it to Findor, who looked glad to receive it. Now they could proceed faster, but trepidation still made them slower than they could have been. Roujeark could sense the growing air of hostility. He guessed that obstacles and hurdles awaited them. For a long time they followed a descending slope which wound and wound round many bends and twists. As they went the air grew noticeably warmer.

After what seemed like an age of walking, they came to a small cavern. Much smaller than the main cavern where Kulothiel had met them, but still a curving open space with a low ceiling. Running around the opposite side of the cavern was a series of doors. They all came to a stop, uncertain what to do next. There were six doors, but no clues as to which way to go. Fear rose and magnified the decision: what if they chose wrongly? A poor choice here could be disastrous, sending them plummeting down into an abyss or into a lair of monsters. The torchlight danced about as Findor trembled noticeably. Steeling themselves, Lancoir and the guards tried each door, and found that every one opened. No locks to narrow their choice.

Roujeark looked closely at each door, going slowly from one to the next and feeling his hands over them. All were alike, heavy seasoned oak with brass bindings and locks. Yet on one the varnish of long-vanished days was peeling, the brass was tarnished and the wood was slightly discoloured. There was even a different smell from behind it, even though all that could be seen through any of them within the reach of the torch was a dank passageway. A memory fluttered in Roujeark's mind and a warning came to his heart. In the long past journey when he had met Ardir in the mountain tunnel, he had learnt then that the most attractive-looking option was the wrong one. The way which had looked worse in fact turned out to be right. Like a caged bird suddenly set free, this memory whirred around inside his head and then was gone, and he was left looking at the odd door out, the door that seemed older and in worse repair. Its contrast with the others was not as strong as it had been on that far-off day, but he felt sure the same lesson still applied. He motioned to the others.

'I think it's this way,' he told them. Curillian looked doubtful.

'What makes you say that?' was his question. Roujeark frowned pensively.

'I cannot be sure, but it reminds me of something I encountered long ago. I feel in my heart that Prélan is leading us through here.' Lancoir looked even more dubious than the king, but he had no better suggestion to make. Curillian looked appealingly around the room, as if they had missed something.

'There is nothing else to guide us. So, let Prélan lead us aright.'

The old door was opened. One by one, they plunged through.

*

II

The Gauntlet

THE Tunnel they entered was much lower and narrower than the one before. Nor was it smooth and well made, but jagged and scarred, full of dents, undulations and imperfections. They ducked and eased past the fingers of rock that blocked their path, making their way slowly onwards. Curillian was up at the front of their file with Roujeark. Suddenly he put an arm out to check Roujeark. He looked forward with suspicious eyes and sniffed the air. Roujeark looked at him questioningly but then saw what he was looking at. A thin, almost invisible silver strand, like a spider's thread, was stretched across the tunnel. Another one like it was at shin height. The torch was brought up, and in its light they could inspect it more closely. Curillian touched it very gently and gave it the slightest twang. They felt, rather than saw, the shower of rock flakes patter onto their heads. Looking up into the still-falling trickle of powdered rock, they eyed the ceiling nervously. They both swallowed hard as they caught one another's gaze.

'Haste yes, Roujeark, but not too much,' whispered Curillian. 'We need to be ultra-cautious.' With exaggerated care, they all ducked under the taut strand, stepping over the lower one in the same motion, and moved on up the corridor. Lancoir was the last armist past, and as he went, the tunnel shook. Their hearts leapt to their mouths, but Lancoir hadn't touched it. Taut as a crouching cat, Lancoir slowly eased himself up and straightened. Then they heard the booming report from somewhere else in the mountain. It sounded far away, but all too near.

'Sounds like someone wasn't as careful as us,' breathed Caréysin.

Recovering their composure, they carried on. There were many more twists and turns and uncomfortably narrow sections to negotiate before the tunnel finally dumped them out in a small sandy chamber.

Their relief at being out of the tight confines of the tunnel was short-lived when they realised that they were in a chamber with no exits.

'Well so much for this way,' exclaimed Aleinus. 'Roujeark, you've brought us to a dead end!' Roujeark didn't answer, but Antaya started back into the tunnel on his own volition. He paused to lean against the tunnel wall and peer back up into the gloom. The portion of wall he was leaning on gave way and sank back into the mountain. An ominous rumbling sound built in volume and tremor. Antaya threw himself backwards only just in time, regaining the safety of the sandy bay just as the roof of the tunnel collapsed. A gust of air whooshed over them, carrying a cloud of rock dust. Choking and temporarily blinded, they all staggered back. When the dust settled, it was all too plain that the only exit was blocked. There was now no going back.

The guards slumped against the wall in despair, but Andil and Lionenn started to investigate the walls. Lancoir, who had taken the torch from Findor, planted it in the ground, and by its light he too joined the exploration. Though they ran their fingers over every face and into every crevice, and though they pored through every nook and cranny, nothing could they find. The mood darkened, and Roujeark felt glaringly conscious of his responsibility for their predicament. *I was sure this was the right way*, he murmured to himself. Aleinus began chucking rock shards at the rockface opposite him.

'There's no way out,' he moaned, 'we'll die down here.' He carried on flinging bits of rock. 'Not much food, barely any water, and the torch won't last long...'

'Shut up, Aleinus,' Lancoir snapped. He had heard something strange and, having silenced his subordinate, he strained his ears. He motioned for another rock to be thrown. Sulkily, Aleinus obliged. The rock smashed into smithereens barely a foot from Lancoir's face, which was flattened against the wall, but the captain didn't care. A faint smile played upon his lips, and he pushed himself away. Slowly, deliberately, he brought his foot down in a powerful kick against the wall.

'Lancoir, what are you doing?' the king asked. 'That's not going to help.' Lancoir took no notice but kicked again.

'It's hollow,' was all he would say. Again and again he kicked, and part of the rock face broke off and fell away. Lionenn caught on quick and used his battle-axe to smash in more of the brittle wall. Others lent their boots to the task and soon large gaps were appearing. Lancoir backed off, and then charged shoulder-first against the wall. It smashed under the impact and fell in pieces around the upended captain. They had to dig Lancoir out of a pile of rock, but he had done his work well. A false façade of rock had disintegrated under his assault and what it had been concealing was now revealed. Behind it was a curious feature. Running up the real rockface behind was a series of tiny little ledges. Upwards they climbed, like an awkward staircase to the ceiling. And there, in the ceiling, was a dark hole. Lancoir rested his foot on the lowest step, bruised but triumphant. It held his weight. Having come this far, he retained the initiative.

Placing both feet on the lowest step, he stretched up to the next step, hands scrabbling at the rockface to help himself up. The gaps between the steps were large and daunting, but progress was possible.

One by one, step by step, they climbed up the wall, leaving the mess of rubble and the apparent dead end behind. Curillian stayed behind with the torch to light his companions' way, but when his turn came, he couldn't climb with the torch ablaze, so he reluctantly extinguished it and tucked it into his sword belt. Roujeark now conjured another light, which was not easy as he balanced precariously on a narrow step. They had all come to a halt because Lancoir had stopped. He called down to say that the hole didn't open onto a passage or tunnel but went upwards in a vertical cavity. Leaving the steps behind, he wedged himself into the narrow space, back to one wall and legs stretched out in front, bracing against the rock.

'Follow me, do as I do,' he grunted. Then he vanished into the hole. Guided by Roujeark's wavering light, they ascended with aching slowness and stomach-lurching uncertainty. The cavity became a vent, a hollow vein in the heart of the mountain that seemed to go on forever. Lancoir gritted his teeth and continued to shuffle, inching his way up. At long last he came to a place where a gap opened out on one side. A breath of air confirmed that he had come to another passage.

Λ

Roujeark's flame was too far below to cast more than the barest glimmer of light here, but Lancoir didn't need sight to know what lay all around him. He could *hear* it. Hear *them*. Sibilant hisses caressed the darkness in every direction. Slithering bodies slunk past each other and rustled through something dry. Lancoir had encountered snakes during his tours of duty to the southern frontiers of Maristonia, and he did not relish the memory. Hastily he dropped back down. He hissed down to the next person below him, which was Findor.

'Snakes!' He heard the guard gulp before relaying the message downwards. After a while another chain-message came back up. Findor reported Curillian's words.

'What's the lie of the land? Can we get past?'

'I can't see a thing,' Lancoir retorted. 'I need light.' He waited, his muscles burning with the effort of holding him in place, every moment expecting a sinuous body to drop down on him. Beads of sweat ran down his forehead. A musty odour of decay filled his nostrils. After what seemed like an eternity, he saw the light from below grow brighter, and then Findor was passing him the relit torch. Steeling himself, Lancoir inched back up. Hissing angrily, the snakes backed away from the flames, but in their light the Captain of the Guard could see now that there were hundreds of them. Twisting fearfully around, he saw that the whole floor around him was a roiling sea of reptilian flesh, writhing around each other like some sort of demonic rope. The light of the torch came back at him from a thousand beaded eyes. Wanting nothing more than to get away, he forced himself to hold firm and summoned the presence of mind to properly assess the immediate vicinity. He was in a sort of bowl-shaped hollow, perhaps thirty feet in diameter. The gentle slopes led up to a wide rim at the foot of the walls, and from that rim was a crooked ramp that led up to a dark door near the ceiling. The entire bowl was full of snakes and worms.

He slunk back down again, fighting hard to control his breathing. His heart pounded as he strained to think clearly. The way back was blocked; this was the only way. But how to get past? Even if he could rise out of the vent without being struck, he could hardly hope to reach the rim or the ramp without being bitten. All it would take was one bite to fill him with venom and end his quest in frothing, seizing agony. He glanced up again fearfully. Something above him had caught his eye. The torchlight was reflecting off something metal. A large circular candelabrum hung down from the ceiling, dangling from a rusty iron chain. It was long disused and looked ready to fall at any moment.

'Pssst,' he hissed to get Findor's attention. 'Get some stones passed up.'

'Stones?'

'Stones. Pebbles. Rocks. Something to throw. Hurry.'

Fortunately, the collapse of the tunnel and the false façade below had provided plenty of suitable ammunition. Lancoir grabbed what came up and stockpiled it in his sleeves. When he had enough, he raised himself to throwing height. One by one, he hurled the bits of rock at the point in the ceiling where the iron chain was fixed. He hoped he could dislodge whatever was holding it in place. His first few efforts clanged off the candelabrum and rained back down on the snakes below. They raised their heads in anger and started to seethe. Lancoir's fears rose to fever pitch but he kept throwing. He managed to hit the chain itself and set it jangling, and the ceiling around the fixing, provoking a shower of rock chunks. The snakes nearest him were leaning towards him, cold fury emanating from them. The corners of his vision were filled with shimmering scales and glinting fangs. He paused throwing to swish his torch about, forcing them to back off. He knew his time was running out. There was no shortage of ammunition, but he had only seconds before he was struck at. His fall would likely doom those below him, and any that survived would still have to face the venomous obstacle. He took a particularly large rock and hefted it. Using all his daring, he spent precious seconds sighting it, and then threw it with as loud a yell as he could summon.

'PRÉLAN!!!' In the confined space the shout seemed deafeningly loud, and it seemed to echo out of the aperture above and spread throughout the mountain. Other contestants heard it and trembled; Kulothiel heard it far above and smiled; the snakes blanched before it. Lancoir's hearing was so taken up with the booming report of his own shout that he scarcely heard the rumble from the ceiling. His rock had hit home, thudding into the loose fixing with ample force. In a flurry of rock and dust, the chain came loose and crashed down into the chamber below. Scores of snakes were crushed beneath it and blinding dust spread throughout the whole space.

'NOW, MOVE!' Lancoir yelled back down the vent. Using the torch, he swept the rim clear of snakes and vaulted himself upwards onto the sloping ground of the bowl. He had no time to think or fear, he only knew instinctively that the fallen metal was his bridge. With terror-fuelled speed he crashed over the candelabrum, snakes hissing and snapping about his ankles. When he reached the rim, he did not stop but powered up the ramp, not caring what lay ahead. Through the throbbing adrenalin haze of his head, he heard his companions following in his wake.

Curillian came last, sprinting behind the flowing robes of Roujeark with the speed of an armist possessed. He brandished his sword like the railing of a sinking ship, drawing strength from its hilt as he charged up the ramp. Vaguely he heard cries up ahead, but he kept going. As he approached the dark door, he thought that once they were clear of the snake den they would pause and take stock, but no such time was given him.

Passing through the door he found himself in utter darkness – the torch ahead had vanished. The last cry he heard more distinctly, a yelp of dismay from Roujeark, whom he couldn't see. His foot reached out and found nothing to rest on. It plunged down, hit something slippery and then flew out from under him. The rest of his body followed, his own momentum thrusting him forward, out of control. He thumped down onto rock slick with water. In darkness that his eyes could not penetrate, he was carried along in a sort of rocky gutter. Moments later he passed under a torrent of water falling from somewhere overhead, gaspingly cold. All of a sudden, the water beneath him was not a trickle but a powerful cascade that swept him away, bearing him into the darkness ahead.

Soaked through and chilled to the bone, he hurtled down a very steep, sloping tunnel. If he had been on a purpose-built waterslide he couldn't have gone much quicker, but no slide in the world was so treacherous. Every few seconds he came to another sharp bend and was hurled round, smacking painfully into the rock walls, only to be righted again and resume his plunging descent. He was whipped back and forth viciously, bruising all parts of his body, but he could do nothing to protect himself. He was completely out of control. Above the sound of the water and his own shouts he could hear the echoing cries of his comrades below, each of whom was having a ride as rough as he.

Roujeark slammed into something hard. In a split second his hands reached out and managed to grab a chunk of rock. The torrent tugged powerfully at him, threatening to carry him away again, but he clung on grimly. He felt movement beside him and realised that he had collided with someone else. He tried shouting to the person, who could only be one of the Royal Guards, but above the roar of the water it was useless. He thought he heard another body go shooting past in the stream, but he could not be sure. Roujeark felt the armist moving, and he feared he was about to be swept away, but it was not so. By chance, the line of their descent had taken them near the tunnel edge where they had thumped into a spine of rock. The spine marked the entrance of another opening, where the tunnel seemed to fork. His companion was not losing his grip, but rather clambering up out of the torrent. He felt boots slide past his fingers, and a few moments later a hand was reached down to him. Glad to let go of the slippery rock, Roujeark clasped the hand. Between it and his own scrabbling feet, he managed to haul himself up. The second hand reached under his armpit and pulled him up.

Next thing he knew he was sitting up in a damp aperture with the underground river gushing past beside him. He took a few moments to rid his ears of water and shake himself off. Blowing water out of his mouth, he looked across to see who his helper was. The armist had to lean close to be seen in the gloom. It was Antaya. He had not been immediately ahead of him in the headlong dash across the snake pit, so Aleinus must have been carried away by the stream while Antaya managed to cling on. Then, more by touch than by sight, he found the protruding knob of rock that had been their salvation. Carried close enough to grab it, they had managed to escape the strongest pull of the current. Without someone else, though, Roujeark felt sure he wouldn't have been able to hold on.

The side-tunnel they were in wasn't exactly dry, with damp walls and puddles underfoot, but at least it didn't have the churning cascade of the main vent. He and Antaya looked at each other.

'Well, we managed to get out,' said the guard.

'Yes, but now we're separated from the others,' Roujeark commented. Antaya looked rueful.

'Should we go back down and try and follow them?' They both leaned over, peering down. They could see nothing but the white froth of the water.

'We don't know what's down there,' said Roujeark, his voice echoing. Somehow, neither of them could summon the courage to lower themselves back into that cold torrent. Reluctantly, they agreed to go on together. Knowing Antaya was an armist of faith, Roujeark encouraged them to stop and pray before going on.

'Guide us, Prélan,' they prayed in the blind blackness. 'Lead us through, and back to the others.'

A

They had to stoop to follow the tunnel, which ran gently down and round several bends. The ground underfoot became gradually drier and the rushing, gurgling sounds of the water died away into the background. They were deep underground, in a capillary of the Mountain, one of thousands for all they knew. They didn't know where they were and certainly had no idea where they were going. After a while, the slope started to level off and then became entirely flat. They followed a faint glow that appeared ahead of them and, rounding a corner, came into a long, narrow hall. A series of wall sconces held waiting torches. It took quite some time, cold and wet as he still was, but eventually Roujeark managed to light one, and once one was lit it was easy to set the rest ablaze. They were suspicious of this sudden provision, but too thankful for the heat and warmth to be deterred. Sitting down to rest, they regarded the hall in the light of the torches.

It was a curious space, natural-looking and yet contrived at the same time. A series of rib-like protrusions stuck out from either wall, demarcating sections between them of roughly equal length that ran down the length of the hall. At each set of ribs, grooves could be seen in floor, walls and ceiling. The bays in between were rough-walled, and each held a torch on alternating sides. It was curious arrangement, like a framework which had once held a succession of long-vanished doors. It seemed they were at the threshold of some kind of portal, with perhaps a significant part of the Mountain beyond. Cautiously they moved forward. The quiet seemed so complete that they could hear the beating of one another's hearts.

Then Antaya unwittingly trod on a weak stone. Only too late did he see that it was slightly raised, and a different colour to the floor around it. An ominous series of grating, creaking noises came from all around them. For a few moments they stood frozen in terror, watching as slabs of rock a foot thick began lowering from the grooves in the ceiling. The grooves were actually gaps through which partitions were now descending, ready to slot into the matching grooves below. At first Roujeark went back, but then realised that would only lead back to the river. He recovered from his panic and followed Antaya, who had instinctively gone the other way. The first partition they passed easily enough, still high overhead, and the second, but by the time Roujeark reached the third one he had to stoop to get under it. Groaning with the strain of suspense, the next few slabs kept lowering. The end of the hall, on the other side of them, suddenly seemed very far away.

They broke into a run, dashing headlong through the hall. Antaya was faster, leaving Roujeark behind and grabbing a torch, but they both had to crouch to get under the fourth partition. Antaya threw himself into a roll to get under the fifth and last one, but when Roujeark got close it was barely two feet off the ground. He dropped to his belly and squirmed frantically through. He pulled his sopping wet cloak through after him, only for the rock slab to come down on it, pinning it fast. With a sound like a sigh of satisfaction the slabs all came to rest in their allotted places, sunk deep in their grooves and unmovable. Breathing hard, Roujeark got to his feet and tore his cloak free, leaving a strip of it trapped behind. In a fit of anger, he tore the rest of the cloak free and tossed it to the ground. It would only continue to encumber him. At least they had a torch, which Antaya had managed to keep alight. When he was able to compose himself again, he said to his companion, 'This Mountain has tricks and traps everywhere, we must be wary with every step.'

The next section seemed easier though, as if the beguiling Mountain was feigning innocence. They followed a flat sandy path that seemed featureless as it led through bare tunnels. At length they came to a room, plain and empty. Once again, there appeared to be no way out.

'Is nothing simple in here?' complained Antaya. Roujeark, though, was beginning to get used to nothing being as it seemed.

'Come, friend, let us search the floor and walls.' Scrabbling around in the sand by the light of the torch, they covered the whole floor until Antaya found something in the far corner.

'Hey, Roujeark, come and look at this.' The other armist hurried over, and together they inspected what Antaya had found. Parting the sand, he had uncovered a small board type object, roughly a square foot in size.

'It looks like a puzzle of sorts,' exclaimed Roujeark, 'but one made entirely of rocks.' He played around with the loose rocks. 'See how these rocks move around. Together they seem to form a picture of some kind, but they're all muddled, so I can't see what it is.' The board had sixteen rocks on it, all fixed to iron sliders so that they could be moved around both horizontally and vertically. They were painted with parts of an overall picture so that when they were rightly aligned, they would depict a scene or portrait of some sort. 'Here, help me move them around. Let's see what it shows.'

Together they experimented with the pieces, which proved to be rusty and unwilling to move, but slowly they explored the different alignments. Gradually they found the right configuration for the pieces, and an elusive illustration began to be revealed. After a few more minutes of fiddling, they gazed down at what they had discovered. It was an ancient motif: a mighty elven prince in glamorous armour, brandishing a twohanded sword overhead. Only a few seconds had passed when, with a sudden snapping sound, the marvellous picture disintegrated and vanished in a puff of dust and tiny stone particles. They both winced, fearing another collapsing ceiling, but nothing happened, so they looked on with amazement as the scattering dust revealed a stone slab with a protruding button of stone. They looked at each other hesitantly. With no better option at hand, Roujeark pushed the button with great apprehension. A long groan filled the room, and then a resounding clang made them both jump. Looking over, they saw a small square hole in the previously unbroken floor.

They scuttled over to see a metal trapdoor hanging down from two ancient, squealing hinges. The hole was big enough for them to fit through, but the vertical tunnel it led to was another matter. It looked perilous, and there was no knowing what lurked inside or where it led to. Yet their fears were trumped again by the knowledge that there was nowhere else to go. Gingerly they lowered themselves down, one by one, dropping again into darkness.

⋏

Curillian shot out of the tube like an arrow from a bow. The jet of water that came with him carried him over a large expanse of water. After a few soaring seconds, he plunged down into the water. When he surfaced, spluttering, he saw that he was in yet another cavern, bigger than all the rest. A low, sinister light illuminated the cavern, emanating from a string of wall-torches that looked like they had been prepared for visitors. Lurking half in shadows were forbidding cliffs, moss-covered walls that rose up sheer all around him. He splashed around, turning in the water to see what the rest of the cavern held, and saw to his surprise a large galley riding high in the water. It was an ancient bireme, a type of ship that hadn't ploughed the main for millennia. It was thirty metres long and had a single mast where the ripped and tattered remains of a sail could still be seen, clinging like bedraggled garments to the rotting wood.

He saw that he was not the first to arrive. Between him and ship were many of his companions, swimming in the direction of the vessel. Lancoir was already aboard, waving. Curillian could see no obvious exit to the cavern so, in the absence of any better options, he swam to the ship.

The bireme had two decks, one below for the rowers and one above, the latter just a pair of fighting platforms running the length of the hull. Arrayed in two columns either side of a central aisle, the rowers' benches ran the entire length of the ship, save for a closed off section in the bow and another raised platform at the back for the steering oar.

The seven armists explored the ship. Andil, who had grown up on the coast, ran his fingers over every surface and grew more suspicious with everything he touched. Everything was brand new, scrubbed and polished. There was barely a drop of bilge-water down among the ballast stones. The smell of pitch was still fresh, and the leather of the slaver's whip might have newly come from the tanner's bench.

'This ship has never sailed in anger, if it has sailed at all,' he told the others. Lancoir was completely in agreement.

'Then I'd like to know what it's doing in the middle of a subterranean lake,' he growled suspiciously.

'And how did it even get down here?' wondered Aleinus aloud. Curillian walked the length of one of the fighting platforms and rested his hands on the polished rail.

'It can only have been set here for a purpose,' he mused.

'A trap of the wizard's...' muttered Lancoir, coming to stand beside him. He continued to mutter inaudible words, his hands gripping the rail reflexively.

'What are you thinking?' Curillian asked him.

'This lake, this ship, I don't like them. I don't like any of it, the whole mountain,' Lancoir grumbled.

'I was just thinking about those rocks over there,' said Curillian. 'It's the only part of the cavern wall that's not solid rock – there might even be a way out there somewhere.' For a while they studied the rocks and nothing could be heard except dripping from all around the cavern.

'Well, we'd better go and investigate,' said Lancoir, but even as he voiced the thought Andil spoke at the same time.

'What?' said the king. 'What is it?'

'I'm not sure, sire, but I thought I heard something.' Suddenly they were all on edge, straining every sense.

'Bubbles!' shouted Lionenn, who was standing at the stempost. Curillian and Lancoir practically catapulted themselves down the ship to stand with him. Together they peered down into the lake. Suddenly it was not so placid. Over a growing area tiny bubbles were breaking on the surface, creating a frothy lacework of foam. Before long the surface was boiling and the deck beneath them quivered. An ominous whooshing noise rose up from the depths and then the lake positively exploded. A monstrous head appeared and reared up like a primordial leviathan, showering the ship in water. After its initial breach it sank down a bit, and a hefty wave smote the ship. As the spray subsided, they found themselves facing an enormous octopus-like creature. Its head was half as large as the ship itself, huge and hideous, scaly contours lining its face. The mouth was a bristling mess of teeth and foul-smelling gunk. Hideous as it was, they had all too little time to study it, for suddenly the air was alive with snakelike tentacles, more numerous than the mind could count. Lined with pulsating suckers and swung with battering-ram force, they attacked the ship in a whirlwind of ferocious flesh.

Recovering from the shock of the beast's arrival, they tugged their weapons free, only to be knocked willy-nilly by the forest of tentacles. Curillian rolled away from a tentacle that seemed to pursue him and retrieved his sword. As the tentacle latched onto an oar, he swung mightily and cut the limb in half. The creature gave a huge bellowing scream that pierced above the thrashing of the lake, but another tentacle replaced the severed one almost instantaneously. Caréysin had managed to fit an arrow to the string of his bow, but time in the water had ruined the fibre and caused the arrow to flop uselessly when he tried to loose it. Lancoir found himself surrounded by the arms, but he was freed by Curillian and Aleinus, who slashed them away furiously.

Hopelessly beset, the seven of them hacked away for all they were worth, but for every tentacle they hewed another took its place. One tentacle caught Aleinus square in the chest and flung him against the ship's side, where he slumped down amid fractured timbers. The others darted and dived to avoid a similar fate, but a bireme's deck was a treacherous place to try and evade pursuit, especially as waves created by the monster's movement kept up a violent rocking motion. Lionenn struggled to keep his balance and managed to get in one good blow before he lost his balance, bashing a tentacle with his mace. Curillian was backed against the forward cabin, slashing all the way, but he ran out of room to retreat. Whilst fighting off half a dozen tentacles in front of him, another one snaked low and wrapped around his ankle. The king was yanked off balance and hauled into the air. Full of dismay, the others watched helplessly as their leader was swung upside down like a ragdoll. But Curillian wasn't finished yet. Lurching to right himself in mid-air, he arched upwards and hacked relentlessly at the tentacle holding him, screaming like a madman. It squeezed him tighter, and he feared it might break his shin, but he kept attacking it until the great sword finally found purchase and bit deep. Another blow severed the limb and suddenly Curillian was falling. He slammed painfully onto the ship's side, the wind driven completely from his lungs. The sword fell from his grasp into the ship and he clung on for dear life. It was surely death to go into the water with that thing.

Lancoir hurled a knife at an encroaching tentacle and smiled grimly when it withdrew. Then, quite unexpectedly, something other than octopus flesh caught his eye. From out of the cavern's high ceiling a square chunk of rock came plunging. Big as a table, it struck the squid full on its head with an almighty squelching smack. Barely a moment later there came a deep groan from within the lake and the whole surface seemed to lurch. As the dazed creature slid below the wild surface, the waters took on an altogether different character. They were whipped into a whirling circle, with some great force from below sucking them down. Like the draining of some colossal basin, the lake began to recede, taking the creature with it. The ship bucked wildly, caught in the grip of the whirling current. Lancoir lost his footing. Out of the corner of his eye he saw two figures plunge from the ceiling into the lake, one red and one in grey and green. Then he saw the king in dire need. Still clinging to the rail, he was being tugged from below. The ship was tilted downward by the weight of the octopus grasping it in an attempt to not be washed away. Also alert to the danger, Findor and Aleinus seized the king's arms and held on tight. Fighting the centrifugal force of the ship's motion, Lancoir staggered across to them. He saw the Sword of Maristonia still lying discarded and scooped it up. Never before had he brandished the fabulous blade, but no time for wonder now. Leaning over the side, he struck at the tentacles holding the king. Sharper than a razor, the sword cut through the grotesque flesh. One, two, and gone! The pressure vanished and they all ended up in a heap inside the ship.

Fighting waves of nausea, they clambered back up to the rail. Looking over, they saw the lake circling down in a spiral towards some hidden aperture. The waters roared and crashed as they were whipped against wood and stone, sending up huge spouts of foam and spray. Suddenly they were shaken from their vantage by a tremendous force. They crashed into the hull as the ship grounded against rocks beneath the surface. Planks were rent and torn as fingers of rock smashed through the keel as if it were a rotten log. For a moment the ship swayed crazily as the waves continued to batter against it, and then it came to rest.

Roujeark felt powerful coils encircle him, crushing his legs in a vicelike grip. One moment he had been falling through the air, having lost his grip in the shaft, the next he had plummeted into a maelstrom of water. He was underwater and could see nothing but boiling chaos, but the tug on his lower half was remorseless. He flailed his arms in search for something to help, and his fingers brushed rock. Somehow his hands managed to get a hold and, for a split second, he was convinced he was about to be torn in half. A heartbeat later he heard a dull whump and the pressure on his legs eased. Kicking desperately, he shook free of his assailant. As soon as his legs were released, he swung them up and away from trouble. The next thing he knew, was water breaking over him and lowering around his shoulders. At last he breathed, gasping deeply and hoarsely.

Beneath him he saw the last remnants of the lake slosh and disappear through a series of long channels set in the cavern's floor. Dead or dying, the hulking mass of a great monster lay half-in, half-out of the giant sluice, a disgusting mass of bunched and slimy flesh. Higher up, stuck fast on the rocks, lay the ship it had tried and failed to destroy. Then, as if in answer to some hidden signal, a gust of wind blew and the torches went out, their fitful luminance extinguished in an instant.

Eerie darkness fell, but in the last moment of the light he had seen Antaya above him on the rocks. He had survived the ordeal too. Wincing with pain, Roujeark hauled himself up level with him. His whole body was ablaze with pain. Then oblivion took them both.

A

It was a shout that roused them.

'Roujeark! Antaya! Are you there?' It was Andil's voice. Slowly they roused themselves, still unable to see a thing. Following the sound of each other's voices, they somehow found their way to each other, slipping and stumbling across the slime-covered rocks. They touched in the darkness, counting to make sure they were all present. Close to Roujeark's ear, the king's voice was full of relief.

'How did you manage it, Roujeark?'

'Manage what?'

'The rock that struck the squid. Did you drop it?' Roujeark thought back.

'There was a room with no exits, but we solved a puzzle that opened a trapdoor. We climbed down into a dark shaft and lost our grip almost immediately, and the next thing we knew we were falling. A small circle of light rushed up to us and then we plummeted down into this cavern.'

'A great rock came down first.' It was Lancoir's voice this time. 'When we first arrived, there were no shafts in the ceiling, so you must have opened one. Somehow, you dislodged that rock. It smashed the monster square on its head. But for that, it would have killed us all.'

'You saved us, Roujeark.' The king's voice again. 'You too, Antaya, albeit inadvertently.'

'You never know what will happen in this place,' said Antaya wonderingly. 'Whatever you touch does something. Everything in here wants to kill you. Still, I'm not keen to repeat that drop, my stomach's still lodged somewhere in my gullet.'

'What do we do now?' Caréysin's voice came out of the darkness.

'Before the squid came, I thought I saw a gap in the cavern wall somewhere,' Curillian said. 'But now the lights have gone out, right on the Keeper's cue. If we could see, we might be able to find that gap and see if it really is a way out.'

Roujeark pulled himself together. 'I may be able to start a light – do you have any wood?'

Findor chuckled for answer. 'There's plenty in the ship, damn thing was nearly smashed to pieces.'

'Well, then go get some,' snapped Lancoir. Findor slunk off unhappily into the pitch black. He had not been gone long when the sound of an explosion filled the cavern. At first they cowered, thinking that the roof was collapsing on them, but when no stones fell on them they realised it was not so. The deep boom had been far off, so too the sounds of crumbling ruins that followed it. It struck fear in their hearts, but nothing like the next sound. Blood-chilling screams, neither near nor far away, a chorus of many voices raised in terror then suddenly cut off.

When Findor finally rejoined the others, he was as shaken as they were. Yet as he slid back down to them, he dropped an armful of wooden splints at their feet. Roujeark took one up and held it in his hands. Forcing himself to concentrate, he tried to reconnect with what he had done before. Long moments passed and nothing happened. Aleinus started to speak, but the king shushed him immediately. Only their breathing could be heard in the darkness as they waited for their friend to conjure something. Slowly, almost imperceptibly at first, a faint redness appeared, like a trick of the mind. Hesitant at first, then waxing stronger, the glow spread and lit up Roujeark's face in the darkness. None of them who beheld that sight ever forgot it: the wizard-to-be, surrounded by blackness, staring enraptured at the flame springing from his hand.

A second later the moment had passed, for Roujeark had transferred the flame to a wooden spar where it caught and grew stronger. Slowly the terror of the noises in the dark receded. They touched other bits of wood to the torch and created a series of brands. Roujeark looked normal again, and a glowing radius of light brought a part of the cavern's back into view: slick rocks and steep walls and a glimpse of gore below.

'Roujeark, my friend,' announced Curillian, 'you're a marvel.' He helped him to his feet and only then, in the flickering torchlight, did Roujeark see the angry red sucker marks that covered both his and the king's legs. Bracing themselves for another effort, they struck off into the gloom, seeking the way out. With much slipping on the treacherous rocks and cursing in the shadowy light, they made their way above the water line and up to the cavern walls. A brief exploration discovered that the rocks led on up the cliff, ascending like a broken staircase. Soon the ship and the sluice were lost to the blackness behind, but in front of them their torches took them up over a crest and into an alcove beyond. The space they found themselves in rapidly narrowed to a rough tunnel, which led away from the cavern. They paused at the entrance, uncertain. But Roujeark stepped past them, going in boldly.

'Prélan is with us,' he told them. One by one, they followed him in, wondering what they would find next.

A

The tunnel was harmless at first, containing nothing more intimidating than a steep slope. The damp floor gradually dried out and then became quite sandy. After a time, they came out into a large room, again conveniently lit with torches.

'Kulothiel leads us to one death trap after another,' muttered Curillian. This latest space was no vast cavern like before, but a smaller, foursquare room carved out of the mountain. Just like the neatly-hewn walls, the room's contents also bore the marks of careful design. The floor was made up of dozens of large, buff-coloured tiles, each with an elven rune painted on. The only opening was in the far wall, but it was covered by a lowered portcullis.

'So, what's the game this time?' asked Caréysin. 'Spell a word?'

'How am I supposed to spell anything?' objected Aleinus. 'I can't even read elvish.'

'I can,' said Curillian, 'but the letters are in no particular order – they don't spell anything.' They stood for a moment, stumped.

'What's that on the far wall?' Andil pointed. 'It looks like faded writing.' They all looked. Sure enough, there were characters on the wall, two words, one each side of the portcullis, but faint and worn by the passage of time.

'It's elvish also,' said Curillian, 'but I can't quite see.'

He stepped closer, squinting. He still couldn't see properly and stepped forward again. This time his foot sank as the paving slab he had stepped on depressed. His whole body tensed, wondering what he had done. Sweat beaded on all their brows and eyes flitted fearfully around. Behind them a second portcullis appeared from nowhere and rattled down over the tunnel mouth from which they had come. They were trapped again. Then the floor beneath them started to quiver and there came a groan of tortured rock from above them. For a few seconds the room became still again, and they all stood riveted to the spot, looking fixedly either at the ceiling or the floor. Then the tremors and the creaking noises returned. This time, to their horror, they saw dozens of tiny iron points piercing the ceiling above. Grating and rending, they slowly pushed through, lowering down like huge fangs. Suddenly the ceiling collapsed under the pressure and rained down in a cascade of dust and rock. But it had only been a false ceiling, a framework hiding the true ceiling, which now came into view. This one was solid, and studded with long, vicious spikes. And it was lowering.

In the same moment that the false ceiling fell apart, Curillian had a blinding flash of inspiration.

'ORON AMULAR!' He shouted back to the others behind him. 'The name of the Mountain! The TILES!'

They didn't understand what he meant, but they soon did when he sprinted to one of the tiles and began jumping up and down on it. This tile bore the elvish 'O' rune, and under the king's onslaught it smashed into smithereens. Beneath it was empty space and the king lost one foot into a hole. The others looked at him in shock, but he waved urgently and shouted at them.

'The other letters – QUICK!' In blind panic, they each ran to a different tile and beat at them, stamping with their boots. Lancoir broke through his first and was almost impaled on the spike waiting underneath.

'NO!' yelled Curillian. 'In order, spell the name!' When they didn't know which ones to go for, he pointed them out frantically. 'R…O…N…' Hurriedly they smashed each tile in turn, opening up a patchwork of cavities below the floor. Lionenn proved more proficient than the rest of them, his mace and brute strength making short work of the tiles. All the while, the ceiling lurched lower. Curillian kept shouting his directions. 'A…M…U…' The tiles were smashed in order, but it seemed to take forever – the descending spikes were barely above their heads now, and in their panic they destroyed some of the wrong tiles, revealing more spikes. With hazards above and below, and gaps all over the floor, they were herded into a smaller and smaller space.

'L…A…' Now the spikes had fallen below standing height, and they were all bent double, preparing to be pinned to the floor and crushed. With their necks bent sideways, they desperately hunted around for the last few letters. Findor and Aleinus gave up and clung to two of the spikes, bracing themselves for the end, but the others kept their presence of mind. The 'L' and the 'A' both disappeared, but by now they were all wedging themselves into the spaces between spikes, doing anything they could to prolong the end. Some were clinging to the descending spikes like monkeys, being carried remorselessly down. There was no room for movement now; the space was so constricted. It fell to Roujeark to attack the last letter, the second 'R'. He struck out with the only thing he had to hand – the torch – and he soon extinguished it in the attempt. Being plunged into darkness once more brought forth screams of terror, the seasoned guards reduced to whimpering wrecks. They were all pressed against the floor now and Roujeark had barely any room to strike. The pressure built on their bodies as the last barrier of air was squeezed away. Pinned flat, it felt like an enormous foot was being forced down on their faces. Roujeark kept hammering with puny little blows, but still to no effect. The cries of terror now turned to groans of pain from compressed lungs. Finally, Roujeark felt the tile break. It gave way under his feebly beating hand. Another second passed, and another, and the pressure above them kept building. Then the grating sound of the mechanism stopped. It was as if a rusty key had stopped turning in a giant lock. Roujeark gritted his teeth and shut his eyes, waiting for the end, but the ceiling remained where it was.

They were still alive, but with no escape. They were held fast in an immovable vice. It was totally dark. They could barely move, much less see the way out. They all heard the portcullis being raised, but they couldn't get to it. Roujeark explored the hole made by the final tile and he found no spike. With just enough room to wriggle sideways, he dropped his legs into the hole. Pivoting awkwardly, he manoeuvred his body down into the cavity. It proved deeper than the others, which gave breathing space at least. He sat wheezing and gasping on the floor, gratefully gulping the dry dusty air. When he had recovered himself, he found that there was more space than he'd thought. He couldn't see anything in the pitch darkness, but he was able to explore, and he found what seemed to be a tiny tunnel leading off. Returning to the hole, he poked his head up and called to the others, though his voice came out in a croak. Antaya and Curillian were nearest him, and they managed to extricate themselves, worming past spikes above and below. For the others it was not so easy, and they had a very unpleasant time squeezing themselves through tiny gaps. Lancoir, the furthest away, had to be dragged from his spot, where he had been stuck fast.

Eventually, sore, bruised and traumatised, they all found themselves in the tunnel. With oppressive blackness all around, they crawled blindly on hands and knees. Roujeark had neither torch nor the state of mind to relight it. But the tunnel wasn't long, and it opened up into a long trench that seemed to occupy the whole length of the far wall. Dragging themselves upright onto shaking legs, they found the doorway by feel. Ducking the downward-pointing barbs of the raised portcullis, they passed through and left the torture chamber behind.

In the tunnel that followed, they did not go far. Still in darkness, they slumped down with their backs to the wall and tried to pull themselves together. Their hearts were only just starting to slow down from a wild galloping beat.

'I'll never be able to use an apple press again,' said Aleinus. His voice was serious, genuinely remorseful, but it sounded so absurd in the situation that the others laughed. The incongruous sound of their mirth helped to ease the tension and bring them back to normal. They regained their feet and carried on following the tunnel.

A

The tunnel grew steadily warmer until it became positively stifling. They sweated in the darkness until a faint red glow broke through. The glow grew brighter and more distinct until the rock walls were clearly outlined in red, like the throat of a dragon. They began to hear strange noises, hissing, bubbling and frothing. Turning a corner, the light became much brighter and a wall of heat hit them like a blow. It was like opening an oven door. Reluctantly pressing on, they came to the tunnel's mouth, which opened out onto another cavern. The heat was fantastic, and they all soon saw why. The path they were on dropped suddenly into a cauldron of fire. They all crowded together, looking down on a gully of lava which lay between two twisted slopes like a molten spearpoint. The path snaked down one slope, clinging precariously to its side.

'First a lake monster and now this!' said Findor wearily.

'There's a whole world in here,' exclaimed Antaya, with awe in his voice.

'Verily,' said Curillian, 'we have come to the very bowels of the mountain. We are so far beneath the earth that we have reached the fires of the abyss. Come, we must follow the path to its end; let us see where it leads.'

With every step they took the temperature increased, and the fierceness of the air was exacerbated by tongues of molten liquid that every now and then would bubble up and spatter through the air. Each one of the armists was pouring with sweat, and as the beads dripped off them onto the floor they sizzled and evaporated in seconds. Noxious fumes made them lightheaded and unsteady on their feet, which made the going hazardous when they reached the level of the lava. Only the slight raise of the path separated them from molten lake. They picked their way with care through a furnace-like defile, round a spur and then out into a wider space. Passing under a cracked and blackened arch, they found themselves in a square chamber of colossal proportions. A giant staircase of hewn rock twisted down from each of the ceiling's four corners, and in the middle where they met was an island-like platform in the middle of a molten lake. Each staircase appeared to lead to an exit, but they were so broken and treacherous that ascending them would be no easy task.

Warily they edged along the perilously narrow path towards the central platform, hoping to avoid the hissing jets of lava and steam that spat occasionally. Caréysin, who had scouted ahead, reached the platform first and suddenly shouted back in alarm. The rest of them hurried to meet him. The platform was not as stable as they would have liked; it dipped and wobbled alarmingly. But it was not the platform that had caused Caréysin to cry out. Looking down, they discovered what had startled him. Dead bodies lay on the platform, half a dozen of them. They wore the motley leather jerkins and tunics of Aranese free-riders.

'These were not men of Southilar's company,' Curillian said, looking down. 'Six men of Aranar. They got here before us, but they will go no further.'

'They must have been overcome by the heat, or caught in a jet of lava,' said Roujeark.

'No,' said Lancoir, 'they weren't killed by heat or lava. They were slain. Look.' Even as he was speaking, Roujeark looked closer and saw the death-wounds. Blades had cut deep into their necks and bodies, and lacerated limbs lay ragged and askew. The six of them had fallen in a small circle that had been fighting on every side, overcome by a hidden enemy. Curillian rolled one over. Horror was stamped on the dead face.

'They died in terror and pain,' the king said. 'Who knows what they came through, only to die here.'

'Which of the other contestants killed them?' Findor wondered aloud.

'It could have been any of them,' said Roujeark.

'Or none,' the king countered. 'There are enemies in this mountain that did not enter with us.'

'Well, whoever it was,' said Findor, kicking a fallen blade into the lava lake, 'they aren't here now.'

A

No sooner had he spoken than they heard the sound of voices. They all jumped, standing up from their examination of the scene and brandishing weapons. Other than the chilling screams, it was the first people they had heard since leaving the first chamber. Following the noise, they saw what looked to be a path identical to their own leading into the chamber from a different direction. The voices, which before had been distorted by fear and crooked passageways, gradually became more distinct.

Out of the passageway stepped an armoured figure, complete with helm and shield. He did not see the armists but stood gaping at the cavern into which he had entered. He had a Pegasus on his shield and on his hauberk. This was a man of Aranar, but not one of the free-riders like those who lay dead at their feet; this man was in Southilar's entourage. After a moment, he turned back and called to others in the passageway behind him.

'Fiery hell, no wonder it's been getting hotter. There's a bloody lake of fire out here.' Others stepped out of the passageway to join him, all uttering violent exclamations of surprise and consternation. Like the first man, all were armoured. The men of Aranar had come fully dressed for war. Among them was the unmistakably tall figure of Southilar, and Theonar, who was taller still.

'They must be absolutely cooking in that armour,' muttered Aleinus. The armists still wore the light mail and travelling clothes in which they had journeyed. Curillian stepped forward and called across the fire.

'Well met again, friends. Welcome to the furnace of Kulothiel.' They looked up in surprise, not expecting anyone else to be in the cavern already. Weapons were raised ready for defence, but Southilar also stepped forward. Raising his voice above the menace of the lava, he called back.

'Still alive, Curillian? You ought to have died several times already, if you've faced anything like what we have. But then you always were lucky.'

The men of Aranar looked uncertain how to reach the armists, but then they spotted the pathway that led out to the central platform. Warily they came across and joined the armists. The first man had been Hardos, one of Southilar's Clan Knights, and he nodded curtly at Curillian and his party. Southilar, sweating like a blacksmith, was more voluble.

'God's teats, Curillian! But what the bloody hell have we let ourselves in for?' He threw down shield and sword and peeled off gloves that were practically steaming. Many of his followers followed suit, only too glad to be free of their burdens. The armists squatted down to rest too, and Caréysin took the opportunity to fit his bow with a new string, which had been in a pouch at his belt.

Curillian had to blow sweat out of his eyes to see the Jeantar properly. 'I tell you,' the big man complained, 'so far we've nearly been crushed, pulverised, ripped to bits, drowned and eaten. And that was just in the first half an hour.'

'You look like you have fared little better,' observed Theonar, joining them, 'but I'm glad to find you yet living, lord king.' Curillian acknowledged his words gratefully.

'And I you, Sir Theonar. And you other knights and lords of Aranar.' In all Southilar had 14 men with him, a couple short of the total he'd had in camp outside the Mountain. Even Caiasan, the irreverent scribe, had made it, looking even more dishevelled than before.

'Strewth,' he exclaimed, 'what a place! Best watch your step here, lads.' He himself tottered and took a swig from a flask at his side.

'This is an evil place,' insisted Sir Lindal, the Unicorn Clan Knight, but before he could expand further, Southilar spoke again.

'I've lost two men getting here,' he told Curillian. 'A man-at-arms ground into mincemeat under a falling rock, and Sir Acil of the Hawk emerged out of the waterslide dead as an anvil. He sank in the lake before we could get to him.'

Off to one side, Caiasan whispered loudly to Roujeark, whom he had sought out. Even above the nostril-singing smell of brimstone, the armist could smell the liquor on his breath.

'He arsed to the left, he arsed to the right, but he don't arse no more.' If anyone else heard, they ignored him.

'How many have you lost?' Southilar asked.

'None,' said Curillian, 'though we too have been beset by many perils.' Southilar looked aggrieved that the armists had sustained no losses, but he said nothing, merely grunted. Sir Romanthony of the Eagle spoke instead.

'What fools we are to have ventured into this wizard's funhouse. Tournament? I'd sooner be back at the Hamid Tournament, or Stable or Rikemord. Men die there, but at least they have a fighting chance. We'll all die in here without ever seeing the prize he spoke of.'

'If it ever existed,' chipped in another. Curillian was unmoved.

'Still, prize or no prize, we must find a way out, and we'll do better together than apart.'

'There's sense,' muttered Southilar grudgingly.

'Have you seen anyone else?' Curillian pressed him. The big horse-lord shook his head.

'Seen? No. Heard? All too much.'

'Screams?' Roujeark asked. 'Explosions?' The Jeantar looked strangely at him, but nodded.

'What's that noise?' Theonar said, breaking into their conversation. He had remained aloof so far, alert and watchful.

⋏

A s soon as he spoke, men and armists alike were on the alert. At first they heard nothing, but then came strange sounds. Harsh, gravelly sounds, like a burrowing through rock. Southilar and Curillian stood back to back, tightening their grips on their blades. They saw nothing, but the odd rumblings continued.

'Whatever this new devilry is, I'm ready for it,' declared Southilar through gritted teeth. Curillian said nothing, but despite the dampness of his skin the hairs on his nape were standing up. Apprehension rippled down through his spine. Then Theonar spoke again in cool warning.

'Look, the walls!' All eyes snapped like clockwork to the wall he was pointing to and took in the horrified sight of grotesque figures emerging out of the rock. Clawed fingers outstretched, cadaverous forms seemed to be ripping their way out of the solid rock. They were skeletons apart from a few layers of thin skin stretching pale over their bones. They carried hammer-headed blades and crooked cutlasses. Seemingly oblivious to the lava, they waded towards the platform with alarming speed.

Even Curillian, a seasoned campaigner, had never seen anything like this. His stomach churned and his limbs quivered. Lancoir did nothing except raise his eyebrows and adopt a defensive stance, but Roujeark could only gape, eyes wide in frightened amazement. Caréysin got off two arrows, each of which plucked its target down into the lava. Then the other skeleton warriors leapt up out of the lava, striving to reach the platform, and they were upon the armists and men before most of them had had a chance to react. Horror slowed their reactions and many were late in bringing up their weapons. The undead corpses leapt upon them and they grappled in a life and death struggle. Those defenders used their weapons to brutal effect, cutting through gruesome skin, cracking fire-blackened bones and severing heads. Curillian's sweeping cut knocked one straight back into the fire where its bones splashed with a vicious hiss. Lancoir, Southilar and Theonar likewise threw back their assailants, but then they all watched with horror as the slain corpses re-emerged. Bones reconnected and scarce skin stretched taut again. Weapons came to hand, and they leapt once more to the attack. Again they hewed them down, but with the same result.

Elsewhere on the heaving platform the struggle raged, blades scything and bodies wrestling. Yells of fear pierced above the clash of steel and the roar of lava jets, only to bounce back off the walls and reverberate around the battlefield. So unsteady did the platform become that one man-at-arms lost his balance and tottered into the lava. Unlike the skeletons, he did not survive, but vaporised moments after his horrific shriek was extinguished. The noise of his passing shocked man and armist all around, and the pause cost two more Aranese dearly. Disregarding weapons, a pair of undead clambered up on their backs and tugged them backwards. Overborne, they too fell into the fire and perished with screams of blinding agony.

Their comrades fought on, but every split limb reformed and every severed head snapped back into place. Not only were their hard-swung blows having no effect, they struggled to keep their feet as the platform bucked and swayed. Then matters took a turn for the worse, as more skeletons emerged from the opposite wall, and still more followed from the other two walls. They closed upon the platform from every direction and looked set to overwhelm the gallant band trapped there. Embattled on every side, Curillian clove another skeleton in two and roared his war cry above the din. His arms were so quick, his thrusts so rapid, that he outmatched even the ability of the attackers to recover from wounds. Side by side with Lancoir, they fought recklessly, keeping a corner of the platform clear.

Nearby, Southilar was surrounded by the skeletons, standing head and shoulders taller than them, whirling in his greatsword in one hand and using his other hand to punch at his assailants. But then they jumped up on his shoulders and grabbed at his legs and he started to lose his balance, swaying dangerously near the edge. He was about to fall when Curillian threw himself at him, kicking one of the skeletons away from his legs and using his own weight to haul him backwards. He and Southilar struggled free of one another and got back to their feet. Curillian kicked another corpse flying and hacked his sword into another, while Southilar caught two by their throats. Lifting them bodily, he threw them into another pair, sending all four toppling from the platform.

Roujeark felt less than useless in the fight and it was all he could do to bob and weave clear of the whirling blades and punching fists. He knew his fire would have no effect on these attackers – even if he'd had the presence of mind to summon it – since the lava had not harmed them. Little skilled with blades, he did not try to attack the skeletons but devoted all his attention to staying alive. Then, in the midst of the melee, he noticed something around the neck of one of the skeletons. A weirdly green medallion, glowing with some fell power. Might it control them? Acting on his half-formed guess, he tried to get close to the bearer. He ducked a wildly swinging blade and ricocheted off Lionenn, who was bludgeoning his attackers. He stumbled over a pile of bones on the floor and tried reaching for the medallion. He nearly reached it when a hilt struck the back of his head, leaving him stunned on the floor.

Through waves of throbbing pain he glanced up, fixating on the bearer of the amulet. Armists, men and undead spun round him in a madcap dance, but he ignored them all. Dagger in hand, he finally closed with his enemy. For a split second he locked eyes with its baleful, unthinking gaze, and then his eyes darted away to warn of the rusty blade swinging at him. Somehow, he managed to parry with his dagger, and in the moment before his foe recovered, he lunged forward and snatched at the medallion. He ripped it free from around the undead neck, even as his legs were knocked out from under him. Staring at the glowing green orb, he felt himself being hypnotised. But he wrenched his eyes away, upended his dagger, and brought it down hilt-first with all his might. He wasn't even aware of the owner's sword swinging down, aimed for his unprotected neck. In the second before it struck, his pommel smashed into the medallion, shattering its fragile glass and spilling green ooze everywhere. In the same moment the sword above his neck disintegrated into ashes. So too did its owner. All across the platform, the skeletons crumbled. Where a heartbeat before had been indestructible enemies, now there were only piles of dust.

Breathing hard and still dizzy, Roujeark rose to his knees and looked dazedly around. The fight was over. The rocking platform was slowly subsiding to stillness. He saw each of his companions in turn, singed, bloodied and harrowed. Most of them seemed not to realise what had happened, but were simply glad to collapse to the ground, exhausted but alive. Only Theonar looked at him strangely. The tall man came over and stooped to inspect both the strange viscous fluid on the ground and the silver chain still gripped in the armist's hand.

'So, they were controlled by a spell locked in an amulet.' A strange look came across his face as he said the words, deep and far-off. 'How strange that Kulothiel should use that trick.'

'What do you mean?' said Roujeark in a frightened voice. The look vanished from Theonar's face as he turned his eyes on Roujeark.

'You found and destroyed the enemy's source of power. You saved us all from certain death. My thanks to you, friend of the king.' Curillian came over to hear the words. Though he was as shaken as the rest, he found it in him to speak lightly.

'Roujeark to the rescue again?' He clapped him on the shoulder, making him wince. 'You'd better leave us to save ourselves every now and then, or what will we do when you're not around?' Curillian in his turn felt a heavy arm on his shoulder as Southilar drew alongside.

'And you have my thanks, Curillian, I would have been toast back there but for you. I'm indebted to you once again.' Curillian stepped clear of the big man, patting his armour.

'Don't talk nonsense, Southilar. I've done it before and I'll do it again, there is no need for repayment. I have no doubt that you will do as much for me someday.'

'Curillian, my lord,' Lancoir cut in. 'Let us leave. They may attack again.'

Caiasan staggered over. Somehow he had survived the fracas, bruised and bloodied though he was.

'How the blazes do we leave?' he demanded. Lancoir said nothing but stared grimly at him. 'Yes, I know you're the strong silent type, but stop glaring at me and answer the flipping question. You see those staircases, do you not see a problem with them?' Caiasan pointed up as he upbraided the captain of the guard.

The company all looked up to try and follow his logic. Three of the four staircases joined one of the corners of the platform they stood on, but they all had gaping holes in them higher up. The fourth one was more intact, but it didn't even reach the platform. Most of Caiasan's companions among the men of Aranar seemed genuinely surprised to find that he had a point. 'There's whacking great holes in all of them, meaning we can't climb them, all except that one.' They looked at the one he indicated. The scribe had spoken truly; it alone was more or less intact, free of the gaping holes which rendered the others completely unusable. But it was far from safe itself, twisted and crumbling, riddled with holes and, worst of all, broken away where it should have met the platform.

'But we can't reach that one either,' said Andil. 'It doesn't reach the platform – it must be twenty, thirty feet above us where it ends.'

Caiasan clapped his hands, exclaiming. 'Exactly! Bonus point to that blighter. We can't reach it, a...' Theonar grasped the overwrought scribe's shoulder and squeezed, silencing him.

'Caiasan, be quiet. Listen for a moment. You're going to get us out of here.'

'I am?'

'Yes. You're going up there.' He pointed at the broken end of the staircase above them. 'To let a rope down for us.'

'But h...' Theonar squeezed again to turn Caiasan's next protest into another gasp.

'We're going to help you.' He turned to the others. 'Right, I need the five biggest men.' Bemused, Southilar came forward, along with Sir Romanthony. The others looked at each other, measuring themselves. 'Come on,' urged Theonar. Eventually two men-at-arms and Rane, one of the Pegasus knights, joined the other two. 'Kneel down next to each other,' Theonar instructed them. They looked at him as if he were crazy. 'Well, go on,' he said firmly.

'Do as he says,' ordered Southilar, as he got down on his knees. The others followed.

'No, not like that,' said Theonar. 'Prostrate, right down, with your noses to the floor.' The men of Aranar complied with bad grace, assuming the position with much muttering. As they were getting into position, Theonar looked round at the rest. 'I need others to stand at the other corners of the platform and balance it out. Roujeark, find me a rope and be ready with Caiasan. Now, another four.' Four more knights and men-at-arms came forward, and Theonar arranged them on top of the original five, each one straddling two of the broad backs below.

'A living pyramid,' observed Curillian. He glanced up at the gap, gauging the distance. 'Hope you've got a long reach, Sir Theonar.' Then he volunteered himself, Lancoir and Lionenn as the row of three. The men beneath groaned and grumbled as the extra weight was applied. In the meantime, Roujeark was fashioning his rope. They had no actual rope, so he, Caiasan and Sir Lindal were lashing together belts and shoulder straps. Antaya and Findor climbed up as the penultimate row, and as they did so, the platform swayed alarmingly underneath them.

'Hurry up!' growled Southilar from the bottom row. Quite apart from the lava which was uncomfortably close, he found that the platform was hot to the touch. The growing pyramid wobbled as the men on the bottom row fidgeted to try and protect their fingers and relieve their knees. When the two armists were in place, Theonar beckoned to Caiasan.

'Got a good grip on that rope? Good. Now be ready to follow me up. The rest of you, do what you can to balance the platform.' Caiasan gulped visibly as he waited, while the others spread out to keep as even a weight as possible on the platform. Already the weight of the pyramid, placed directly below the targeted staircase, was dipping the platform dangerously close to the lava line.

Sure-footed as a mountain goat, Theonar sprang up the pyramid to the top. Only now did they see quite how tall he was – almost seven feet in height – and he went a long way to bridging the remainder of the gap. He called down to Caiasan, letting him know he was ready. Roujeark feared that it wouldn't be enough. He didn't think the scribe could reach the lowest step, even perched on Theonar's shoulders. Caiasan clambered up with considerably less elegance than Theonar, kicking several comrades as he struggled upwards and nearly pulled the whole shaky edifice down. At last he reached Theonar, who crouched down ready. With breathtaking poise and balance, he lifted the shrieking scribe upward. The whole pyramid quivered with the motion and the noises of discomfort from lower down rose to a whole new pitch. Caiasan strained upwards, but he was still out of reach.

'I can't reach,' he yelped.

'Stand on my shoulders,' said Theonar.

'What? No chance.'

'Do it, or we'll all burn!'

'Can't hold much longer!' came a grunted shout from below.

Somehow Caiasan managed to place his feet on Theonar's shoulders instead of his thighs, where the knight gripped them firmly. Crying for dear life, he straightened up uncertainly and reached again. Still the step was an arm's length too high. The watchers below held their breath.

'Should we add another layer?' asked Sir Deàreg.

'No, the pyramid would be too heavy, and tip us all into the fire,' said Roujeark.

'But he can't reach!' said a man-at-arms, panic rising in his voice.

'Get it done!' growled Hardos from the second row. 'We're about to collapse.'

Roujeark saw every braced arm shaking with the effort and knew he had to act. If they didn't accomplish this, they were trapped forever in this furnace. Shutting out the noise around him, he concentrated all his mind on the swaying figure of Caiasan. Nothing but fire had ever come to him before, but now he envisioned a wholly different power. Nothing happened, but he kept his focus. The pyramid was at breaking point when Theonar crouched down again. Keeping tight hold of the scribe's ankles, he shot upward, this time heaving his burden into the air. With nothing left to hold onto, Caiasan found himself flying through the air, screaming one long continuous exhalation of terror. He had reached the end of his trajectory, about to fall back, with his outstretched fingers barely inches from the step, when something took hold of him. An invisible force lifted him the last few inches, even as Theonar got ready to try and catch him. With feverish intensity, his fingertips gripped the elusive step, knowing his dangling life was on the line.

At the same moment he took hold, the pyramid collapsed. Men's arms finally gave out, and they fell in a heap. It was many confused seconds before they managed to extricate themselves, several of them coming close to falling in the lava. But when they forgot their own privations and looked up, Caiasan was still dangling.

'He made it!' exclaimed one,

'But he can't get up!' said another.

'Come on, Caiasan,' they all yelled. 'You can do it.'

'HEAVE!' bellowed Southilar, as if he might lift the dangling man by the power of his voice alone. No one noticed Roujeark, standing like a zombie, his outstretched arms rigid as he poured his attention into what he was doing. When Caiasan's leg came up and wrapped around the step, they thought it was by his own efforts. Now with enough purchase, and with raw ability lent from his survival instinct, Caiasan managed to wriggle onto the step. He collapsed on his back, panting fit to burst. At the same moment Roujeark slumped down, even as the others cheered about him. Only Theonar noticed him. The tall knight came over to check on him, full of concern.

'You're one of them, aren't you?' he said. 'One of the wizards?' Roujeark nodded silently, quite exhausted.

'I'm not sure I want to be, if this is what it takes.' Theonar pulled him up and gazed at him with his intense blue-eyed stare.

'Whatever your heart says now, Prélan has destined you to be a saviour of others. Because you are here, this isn't the end for us. But for you, this is only the beginning.' Another cheer interrupted them, and they turned around to see that Caiasan had recovered enough to let down the belt-rope.

'Here we go,' Curillian said, coming to join them. 'On to the next challenge.'

One by one the party pulled themselves up on the rope. As each man or armist reached the lowest step, the one before moved upwards, and so the party inched up the twisting staircase. It was a nerve-wracking experience, being so high up on so perilous a path with neither rail nor bannister to keep them from falling into the fire. It might once have been even and regular, but the staircase now was rough and unsteady, full of holes and crumbling in places. They picked their way carefully, scrambling more than walking. In places they had to leap across gaping holes with their hearts in their mouths. But each time they got past such an obstacle, and looked over at the other staircases, which had much larger gaps, they were silently thankful. If anything, it got hotter as they ascended, but they kept their eyes on the dark hole where the staircase disappeared into the ceiling.

Lancoir let the others go first. He brought up the rear with the belt-rope coiled round his shoulders. He kept one eye on the treacherous path and one on his king, who was immediately in front. Above them the other members of the party vanished one by one into the ceiling, leaving the furnace behind. Just as Lancoir came to the hole and was about to do likewise, he stopped, obeying a sudden instinct. He turned round and looked back down into the fiery chamber, cuffing the sweat from his eyes. For a moment all he could hear was the seething of the lava, but then he heard distant voices echoing from one of the approach tunnels. He paused long enough to see the first figure emerge out into the open. By the fur garments he knew him to be a man of Ciricen, one of Earl Culdon's following.

'Prélan save you,' he muttered. Then he was gone.

A

He found the others bottled up in a narrow tunnel that wound upwards in tight spirals. After a while of following this, he heard a frustrated cry and soon after came to a halt, as the men in front had stopped. Gradually the word filtered back that they were stuck on the wrong side of a locked door. At least it was slightly cooler in here. The armists waited patiently while the men of Aranar argued uproariously, until Southilar's voice subdued the others. They heard him pushing through to the front, then a few moments of strained silence. Next came a slow, rhythmic banging. Southilar was trying to kick the door down. Even his great weight and strength couldn't budge it, and he heard him bang it with his fists in frustration.

'Give me room!' Lionenn's voice growled in the dark. Repeated hammer blows crashed in the darkness as mace and door met. Evidently the mace prevailed, for shortly afterwards there were cheers of success and they were able to move again. But the cheers soon faded, and the armists followed the men out into an open space in awed silence.

They were in a tall smooth-sided atrium. In front of them was the longest staircase any of them had ever seen, stretching upwards out of sight. As different from the one they had just climbed as could be imagined, its smooth masonry was flawlessly straight and level. All the way up it was flanked by frescoes of ancient scenes and lines of sentinel statues. From somewhere up above there issued a wan bluish light, the faintest shards of which just touched the place where they stood. The door by which they had broken in was one of three, but the other two, towering up to left and right, were quite different. Tall, tapering and richly ornate, they gave onto twin passageways altogether more wholesome than the ways had followed up to this point.

'It seems we came by the hard way,' Southilar observed gruffly.

'Verily,' said Curillian, 'but that was surely intended. Unless I'm mistaken, we are come now to the habitable parts of the Mountain.'

'Yes,' agreed Theonar. 'I think our experience from now on will be quite different to what we've just had.'

'So we've crawled through the sewers and fought through the bowels of the place?' Hardos complained, his voice sharp with resentment.

'Maybe,' Curillian allowed, 'but from what I've heard, I wouldn't necessarily call them sewers. Legend has it that Oron Amular had vast caverns for the training of its acolytes, places designed to be difficult and uncomfortable. If that is so, then what we've come through are the same challenges once used to test warrior-wizards.'

'All very interesting,' said Sir Deàreg, 'but I for one am glad to have got the hard part over. I'm looking forward to an easier stretch.' The Aranese made to start moving forward, but Roujeark's voice halted them.

'Don't count on that, sir knight. The higher we go now, the more potent the magic will become around us. This is the very birthplace of magic, is it not?' He caught Theonar's eye, but the tall knight gave nothing away in his face. 'Everything we see here could be dangerous. Hard part over? I doubt that very much. Nay, the closer we come to the prize, the more Kulothiel will test us.'

His words cast a dread over the lords, knights and men-at-arms of Aranar, and when they walked forward now there was significantly less confidence in their steps. Curillian encouraged his armists.

'Come, friends, what Roujeark says is probably truer than he knows, but we've come this far together, and we'll go on together.'

His party followed the men and Curillian himself was striding towards the lowest steps when he noticed Sir Theonar hanging back to catch him. The tall man came close and whispered in his ear before hastening up to rejoin his companions.

'Before your Konenaire broke the door down, we heard sounds out here. It was empty when we came out, but I am convinced that someone was here just before us. Watch your step, my lord king.'

Curillian let him go on ahead and hung back until his comrades were well above him. Then he turned, making no noise, to watch the atrium. Several long moments elapsed, then a shadow moved. Out of the left hand passageway, a tall figure materialised. From the other side came two others, elves all. Elrinde of Ithrill nodded in wordless greeting. Curillian returned the gesture, holding his eye for a while. When neither he, Astacar nor Linvion moved, Curillian turned and continued on his way.

The staircase proved to be even longer than it had appeared from the bottom. The whole way up they passed scenes of history and legend painted on the walls, though in the gloom they couldn't guess at their subjects. At regular intervals the steps were interrupted by wide platforms, each with a brace of tall marble lampstands, their lights long since extinguished. As they climbed, the ghostly luminescence from above grew gradually brighter. They were almost drenched in it when at long last they reached the top. The stairs gave onto a vast room, cathedral-like in its proportions and layout. Rows of enormous carved pillars supported a vaulted ceiling whose painted details could not clearly be seen.

Right in front of them was a metallic gateway, gleaming silver-blue in the light of whatever lay beyond. Two great statues flanked the opening at its centre, intricately sculpted into the likenesses of ancient mage-lords. Their outstretched staves barred the way, and though no barrier was in evidence, all beyond them was obscured as if by thick glass. They all walked up to the forbidding obstacle, mesmerised and chilled at the same time by the eerie light. Lancoir was foremost now, and he strode towards the crossed staves. After gazing up for a moment at the ancient engraved faces, he reached out and touched the staves. A blinding moment of pain and the next thing he knew he was picking himself up from the top of the stairs, having been hurled back fully thirty paces. His companions, who had been knocked willy-nilly by his backward flight, were just getting to their feet again, marvelling at the flash they had seen and the glowing blue forcefield that had momentarily been revealed.

'I…don't think we should touch them,' Caiasan said, overlate.

'Now he tells me…' Lancoir muttered. Dusting himself off, he returned to the statues, this time to inspect them, in company with Curillian, Roujeark, Theonar and Southilar.

'Who are they?' asked the Jeantar, looking up in awe, his face bathed in the spectral glow.

'I know not,' said Roujeark. 'Some long-past champions of the League, I would guess, defending their realm even in death. But these are not pieces of art. Did I not say everything here could be dangerous?'

Aleinus, standing behind them, overheard and muttered aloud, 'Great, down there everything we pressed triggered some booby-trap; up here, anything we touch is likely to give us a shock. I like this place more and more.' Caiasan shrugged expansively in sympathy, but everyone else ignored him. Back in the leaders' discussion, Sir Theonar made his contribution.

'It matters not who they are. All we need to do is find a way to get past them.'

'Any suggestions?' growled Southilar. Theonar had none to make, and nor did any of them. After a while they tired of their inspection and sat down to think.

'Kulothiel isn't giving up this last stage so lightly is he?' said Caréysin with a rueful smile. Curillian nodded agreement and sat back, propped up against a pillar. He felt wearier than he had in years.

For some while they sat about, racking their brains for a solution, but none came. Then Roujeark felt a strange sensation surge through him and, when he looked again, there was no one about him. Gone was the pale blue glow, replaced by the blaze of a hundred lamps. Then he heard footsteps coming up the stairs, which now looked resplendent in golden light. A wizard strode energetically up and passed him by. He took no notice at all of Roujeark. The wizard went straight up to the statues, which stood staves crossed as before. Roujeark followed, full of curiosity. Head bowed reverently, the wizard uttered a strange word, so softly that Roujeark couldn't catch it. However, there could be no mistaking the effect of that mysterious word. The staves separated and snapped into an upright position. The rest of the statues hadn't moved, but now the way was clear.

Roujeark saw the opportunity and hurriedly made to follow. He passed through the barrier hard on the wizard's heels, moments before the staves came back down. With a faint hum the forcefield came back into operation.

A cry of amazement from his companions tugged him back to reality, and he shook his head with a start. The blue light was back, shining softly all around him. He looked for his comrades, and there they were, on the wrong side of the magical portal. They had leapt up in astonishment when they saw him scurry through, and now were looking at him in amazement, their faces somewhat distorted by the intervening barrier. One of the Aranese knights chucked a ration-biscuit at the barrier to test it, and sure enough the object was hurled back, spraying across the dusty floor in a thousand pieces.

'Roujeark!' The voice was Curillian's, though it was muffled by the forcefield. 'How did you do that? You walked straight through. The staves came up, let you through, and then slammed back into place. What did you do?' Roujeark was no less bewildered than the king.

'I don't know sire. I had a kind of vision, and I watched a wizard approach this very spot. He spoke a password to open the gate, but I couldn't hear what it was. I was up before I knew it, following him, and no sooner was I through than the vision faded. Now here I am.'

'Amazing,' exclaimed Caiasan, pushing forward. 'It's like the Mountain recognises you as one of its own. You truly are a wizard!' There was awe in his voice.

Sir Hardos was less impressed. 'But that still doesn't help us! Unless he's going to finish the Tournament by himself, how do we get through as well?' There followed a loud, futile argument with lots of wild suggestions thrown around, but somehow Theonar's soft suggestion cut through it and silenced them all.

'Search the statues. There may be a clue.' He stepped away and let them search, but through the forcefield Roujeark caught a strange look in his face, a glimpse of withheld brilliance.

The search was conducted gingerly, the examiners fully expecting to get zapped at any moment, but it seemed that the defensive power was only in the space between the staves, not on the rest of the statues. Ornate though the statues were, no words were written upon them.

'There's nothing here,' Andil said dejectedly.

'Wait…wait a minute,' contradicted his fellow-guard Findor, 'there's something inscribed on this ring here…only I can't read it.'

'Let me see.' Curillian pushed in. What Antaya had found was tucked away on the finger of the right-hand statue, the hand not holding the staff. A word was set on a stone ring, on the side facing away from the staircase. Craning his neck, Curillian peered at the elvish script.

'*Nahtiere.*' He breathed the word to himself. He extricated himself. 'It's no word of elvish that I recognise, but here goes.' He turned back to face the barrier and bowed his head. '*Nahtiere.*' He did not look up but heard the swish and eerie whisper as the two staves slid smoothly up and shuddered to a halt by the wizards' sides. Awed gazes were replaced by hasty steps as everyone began moving forwards. Curillian led them through, while Sir Theonar stood under the barrier to keep it open until all had passed. And so they stepped over the threshold, into the very heart of the mountain.

⚔

Now, with nothing in the way, they could at last see the source of the light. In the middle of the pillared hall was a strange edifice, shaped in the likeness of the Mountain itself. The inexplicable glow emanated from a plinth at its top, filling the hall with unearthly light and scattering the shadows into recesses between the pillars. With dread and awe they slowly approached, but only a few dared go close. Curillian, Theonar and Roujeark. They were deaf to the imprecations of Southilar, urging them to remain.

The sculpture was star-shaped, like the mountain it evoked, with four out-flung spurs. Between those spurs were four sets of steps ascending to the high platform. Reverently, the three questers climbed them and met at the top. The structure was fashioned of a material like nothing any of them had ever encountered, obsidian-dark, smooth as marble, cold as the stars. In the steps and on inlaid panels to either side were runes of power, glowing with their own unquenchable fire.

On the platform was a font, a carved pedestal of perfect white stone. Like everything else in the vicinity, it was bathed in the blue light. A shallow pool in the font held crystal clear water, fresh as mountain dew. And in the pool was a marvellous gem, though so incandescent that they could not tell what it was. Brighter than all the stars of the sky gathered together in one place, it was beautiful and terrible. They could not look directly at it, but it seemed to be curved in a graceful oval, as large as the egg of some giant bird.

'It is the Tear of Mírianna.' Curillian and Roujeark stood entranced, robbed of the power of speech, and they were barely aware of Theonar speaking. Had they known it, his voice was strangely changed, grown in power and dignity. 'No less than the greatest treasure ever wrought by elven hand. If wrought it was; some say it was one of the few heirlooms Avatar brought with him to Astrom from the stars. Undimmed by all the years, the League may have passed into the night, but the Tear still shines. If all else is conquered, can any evil ever draw nigh so heavenly a radiance? Let the shadowy heart of the Fire-demon himself be illumined if ever he gazes hither, and let no mortal eyes ever forget the sight.'

'Avatar.' Curillian mindlessly echoed the name, gripped with unthinking awe. Somewhere in the back of his mind, Curillian remembered what Theonar was talking about, but it was beyond him to articulate it. Avatar was the High King of all elves, the eldest member of that ancient race. Legend had it that he and his spouse, Mírianna the Star-Queen, had crashed to Astrom in a fallen star, sent along with two others from *Eluvatar*, the Holy-Star and dwelling place of Prélan. The other two stars contained the kings and queens of the sea-elf and wood-elf kindreds, just as Avatar and Mírianna ruled over the high-elves. Legend it might have been for all that any mortal knew, but Curillian had spoken with ancient elven lords like Lancearon who swore to it as a Prélan-given truth.

'The High King discovered Oron Amular and its Pool of High Magic,' Theonar went on. 'He founded the League of Wizardry here before he departed these shores, creating an institution which for seven thousand years has protected and enlightened the Free Peoples. This tear he bequeathed to the Mountain in honour of Mírianna, a light to grace the threshold. And verily these are his parting words, engraved in a circle around the rim of the pool.' As his companions stood still transfixed, the tall knight circled the pool, reciting the ancient script as he traced the words with his finger.

Though I leave these shores,
This legacy of light I leave forever
To shine by the grace of Prélan in
The heart of His hallowed Mountain.
Here let the Tear of Mírianna dwell,
A token of hope to all who behold,
And a promise of deliverance
To all who believe that He shall come again.

Just as they both marked but could never remember afterwards the change in his voice, so Curillian and Roujeark both saw but couldn't grasp the look in his face. Theonar stood rapt in the holy light, his face displaying wonder and intimacy mingled. Adoration and long-harboured pain swirled through his eyes, quivered in his lips and rippled in his skin. Or so it seemed to Roujeark. Then the moment passed, and he turned away.

'Be released. Let us go.' Suddenly the armists were loosed from the spell. Dazed, they followed Theonar back down the steps. On their way back to the others, both chased after elusive thoughts that flittered ahead of their groping minds, refusing to be tied down or retained. Whose voice did we just hear? How does he know such things?

Their comrades waited for them with fearful expectancy in their faces, wary of what dreadful magic might have rubbed off on the explorers.

'Curillian? Is all well?' Lancoir asked, but his question was overtaken by others.

'What is it? What did you see?'

'Whence comes the light?'

'Is the Tournament over? Have we won?'

Curillian looked at them, blinking. He still felt foggy-headed and disorientated by the dazzling light. The glistening Tear still seemed to fill his vision.

'It is a tear,' he said slowly. 'Left here by Avatar. His bequest to the Mountain.'

Caiasan burst forth in excited response, sounding more cogent than any had heard him for a long time. 'Avatar? The same Avatar who founded the League of Wizardry? Who was the first forefather of King Lithan of Kalimar?' Curillian could only nod. 'The same Avatar who slew the Fire-demon and singlehandedly vanquished his great armies? The noblest and greatest being who ever was or shall be?' The young scribe was suddenly showing off his knowledge, reminding his countrymen why they had put up with him all these weeks. Curillian and Roujeark could say nothing in response, so Theonar spoke instead, in gentle correction.

'Verily, that is he. Avatar. High King of the elves, first and eldest. But he did not slay the great demon, only defeated, banished him;

a feat which nearly cost him his life. Next to him Lithan is but a child, he who outshines all others that remain today. Avatar was the greatest and fairest of all the elves, for in him was found the sum of elven greatness: strength, beauty, power, wisdom, kindness and grace.' Southilar could contain his curiosity no longer.

'Sir Theonar!' he barked. 'How do you know such things? You speak of this long-dead elf as if you knew him personally!'

Theonar shook his head sadly. 'Not dead, only gone. And no, I did not know him, though I would that I had.' Raising his head, he looked his lord in the eye. 'It is my fate to know what others know not, and to have seen what others cannot conceive.' All were now looking at the two tall men, locked in confrontation.

'No, that's not good enough,' snapped Southilar, spitting his words in sudden anger and pointed a gloved fist at his subordinate. 'Enough evasion; no more of your oh-so-humble dissembling and wordsmithery. You'll tell me, your lord, exactly who you are and where you come from, right now.' The contention between the two men, which before had been concealed like glowing embers under ash, now burst forth in flame, plain for all to see. On the one hand, Southilar's bristling anger and brusque demands; on the other, Theonar, standing in quiet defiance.

'You would be wise, Lord of the Pegasus,' Theonar said, still not raising his voice, 'not to insist here and now. Whatever you guess, however much you fear, you must lay aside your demands of me. Greater things are at stake. My identity and my past are for me alone to know. You need me, not so much to win this Tournament, but to help get us out of this Mountain alive. With your questions unanswered you will have my help, or not at all.' The two men's eyes bored holes in each other, waging a silent war of wills.

Curillian intervened. 'Come, Southilar, Theonar, we need you both. Lay aside your quarrel for the time being. There will be plenty of time for you to resolve it later. For now, there's a tournament to win, and a wizard's lair to escape.' The tension prevailed a moment longer and then Theonar turned away, striding off down the hall.

'Come then,' he called over his shoulder. 'Let's get this done. The guardsman's question I can answer. No, it is not over, we have not won. This is merely the start of the next stage.'

❊

III

The Wizard's Lair

THEONAR Strode off down the hall, leaving the monument and its light behind. The rest of them followed him, plunging into what seemed to be utter darkness. They had no more torches, and no more means of conjuring light, so they braced themselves for a dark journey. But as the radiance fell further and further behind, they came to realise that the halls in which they walked were otherwise lit. The great wall-braziers were out of reach and without fuel, but from mysterious apertures high overhead filtered the soft radiance of starlight, as if from window slits in the mountainside. In that celestial light they saw that though their path wound much round corners and up and down stairs, the grand ecclesiastical feel all about them remained strong. Rarely were they without pillars and statues on either side, and never once was the high ceiling anything but ornate, filled with the adornment of many years' abiding.

What did change was the feel of the air. They all marked it to one degree or another. The air seemed thicker, somehow charged. It seemed to tickle their nostrils and eyelids, and ever and anon they would feel strange sparks about their person. To their ears came faint voices in tongues unguessable, whispering of enduring secrets and deep knowledge. An acrid taste was on their tongues. Bittersweet, like the aftermath of perfumed gunpowder, the odours of long-cast spells filled their noses and infused their imaginations with peculiar thoughts and strange imaginings. They all walked in a daze, suffused with sensations they had never felt before, at once wondrous and unsettling.

Now there was a carpet beneath their feet, a long, unflinchingly straight carpet of a shifting midnight blue that never seemed the same colour twice. To match the carpet, the bare walls were hung with gigantic tapestries that went on as far as the eye could see – huge, fantastically coloured needlework that must have been centuries in the making. In the imperfect light they could not discern them clearly, but they portrayed scenes of myth and history. They were in an immense corridor of tapestried history. The skilful threads showed wars waging, nations rising and falling, people toiling, monuments lifting and tragedies unfolding. Elves and men were shown, armists, dwarves, orcs and trolls. Kings and wizards were depicted, serfs and merchants, diplomats and warriors, traders and priests. Good and evil intertwined, joys and sorrows.

'It cannot be,' gasped Antaya. They all looked and saw what he saw. The very end of the tapestry showed their own exploits in the Tournament so far. The slaying of the great beast and the wreck of the bireme, the travails of the men of Aranar; the tapestry was alive, growing still further. Its newest threads wove themselves before their very eyes with no hand visible, and they saw other parties of men and dwarves struggling elsewhere in the Mountain. There was the Hendarian bishop, puzzling over a riddle in the rock while his king waited impatiently; there were the sun-darkened men of the south, treading warily down a rodent-infested tunnel; and there were the dwarves, toiling to clear a blocked doorway. Their deeds were being recorded even as they performed them.

'Surely Kulothiel is up there somewhere,' wondered Roujeark aloud, 'sitting with a pen and dictating this magic.'

They rewalked the corridor with necks craned upwards in awe. Each was astounded to find his own life recorded, and they became strung out as every man and armist stopped to gaze at his own story. A strangled sob rent the air, but they were all too sunk in their own little worlds to heed each other. The wondrous hall suddenly became a place of nightmare where painful memories from the past rose up to assail those who thought they had left them behind. Roujeark was full of suppressed anger when he saw the many wasted years of waiting in the threads, but his anger turned to tears of anguish when he traced them back to the night of his father's death. Through blurred vision he saw the fallen Dubarnik, and his wrathful killers standing over him. When he managed to wrench himself away, he almost stumbled into Lancoir, who stood still as stone, gazing up at the tapestry. He had found his own portion, and now he was rooted to the spot, emotion seizing his face and making his body quiver. Roujeark stood by him and looked upon the valiant knight unjustly slain by envious rivals. He shuddered, remembering the tale of woe Lancoir had told him under the eaves of Tol Ankil; he never thought he would live to see it retold with his own eyes.

Curillian walked further than any of them to find the beginning of his tale. When, much later, Lancoir and Roujeark reached him, they found him transfixed. They had seen his great deeds as king; the warrior armist crowned at the peak of his powers; his legendary deeds in the Second War of Kurundar made real; his service to Lancearon and the strange paths of his youthful exile. Yet, in the end, his story also began, just as theirs, with the loss of a father. They stood in solidarity with him for a while, sharing his pain. When at last they moved on, unspeaking, they all felt a much closer connection with the armists beside them.

Curillian's life, long as it was, came and went, yet it was still but a breath in the great tale of years. Using the intermittent light, Curillian interpreted the scenes for them.

'Look,' said he, 'see Lancearon's campaigns and the rise of the Silver Empire...the days of the Great Union...the First War of Kurundar, and the final battle at the feet of Oron Cavardul.' And so they walked back in history, back to where the knowledgeable king's lore faded and his identifications became guesswork. They passed back beyond the Great Betrayal and the dawn of men into the days of the Second Chapter, further back than any mortal could peer with certainty. The scenes became the stuff of distant legends, of ancient plagues and mythical wars. They walked on, overwhelmed by the weight of years, stepping into primeval chapters of the world when the elves were young and first walked on Astrom.

Finally, when it seemed like they had been walking for years, they reached the beginning. That tall, impossibly beautiful pair of elves, must surely be Avatar and Mírianna, rising out of a fallen star to become the first living souls to inhabit the world. Then they saw something that none of them could understand. Serene, majestic, unfathomable, it stood at the very beginning, hovering over the waters, though whether it was a person, a storm cloud, a star shining, or something else altogether, they could not tell.

'It is Prélan,' Curillian said at last, his voice thick with awe.

'How do you know?' whispered Roujeark, equally awestruck. Curillian pointed.

'He is at the beginning, but He has been there all along, all through the tale of life...' Roujeark looked and saw that the upper edges of the divine depiction swept into the topmost reaches of the tapestry. What he had taken for a decorative border was in fact the unsleeping presence of Prélan. Roujeark fell to his knees, unable to move for the moment. He wept uncontrollably. They all wept, without knowing why. When at last the tears subsided, Roujeark spoke.

'If nothing else awaits me here, I would have come just for this.'

Curillian rose, and then raised him up too. 'The Almighty Father is not just in the tapestry, Roujeark. He's all around. He's in here.' He tapped Roujeark's chest. 'He has always been with you, and always will be.'

Roujeark stared at his king, marvelling at how attuned to Prélan he was, how much he knew, how deeply he believed. The king reached out both arms and clasped both Roujeark and Lancoir by the neck. They linked arms with him and with each other. In a triangle, they summoned fresh strength.

'We have glimpsed the glory of the One and Only and have not perished,' Curillian declared. 'We will go on. Let us finish this.'

Having now come to the end of the tapestry, they noticed for the first time that Sir Theonar was still ahead of them. It seemed he had not stopped, nor been affected as they had been. He stood, leaning against a great doorway, which stood at the end of the hallway. All this time they had been wandering down the same great corridor. The doorway was immense, covered with gilt inlay a foot wide and set with glowing red runes that none could read. Yet whatever they said, the great gates stood open, and so they passed through. They found themselves in another corridor, full of closed doors. They were about to press on when they saw one door that was open, on the left-hand side of the passage.

Walking through it, they stumbled upon another marvel. From a viewing platform they gazed down on a huge, living map that filled the chamber. There was Astrom, with all its mountain ranges, rivers, valleys, forests and plains. There too were the great nations, full of cities and roads and all the handiwork of mortals and elves. And what was more, they could actually walk down and tread the fields and coasts. It was in there that the others caught up with them, having finally broken free of their own private reveries in the hall of history. The men of Aranar found their own lands where horses foaled and clans vied; the armists explored the long coastlines and mountainous backbone of Maristonia. Curillian paced across to Kalimar, tracing out their journey with giant steps. He came to stand by Oron Amular, so obvious now he knew where to find it. It stood up tall amid the Black Mountains like a spire of pearl out of crumpled rock.

'What did they use it for?' called Sir Lindal from his Unicorn lands.

'If not merely to marvel at,' answered Curillian, 'a map like this could be of great use in planning out campaigns and considering policies.' He was thinking of his own strategic maps, which until now he had thought large and unrivalled. 'All this time the wizards bestrode our world, and we knew it not,' he muttered to himself.

⋏

Reluctantly they left the map chamber and continued on down the passage. It reminded Lancoir of the imposing corridor that led to the royal throne room in the palace at Mariston, with its alcoves and high ceiling, but this place was altogether more unnerving. A cold draft came down to meet them from somewhere up ahead, and they perceived another great doorway. Passing through it, they had their breath taken away again.

They were in another colossal chamber, through which the path ran straight like a highway. About the road were strange shapes, like waves in the rock. There were four of them, each issuing from a gateway above and each running down to meet the main road with tributary paths. The lowest was also the broadest, as if designed to accommodate many wizards marching abreast, and each successive one was narrower and descended from a higher starting point.

'It's the strangest group of paths I've ever seen,' exclaimed Roujeark. Curillian moved past him, clasping his shoulder.

'Indeed, but can you imagine it when they were in use. These roadways full of warrior-wizards and mage-lords marching to war against the enemies of the League,' he paused, overtaken with awe at the picture he had painted. 'What a sight that must have been.'

A

The main path squeezed through a narrow section between the raised areas on either side, shepherding the party into a short tunnel. When it opened out again, they saw rock walls smooth as masonry running towards the cavern's end, which curved like the rim of a goblet. A great closed gateway awaited them there, but between them and it the walls of the cavern narrowed again to form a bottleneck. Standing guard either side of that bottleneck were two titanic figures. Immense figures of stone, they stood with their backs and shoulders braced against the curved ceiling of the cavern, as if they were holding it up. Unarmed and unadorned, they gazed down on the trespassers who approached their feet. The men of Aranar quailed under the baleful stare of the guardians, and hung back. Even Curillian's followers were unnerved, so that he was alone when he drew level with the giants. He came up only to their shins.

They watched as the king stopped, laying hand to his sword hilt as if warned of peril by some extra sense. Curillian drew his great blade and held it down by his side. Then he moved off again. He passed over a delicate red line on the floor, and straightaway there was an ominous grating sound. Far above, stone eyelids snapped open and the previously immobile arms flexed and started to move. The men of Aranar fell over themselves trying to get away, Roujeark cowered back, and even Lancoir stood aghast, but not Curillian. He was already moving, sword up and ready to fight. He sped past the feet of the giants and into the open space before the doorway. He took up a defensive stance, sword brandished, but the giants were only just lowering their arms. With slow stiffness they reached down, as if to grasp at the intruder, but then their fingers detached and dropped to the floor.

Only they were not fingers at all, for they took on a new shape as soon as they hit the ground. What rose up were small warriors, faceless and terrible. They wore no clothing or armour but seemed to have jet black skin of some malleable metal. There were ten of them, five from each right hand, and all were differently armed, sporting everything from nets and tridents to cutlasses and flails. As one they faced Curillian, standing between him and the door. He had just long enough to stare into their unseen eyes before they leapt into action. To the terrified onlookers it seemed as though Curillian must be overwhelmed by that first onslaught, but somehow he slewed his way through them, hewing left and right as he passed them. The metallic warriors veered away from his blade and jumped through the air, fluid as molten metal and agile as tumblers.

'CURILLIAN!' Lancoir bellowed, running to join the fight. For a few heartbeats the rest of them could only watch, mesmerised by the sight of the two armist warriors doing battle, all alone and beset by faceless foes. Then the other armists plunged into the fray, and some of the men of Aranar would have gone too, had Southilar not held them back. He thought all had obeyed his craven order, but Theonar went forward regardless.

'Sir Theonar! Get back here!' Southilar shouted after him, but he was ignored. Yet Theonar went not to the fight, but to the right hand of the two guardians, who, having deployed their fighting denizens, had straightened up to resume their vigil. Using any crack or hold he could find, he shinned up the great leg like a squirrel. His countrymen were agape, not sure which spectacle to watch: the whirling fight or the dauntless climb. Curillian and his comrades were hard-pressed, unable to land a proper blow on enemies who moved like greased smoke. Only the king's fabulous blade found its mark, and though it came away unscathed, it had done no damage. The other blades did not fare so well, being chipped or turned by the devious metal their foes were made of. Roujeark aimed a blast of fire at one of them, but his victim just soaked up the fire, almost revelling in it, before hurling it backward with redoubled fury. He dove out of the way, robes singed and face scorched, and then had to get up and flee as his adversary pursued him.

Lionenn was swinging his mace with might and main but couldn't seem to land a blow. Instead he himself took a pummelling, but each time he somehow managed to get to his feet again. Caréysin's arrows had no effect whatsoever, even those that hit their marks, and his firing was put to a stop when a black metal figure hurled him bodily against the wall. Andil was bleeding from a dozen cuts and retreated out of the fight. Findor took a sword-thrust in his arm and cried out, but Lancoir came to his rescue by bulling over the warrior who had wounded him. Then Lancoir himself went down, cracked round the back of the head by the haft of a trident. Antaya found himself without a sword and Aleinus was backed into a corner; it was looking bleak for the armists, and only Curillian fought on unimpaired.

Death was staring the Royal Guards in the face when suddenly Theonar leapt down from on high. Landing in their midst, cat-like, he took off at a run and nimbly somersaulted over the enemy. He ran for the closed doorway, and the ten warriors suddenly stopped in the middle of their attacks. It was as if they were alerted to some hidden peril. Forgetting the armists, they chased after Theonar with terrible speed. Theonar reached the doorway and slotted home a giant key. The ten were almost on him, weapons outstretched, when he turned the key with an almighty clunk. Some giant mechanism had been set in motion, and hidden wheels turned. The ten warriors stopped dead in their tracks, then turned and scuttled back to their parent statues. They clambered up the stone guardians like dark monkeys in the forests of the south. When they reached the right hands, they seemed to fuse back into the stonework, and lo, they were fingers again. In eerie silence, there was no hint that they had ever been anything but inanimate.

The sounds of their retreat echoed round the chamber and slowly died away. The men of Aranar looked on speechless, unable to believe what they had witnessed. But when they looked away from the stone statues, they saw Theonar standing by doors which were swinging open. His countrymen came towards him fearfully, half-expecting the grim warriors to leap down again when they passed the red line, and wary of Theonar himself, who seemed to have become virtually superhuman all of a sudden. Theonar stood aside respectfully to let the Jeantar past. Southilar eyed him darkly, more suspicious than grateful, but Caiasan blurted out, 'How...how did you do that?' His voice was laced with amazement. The tall knight shrugged modestly.

'I saw the key hanging from the right-hand statue. I guessed, rightly as it turns out, that it would open the door.'

'But the way you climbed...' Caiasan persisted, as his companions filed past behind him. Theonar turned him by the shoulder and prodded him onwards.

'Caiasan, my friend, when a man is pressed, he can do things he would normally think impossible. Necessity is a great means of redefining your limits.'

Back in the cavern, Curillian was tending to his armists. Andil had light wounds, not serious, but both Caréysin and Lionenn were battered and shaken. Roujeark, Aleinus and Antaya were unhurt, and Lancoir was just groggy from his head-blow, yet Findor was in a bad way. Covered in blood, he was helped to sit upright by his friends. A sword had torn a huge gash in his arm. Nerveless, it now hung uselessly by his side. Roujeark tore a strip of red-brown linen from his robe, which Curillian then tied above the wound to stem the bleeding. Findor looked pale and shaken, and they had to haul him to his feet and support him as he walked.

'It's a miracle we didn't suffer greater loss,' said Antaya as they paced slowly.

'Indeed,' agreed the king. 'If Theonar hadn't acted when he did, then we would all be dead.' Roujeark swallowed hard as that realisation hit him. The Aranese knight was waiting for them inside the elaborately fashioned doorway.

'That was a mighty climb, sir knight, and a daring leap. My armists and I are beholden to you.' Theonar bowed low, graciously accepting the thanks.

'Come,' said Lancoir. 'Let's see where the horse-lords have got to.' He led the way and the others followed him. Curillian motioned Theonar on ahead.

'Go on ahead, friend Theonar, we will only be going slowly with Findor here. Feel free to leave us behind and join your comrades.' Theonar shook his head in declination.

'No, lord king, by your leave I'd like to stay and walk by your side. I can no longer abide the company of the Jeantar.' Curillian nodded his consent.

'Sire,' said Andil, plainly concerned, 'we cannot let the men of Aranar get too far ahead. What if Southilar should reach the finish line before us? We've come so far, I couldn't bear to lose now.'

'We can go only as fast as our slowest armist,' replied the king. 'But fear not, Antaya, it's not over yet. Let Southilar try and fail. Then it will be my turn.'

They were on a broad, well-made staircase that led up from the door. Wall torches burned, as if in welcome, and illuminated their way. When the stairs levelled off, they walked down a passageway filled with doors and side passageways. They smelled the musty aroma of dormitories, classrooms, armouries, refectories and storehouses long disused. They caught glimpses of the ordinary day-to-day life of wizards, but they had no time to stop and explore.

They could hear the sounds of Southilar's party up ahead, and they were content to not hurry until those sounds took on a different note. Suddenly they heard alarm, and they picked up their pace. They hastened up some more stairs, and along more passageways. They heard swords being wielded, but when they came upon the men of Aranar, they saw no enemies. Southilar's party stood on the far side of a great fissure, across which stretched a flimsy-looking bridge. The sword strokes they had heard were not aimed at any foe, but against the bridge itself. They caught Sir Hardos, Southilar's right hand man, in mid-swing as he hacked at the bridge. He looked up, red-faced, and seemed momentarily ashamed of what he was doing.

The armists and Theonar came up short, appalled by what they saw, but Southilar did not relent; in fact, he added two more men-at-arms to help Hardos in his work. Together they hewed at the bridge and succeeded in breaking it asunder. Shorn off from its shorings, it groaned and toppled into the chasm. Above the rending and the clattering of its fall, Southilar hailed them.

'Thank you for all your help so far Curillian, but I go on alone from here. This is a tournament after all, and I'll not share my glory with you.' With that he turned, and he and his party hurried away.

The armists and Theonar stood aghast on the wrong side of the chasm. The treacherous Aranese soon disappeared into the gloom, while below them nothing could be seen of the bridge they had destroyed. Peering over the edge, they could see no bottom, for the light of the wall-torches was soon swallowed up in the black emptiness.

'Treacherous scum!' exclaimed Theonar, with surprising vehemence. He faced his companions. 'This, my friends, is why I no longer wish to serve that man. What a coward – he is so afraid of losing to you, lord king, in a straight contest, that he has stooped to this perfidy.' The tall knight turned his anger upon himself. 'I heard him speak of you as unbeatable so many times – I should have seen this coming.'

Curillian, taken aback by the revelation, patted the knight's shoulder. 'Don't berate yourself, my friend, this betrayal was not your doing.' Theonar balled his fists, staring after his vanished master.

'I will make amends for this,' he promised. 'Curillian, I will challenge that man for the clan lordship and depose him if it's the last thing I do. I should have done it long ago; now it's well overdue. Then, when I rule in Jaglalir, I shall make good Southilar's actions and clear the stain of this betrayal.' Curillian looked out over the chasm with him.

'My friend, I wish you success, but let there be no debt between us.' Theonar looked down at him with fierce earnestness.

'Lord king, be it debt or unprompted kindness on my part, you will need my help soon. This Mountain Tournament is just the beginning. Greater tests lie ahead. And if ever I become Jeantar, the better shall I be able to help you.' Curillian clasped his hand and shoulder.

'Let it be so. Sir Theonar of the Pegasus, you shall ever have the friendship of Maristonia, and whatever challenges lie in the future, let us face them together. But first, let's find a way to get across this gap. There's a tournament to be won, and Southilar must be stopped.'

While the two of them had been talking, Lancoir and the others had formulated a plan. The captain ducked out of the belt-rope still coiled over his shoulders and dropped it on the ground.

'Apparently no one stopped to get their belts back,' he said tersely, with a savage grin.

'So let us use them,' said Roujeark. 'We must be able to get across somehow with these. Look, the posts of the bridge are still there – can we loop the end of the rope across one of them somehow?' Antaya took the rope and hefted it doubtfully in his hands. Andil, who had a much better throwing arm, took the responsibility instead. Sighting the post, he cast the rope out over the chasm. He missed his mark the first time, but second time around he succeeded in looping the end belt around the bridge-post. He gave a firm tug, and it held. He then gripped the rope's other end hard, preparing to swing himself across.

'Wait!' barked Lancoir. Taking the rope from Andil, he tugged again, much harder this time. The bridge-post cracked, snapped and fell into the chasm. Grim-faced, Lancoir hauled the rope back in, wooden spar and all. He dumped it back in Andil's hands. 'You're welcome,' he grunted. Andil just stared dumbly down at it as he held it in shaking hands.

'To think I nearly trusted my weight to that,' he whispered to Aleinus beside him.

'Now what are we going to do?' demanded Aleinus pleadingly. Lancoir cuffed him over the back of the head.

'Shut up and let me think, that's what,' he growled.

'Let me try something,' Roujeark volunteered. He took the rope and had his companions tie it underneath his armpits. He looked at Curillian, smiling bravely. 'Swing me across,' he said simply. Curillian hid his surprise.

'Are you sure, Roujeark? It's not enough just to get across – you also have to swing the next armist over by yourself.' Roujeark nodded resolutely.

'I have newfound strength I never knew I had.' Curillian considered for a moment, then nodded assent. He took up the end of the rope as Roujeark steeled himself and sat on the edge of the abyss.

'Let me,' said Theonar. 'I'm stronger.' Not many could have said that to the King of Maristonia, still less been willing to actually say it, but Curillian acquiesced. Theonar took up the rope in strong hands and paid out plenty of slack into the darkness.

'Whenever you're ready, master wizard,' he said. Roujeark nodded, gulped, and slid himself off into thin air. With a stifled yelp he dropped suddenly for a few feet and came up hard as Theonar caught him. Gasping, he took a few moments to come to terms with dangling above the unguessed depths, and then he turned and kicked off the wall, launching himself further out. Theonar followed him with the rope, paying out extra length as was needed. Gradually Roujeark gathered momentum until he was swinging wildly from one side to the other. Fearfully, Roujeark let go of the rope, which he had been clutching for dear life, and reached for the rift's far lip. There was still a bracket of wood where the bridge-post had once been fixed to the rock, and he aimed for that. Coming close, he snapped his hands on thin air before swaying back out of reach. The next time, he seized it and held fast to it against the backward tug of the rope, which was almost at its full reach. He let out a shrill yell of triumph, his heart pounding in his own ears. Gathering his wits and his strength, he found tiny toeholds with his boots and started to climb up. The rope was stretched taut when he wriggled up onto the level ground, and he lay precariously on the very edge, lest he pull it out of Theonar's reach on the far side. Slowly, his breathing calmed.

His companions cheered his effort then prepared to follow. There wasn't enough rope left on their side to tie around themselves, so Aleinus, the lightest of them, just had to cling onto it for dear life. When he propelled himself off the edge, his weight nearly pulled Roujeark down into the void, but he just about managed to steady himself. Aleinus' weight carried him across the blackness to ricochet off the wall on Roujeark's side. Bracing himself, Roujeark strained against the weight and waited until Aleinus' momentum expired and left him dangling. Then, concentrating mind and body, he hauled upwards. At first the effort was too much, and he slipped forward himself, but digging his boots into the broken bases of the posts, he stopped himself and strained again. Hand over hand he hauled, and then suddenly the weight lessened, as if new strength suddenly flooded into his system. White-faced, Aleinus came above the rim and latched himself onto the side. With relief, Roujeark felt the strain disappear and he switched his effort into helping Aleinus up and over. The two of them lay panting side by side for some time before they could muster the energy to think of their stranded comrades.

Roujeark now untied himself, and holding one end jointly with the guardsman, they flung the rope back to Theonar's waiting hands.

The knight seized it and jumped out into the chasm without a second thought. With two of them now hauling, the job of bringing him up was much easier, and when he was beside them it became even easier still. Antaya came next, followed by Lancoir, Caréysin and Lionenn. Curillian stayed behind to help Findor, whose left arm hung useless by his side. Praying to Prélan for extra strength, the king took his wounded comrade under his arm, gripping him tight about the waist. With his other hand he grasped the rope and launched them out across. Many willing hands brought them safely over, but even so Curillian's arm was burning by the time he let Findor go.

And there they all were, safely across the chasm. They gave themselves a few moments to recover, then went on again. They met further obstacles as they went, other gaps and holes in the tunnel with dreadful drops beneath, but none so wide that they couldn't leap across, albeit with their hearts in their mouths. Other times they had to inch along narrow ledges, not wide enough even for the length of their boots. Slowly but surely, with hearts thudding, they traversed the hazards. They had only just negotiated the longest of these when a cracking sound split the still air of the tunnel. Curillian looked down at the floor beneath his feet, which was already starting to crumble into the gap.

'RUN!' he shouted. They all took off with the speed of terror, yelling at the tops of their voices as the floor gave way behind them. The gap was widening as it swallowed the tunnel floor, snapping at their heels even as they sprinted. Most of them succeeded in reaching a point of safety where the ground held firm, but Lancoir was hindmost and in real trouble. Curillian saw the gap catching up with him and hung back at the edge of the solid ground to help him. The captain of the guard was only too aware of his peril, and he put on a burst of speed…but it wasn't enough. With a great yell he threw himself into a despairing dive as the ground gave way beneath him, and at the very same moment Curillian lunged back towards him. Lancoir tumbled into the blackness, an uncharacteristic look of fear etched into his face, but their outstretched hands met. For a split second they fell together before they came up hard. Theonar's long arms had caught Curillian's feet. The tall knight had been dragged well over the rim himself, but his legs in turn were held fast by Lionenn.

'Hurry,' called Roujeark. 'I don't trust this ground.' The king's grip was unshakeable, and slowly the fear left Lancoir's eyes as they were hauled up together. Muscles bulging on his tattooed arms, Lionenn barely needed help from the others to lift his comrades out. Wearily they were hauled onto the firm ground and lay there, panting. Sweat poured down their faces. Slowly they dusted themselves down and waited for the ringing of their own cries of fear to recede from their ears. Willing hands helped them away from the edge and then, stumbling, the whole party put as much ground between themselves and the gaping chasm as they could.

⋏

'**W**e should get out of this tunnel before it gives way again,' said Roujeark fearfully.

'Do you hear that?' said Theonar, checking them. Faint but unmistakeable, there came the sounds of combat from somewhere up ahead.

'It sounds like Southilar's reward has been to run headlong into trouble,' remarked Curillian. 'Let's see what's become of him.'

Soon they could see a fringe of ruddy light which marked where the tunnel came to an end. The clash of swords and cries of pain came louder now, but when they came to the doorway, they found it led only into a narrow space. Almost immediately they were brought up short by a smooth curving face of rock rising high above them. To left and right were narrow pathways squeezed between this obstacle and the cavern walls on the other side. There was only room for one to walk abreast. A few more clashes of steel, some thudding noises, and then the din ceased. After that, all they could hear was some faint whimpering. Curillian held them back from rushing.

'We do not know what lies ahead,' he whispered. 'Just be ready.'

They all brought up weapons and cautiously trod forwards. They branched left and right in two groups: Curillian, Lancoir, Caréysin and Findor to the left; Theonar, Roujeark, Andil, Lionenn, Antaya and Aleinus to the right. Slowly they followed the curving rock wall round until it started to lower. When they had reached the end, and it had come down nearly to their own height, Curillian paused and peeked round the end. Glancing across the cavern, he saw Theonar looking out from the opposite side. They were behind a great amphitheatre, whose immaculately carved tiers of seats swept back and above to the top of the wall that faced the tunnel mouth. Yet they both ignored the amphitheatre, for their eyes went immediately to the armoured figure standing at the edge of its central platform. It appeared to be only the statue of a mighty warrior, wrought from black iron, helmeted head gazing down at the floor as it rested upon a great two-handed sword.

Commanding the platform from which a speaker could address the whole amphitheatre, the warrior stood unmoving, except for a wisp of unseen wind which stirred the red plume atop his helm. He barred the way to a great doorway in the cavern wall behind him, which could only be reached by a narrow bridge connected to the platform. Between door and platform was a gulf of nothingness.

Curillian stepped out of cover, moving out onto the platform. Only as he did so did he notice the men of Aranar, lying about as if flung asunder by some great force. They all looked much the worse for wear. Some had scored mail or dented swords, others had helms knocked askew and the wind driven from them. Yet no sign was there of what had caused their discomfiture. It was as if a band of enemies had descended, smashed them about and then vanished. Only Southilar yet stood, occupying one of the lower tiers. Sword drawn, he glared at the warrior. His face was suffused with a mixture of anger and shame. Only slowly did he become aware of the armists' presence as Curillian's followers filed out behind their king and Sir Theonar. The Jeantar tried defiantly to meet the armist king's gaze, but he soon broke down and looked away.

'What happened here?' asked Roujeark, going to where Caiasan the scribe lay crumpled against the stone, quite subdued.

'We tried to get across,' he managed to whisper through bruised lips, 'but he denied us. We none of us could get past him.'

As he was speaking, barely heard by anyone other than Roujeark, Curillian had been slowly approaching the immobile warrior. He still showed no signs of life. Blade in hand, Curillian stepped closer still. Suddenly the helmeted head snapped up as if some mechanism had just kicked into action. Through a thin slit in the visor, his dark eyes glared out. They were like no eyes Curillian had ever seen before, and he had faced many kinds of enemy. Yet where the eyes were dark and hostile, the voice was fair and courteous, despite being given a metallic edge by the helm.

'Hail noble competitor, my master's congratulations on passing the challenges and reaching this place. Victory is within your grasp, if only you can overcome the final test.'

'Beware Curillian,' croaked Caiasan's voice in warning. 'He spoke even thus to us, before attacking us.' Curillian tightened his grip on his sword but stared levelly at the guardian.

'And what, pray, is the final test?' he asked, even though he knew the answer.

'You must defeat me,' the warrior declared. With those words, he brought up his greatsword and adopted a defensive stance. Lancoir and Theonar came up, weapons ready, but Curillian waved them back.

'No, my friends. Leave this to me.' Looking back at the knight, he spoke to him, 'Come, stranger, you don't want to fight me. I've reached the end of this accursed Tournament. There is no need to fight.'

'Nevertheless,' said the knight, 'there are times in life when one must fight. Now is just such a time.'

'Look,' snapped Curillian, 'I've been nearly drowned, crushed, incinerated and slaughtered, and I'm angry. I'm in a mood to speak to Kulothiel and claim my prize.'

'Don't be a fool, lord king, who but my master bade me hold this bridge against all comers? The Tournament is not over and remains unwon while I stand here undefeated. You've slain great beasts, unlocked many doors and survived all the wizard's snares, but conquer me or it's all for nothing, and you can go back to Maristonia with your tail between your legs.'

Swift as a striking snake, the knight brought his greatsword down in a great arc upon the armist king's head. All those looking on thought he would be cut down where he stood, but at the last moment he brought the Sword of Maristonia up to parry. There was an explosion of light and sparks as the two great blades met, each a match for the other. The two combatants recoiled from the force of the encounter, and then began to circle one another slowly. Curillian tested his opponent with some probing feints, looking for an opening, but the knight was equal to it, agile and watchful. Then suddenly the knight struck again, darting forward in a quick thrust which Curillian had to turn aside. A third and a fourth time their blades clashed, and still neither managed to gain an advantage. Roujeark was struck by how similarly they moved.

Lancoir looked on anxiously. Curillian was the finest warrior he knew, stronger and faster than any, but he was not at his best. He was tired and moving slowly. The Tournament had taken its toll. Curillian still moved well, with the customary footwork of a lifelong swordsman, but there was none of the dazzlingly swift ferocity with which his king normally destroyed his enemies. Suddenly, as if to disprove Lancoir's silent doubts, Curillian leapt into action, abandoning his watchful stance and throwing himself into an attack. He feinted left and struck right. Peeling away in the blink of an eye, he ducked under his foe's elbow and made to cut at his back, but the knight had turned. The manoeuvre would have been the end of any ordinary warrior, but the knight anticipated the move. He blocked the killing blow and threw the armist back. Curillian came again in a blur of blows, but each one was warded off. Back and forth they fenced, blades working so swiftly that the onlookers could barely follow them. It was a mesmerising display of swordsmanship, but at the end of it Curillian was no closer to winning.

At last the fighters separated again, stepping back and regarding one another.

'You cannot defeat me, armist,' declared the knight, 'for I am the equal of any swordsman.'

Curillian refused to be drawn. He just glared at his foe, breathing hard. The knight swayed slightly but was unhurt and watchful. In much less time than this, the knights of Aranar had been beaten down one after another, and the watching armists knew with a chill certainty that if Curillian could not prevail, then none of them would.

Roujeark knew that as well as any of them. He considered wading in and trying to use his magic, but some intuition forestalled him. Magic would not win this contest. No, this was Curillian's moment, and he would have to win with his sword or with his bare hands.

Curillian stared wearily at the knight, summoning up the energy to try again. He could not remember a challenge like this. How long had it been since he'd met his equal? Not since the darkest days of the Second War, when Kurundar's fell champions had yet walked the earth. He was unnerved by how easily the knight was anticipating his moves, almost as if he knew what he was thinking. Pushing the thought aside, he launched himself forward. Running at the knight, he jumped high to one side of him and swung down a killing blow with all his might. Yet the knight danced back knowingly, and all Curillian's momentum went to waste. Caught off balance when he landed, the knight's counterstroke came fast. Curillian was only just able to fend it off, but the force of it sent him sprawling.

'Get up, armist king,' the knight said. 'We're not done yet.'

Now Lancoir was really worried. To see Curillian worsted was so rare he could not remember the last time. Going into every battle alongside the great king, he had had the utmost confidence in his survival and victory - but now? He felt a sharp twinge of doubt ripple up his spine like a shiver. With a knot in his stomach, he knew he would have to fight next if Curillian failed, and how could he hope to succeed where his king failed? He might intervene and save his master from death, but they would be defeated, now, at the bitter end. To come so far and fail in the end was unbearable.

Curillian picked himself up, ignoring the screams of his weary muscles. He dug deep into his vast reserves of stamina and attacked again. But whether by hacking and bludgeoning or by trickery and guile, he could not find a way through. After every attempt, the forbidding guardian of the bridge still barred the way. Was he even weary? He showed no sign of it. *Damn it,* thought Curillian, *I will not be beaten.* He struck with hellfire fury and drove his opponent back under a rain of blows. The two warriors were locked in a struggle that was much more than just a swordfight, but a mental clashing of wills. Curillian felt as if he had transcended to a new plane of reality, where every aspect of his being was bound up in the fight. Finally, he succeeded in getting a thrust behind the knight's guard, but there was no force in the blow. He only managed to slice the wrist, cutting just deep enough to get through the armour. But even as he did so, he felt a sharp pain in his own wrist. Crying out in shock and fear, he looked disbelievingly at his hand. It was cut and bleeding, even where he had hit his enemy. Reeling away, holding his wounded hand, Curillian felt an unfamiliar panic rising. *Prélan help me.* Out of the corner of his eye, he saw Lancoir dashing in to attack the knight, all anger and passion. There was a brief flurry of swords, but then the knight's elbow smashed into Lancoir's face and sent him lurching away.

Prélan help me, Curillian thought again, praying this time. *How do I beat him? He fights like...like me...* Sudden suspicion flooded into his mind and gave birth to a flash of insight. Wiping a hand across his bleeding mouth, he smiled grimly at his opponent.

'You'd beat anyone who came here, wouldn't you?' he called to him. The knight stared back impassively. 'You bleed, I bleed, eh? Man, woman, armist, elf, dwarf – you'd defeat them all. How can anyone defeat themselves? Bravo to the victor, who in winning slays himself. I don't know whether you be a living being or a phantom of wizardry, but Kulothiel has surpassed himself in this last challenge, hasn't he? Maybe this Tournament is unwinnable? Well, you may be my equal, but no one is the equal of Prélan, the lord of battle, and *He* is my strength.'

One last time he ran at the knight, legs pumping in reckless speed. The knight took up a stance ready to deflect him, but at the last moment Curillian flung his sword up in the air. The spectators gaped open-mouthed in awed surprise. The knight was distracted by the unexpected abandonment of the sword and Curillian seized his split-second opportunity with both hands. He cannoned into his enemy, knocking him flying. With a crash they landed together near the bridge. The force of the impact and the unforgiving armour nearly did for Curillian, but he somehow kept his focus. On his back, the knight's heavy plate armour put him at a serious disadvantage, whereas Curillian's cunning mail fitted him like a second skin while losing nothing in strength. Awkwardly the knight tried to strike with his sword, but Curillian wrenched it from his hand. Then he seized the black helm and tugged it free.

The shock of what he saw nearly stopped him from following through with his desperate plan. The face staring back at him was familiar from many palace mirrors and the reflection of his own sword. The craft of Kulothiel had made his last challenge the very embodiment of whomsoever should approach. Curillian steeled himself, knowing it was a trick of magic. His face a rictus of determination, he reached inside the protective mesh coif and wrapped his fingers around the exposed neck. Swordless and encumbered by his armour, the guardian knight could only move his arms and legs in feeble blows, which Curillian easily subdued. He kept squeezing, applying more and more pressure until his hands were white. The knight suddenly croaked in submission. He raised a gauntleted fist in surrender.

'Enough,' he gasped, barely audibly. Curillian relaxed his death-grip slightly. 'I yield,' said the knight. 'Advance, victor, and claim your prize. The way is clear, and the door is open.' Curillian glanced up, and the door beyond the bridge which had been closed now stood ajar, inviting yet repellent. Swiftly the bloodlust drained from him as relief and weariness swamped him in equal measure. All of a sudden, the black armour under him became very hot. He scrambled back and off as the whole body, armour and all, melted into a puddle of steaming liquid. Then a sudden gust of wind blasted through the chamber. It knocked them all from their feet and blew the liquid away into the void like dust and ashes. Curillian slumped onto the floor. He had done it. He had won the Tournament. But he felt not even remotely triumphant.

IV

Power Unimaginable

CURILLIAN Retrieved his sword and used it to help him back to his feet. Leaning on it, he stumped back to his companions, who were waiting, wide-eyed, at the foot of the amphitheatre. Lancoir came to him, nursing a bruised face, and soon all the armists had crowded around.

'No, my friends,' he said, 'all is well, I'm just tired.' They backed away again to give him some room. 'It's over, but never have I been so tested.'

'Curillian, you're hurt, we must tend you,' insisted Theonar, full of concern, but the king waved him away.

'He's right,' Lancoir said flatly.

'No Lancoir, it's nothing.' The captain of the guard swallowed hard and acquiesced. 'Now I must finish the Tournament at last,' Curillian went on. 'Only one can go.' He looked over the bridge to the forbidding door. 'I shall go and claim the prize on behalf of you all, and in the name of Maristonia. Stay here and see to it that no one follows me.' Then, walking slowly but stiffly, he left them and moved towards the bridge. As he went, he passed Southilar, who stood agape, amazement and jealousy vying in his face. Curillian glanced contemptuously at him and went on by.

Cautiously he stepped onto the bridge, trying hard not to look down. Feeling faint and dizzy was not the best time to attempt such a perilous crossing, but he took his time and passed over safely. Cold airs eddied about him, chilling him, and a hostile presence seemed to issue out of the door to confront him. Curillian hesitated, looking up at the door. It was more intricately carved than any he had yet passed through, but the details were lost on him, for his head was spinning. He bowed his head, spoke a quiet, fervent prayer, and then plunged in. His nervous companions watched as he was engulfed in the shadow and lost.

The tunnel was much like those he had already passed through. He found to his relief that there were no overt dangers, but there was a latent menace in the air. Sweet saccharine odours hovered in the air, redolent of bygone spells, and the air itself felt abrasive, as if it prickled against the presence of a stranger. It was a peculiar and unnerving sensation that Curillian would never forget.

Like the passage with the bridge that Southilar had treacherously thrown down, there were many side-tunnels and openings to both left and right. He was overtaken by visions of dusty old scholars bent over ancient volumes and expectant faces reflected in the surface of sinister liquids. Though the passage and its side chambers were cold and empty, he felt that some other will was showing him glimpses of what they had been used for in days long past: workshops, classrooms, infirmaries and apothecaries. The tunnel ended abruptly at a broad balcony which overlooked a vast octagonal cavern. In the darkness Curillian could not discern much, but he held onto the rail of the balcony for fear of falling. Breathing hard, he was unsure what to do next, but then suddenly a great gust of air blew through the cavern. With its passing, a hundred torches were lit as if by magic, and suddenly the great chamber was revealed in all its glory.

Each of the eight walls were cut into a honeycomb of rock shelves. The shelves were full of manuscripts and scrolls, thousands upon thousands of them; tomes and volumes of all kinds, the collected knowledge of the League of Wizardry accumulated over long millennia. On the floor of the cavern were long tables set with chairs for study, but Curillian could see no means of getting to the higher books, no steps or ladders. Curillian's own library was impressive enough, but nothing compared to this. Every secret in the world might have been captured on parchment in this chamber, but no one was there to read them anymore. All was covered with a thick layer of dust, untouched for decades. He found himself suddenly filled with a fierce desire for erudition, to listen to the words of ancient masters and to be considered a loremaster himself. The names of every mountain, the number of feathers in an eagle's wing, the deepest teachings of Prélan – what could he not learn in this place?

With the light of the torches, Curillian could now see that spiralled stairwells led down from the balcony to the library's floor. He descended and traipsed across the floor, full of wonder. Gnawed with helpless curiosity, he forgot his business for a while and inspected the books. He could not make head nor tail of the runes on the cracked leather bindings, which were obscured by dust and spiders' webs. Yet when he reached out to touch one of the spines his hand leapt back as if burned, and another vision blazed into his mind, vicious as an angry bird of prey. He saw the scenes of a terrible and nameless battle in a frozen wasteland, of dying wizards and the air alive with bolts of fire and coils of mystical power. He heard infernal blasts, horrendous screeches and cries of pain so dreadful that he had to cower to the ground, covering his ears and shutting his eyes. The vision passed, and he straightened up to see an empty library again.

The silence was oppressive after the sudden sharp sounds of a faraway tragedy, and sadness hung in the air like a pall, impregnating the very fibres of the rock. His mind struggled to comprehend what terrible secrets he was being exposed to, but it seemed that a cataclysmic doom had befallen the League of Wizardry, reducing the once teeming mountain to an empty husk. With some extra sense he felt their pain and sorrow, even though he did not know the facts. He quickened his pace to get away from the oppression of it and exited the library by an archway in the far wall. He came into a triangular atrium with three passageways leading off from the three points. Drawn by what power he knew not, he entered into the passageway straight ahead of him, which led up wide, cold steps. As the library had been, so this staircase was dark and menacing. All that could be seen at first were endless rows of glowing runes, one at both sides of each step, ascending into blackness. Another pulse of magical energy throbbed through it. Curillian was thrown onto his back by the passing of what felt like a moving wall. Looking up from his fall, he saw that countless wall-sconces had been kindled to life so that the way up was now illuminated. This time a voice spoke audibly to accompany the striking change in his surroundings. Kulothiel was speaking to him from somewhere far above.

'Welcome Curillian, victor of the Tournament. Long have I waited to meet you. Ascend to my chamber, and we shall speak.'

Aching and weary, Curillian picked himself up and climbed the stairs. The sconces were filled with uniquely beautiful flames like dancing fountains of liquid gold, but the air was still hostile and coarse, in seeming contradiction to the sorcerer's welcome. He came to yet another cavern, smaller than the library yet still cavernous in its own right. This one was already lit by great wall-braziers whose light was conveyed to the furthest corners by a series of burnished mirrors. On a raised dais stood a vast table lined with dozens of ornate, gilded chairs. Curillian approached and saw that each one was a masterpiece of craftsmanship, the carving and embroidery far surpassing anything that mortal skill could produce, but the plush upholstery was moth-eaten and sunken, the gilt woodwork chipped and peeling. He ran his fingers over them, and through the deep covering of dust on the table top. From the centre of the great table issued a glowing light, as of blue flames kept perpetually alight. They emanated from an enamel hollow, about which was a golden band inset with runes he could not read. Kulothiel's voice spoke again, providing the wording.

"'May Prélan grant us the wisdom to use His gift for the good of His people and for the glory of His name." The very words we lived by...'

Yet of Kulothiel himself there was no sign, so Curillian surmised that he must go on, penetrating further into the highest and most lordly parts of the mountain abode. His footsteps took him to a great archway crowned with a glowing halo of sapphires, in which was set a portal like no other. Spiralling ribs of glistening metal swirled from every edge to meet in the middle at an enormous blue diamond. It blazed with its own inner light, resembling the eternal flame on the table in colour and heat. Curillian could see no handle or knob, but when he brought his fingers close to the diamond it suddenly retracted and disappeared. As it did so, the spirals of metal unlocked and separated, gliding away from each other with the smoothness of oiled hinges. Without a sound they vanished into hidden recesses, allowing him to step through. No sooner had he done so than the same mechanism kicked into reverse. The spirals hissed shut, clasping around the diamond and locking the door securely behind the intruder.

Trapped, he found himself in a narrow circular space which was bathed in warm blue light. There was no way out other than the eerie portal behind him, but when he tried to open it again it would not budge. Fighting down panic, he looked around for some means of escape, but there was nothing. He was on a perfectly circular panel of flooring and above him was a gaping chimney of nothingness. Suddenly the floor moved and he found himself shot upwards into empty space. Quite disorientated and full of terror, he lost his footing and sat in an ungainly heap as the disc whisked him upwards through the bluish shaft. Just as suddenly as it had started, the disc came to a silken stop at a platform which opened out from the top of the shaft. Giddy and feeling sick, Curillian staggered off the disc and onto what he hoped was less treacherous ground.

As he recovered, he saw one final staircase leading up into what seemed to be the very roof of Oron Amular. Stabbing through his waves of nausea was an overwhelming sense of power. The atmosphere swamped him like a blanket. It throbbed through his ears, dazzled his eyes and baffled his brain. It was a most extraordinary sensation that left him feeling like a spirit gliding through a pool of floating particles. His head swam and, but instead of fighting the alien feelings, he allowed himself to be pulled upwards by the magnetism of what awaited at the top of the stairs.

Ever after he could remember very little of his time in that place, his memories being of an incredible variety of sensations, only blurry like a smudged collage. He ascended the stairs in a sort of daze. What he saw from the top took his breath away.

There, in all its eternal glory, lay the Pool of High Magic. He had never seen it before, but what else could it be? Of all the secret waters in the deep places of the world, there was surely none like this. All the legends spoke of it, a great pool at the very pinnacle of the Mountain, an energy source and the beating heart of the world's magic. And here it was, spread before his mortal feet. The pool dominated this topmost cavern, tranquil as a millpond and glowing with an ethereal light. Looking up, he saw that the gnarled ceiling and walls, which no hammer or chisel had ever touched, were bathed in the bluish radiance like some primordial grotto. He could well believe that only just above his head was the uttermost crown of Oron Amular. He shivered slightly. Although it was cold, it was nowhere near as cold as it should have been. Vitality seemed to exude from the pool as if power were constantly evaporating from an inexhaustible source and it warmed the otherwise frosty air, though it also made it heady and beguiling.

Entranced, he tottered towards the shore of the pool, treading close to where the limpid water lapped gently at a glistening slope of rock. Intensely curious, he leaned forward and peered into the depths, wondering how deep it was or where it all came from. He was amazed to see currents and eddies contorting the great body of water, as if its own power kept it constantly writhing in motion, and yet the surface was completely still, like a lid of crystal over a tempestuous receptacle.

'Do not fall in,' said a voice, just as he was beginning to lean dangerously far. It seemed both near and far away, quiet yet gaining strength in a long series of echoes. 'Only the staves of the wizards were ever dipped into the pool. Twice only in all its history have unfortunate souls have fallen in: one never came out, his life-force consumed by the pool; the other was fished out almost immediately. Nevertheless, he emerged scarred but with superhuman strength, and much woe befell us before he was subdued.' Curillian jerked away from the pool and looked around for the source of the voice. For a while he could see nothing, but as he trod carefully around the edge of the pool and as his eyes adjusted to the strange light, he glimpsed a raised area beyond the pool's far edge. A brilliant object was shining there, like a sun veiled by gossamer clouds. He made his way slowly towards it, feeling very small and insignificant. He had never felt so completely immersed in the presence of Prélan, and it awed him to his core.

It seemed to take him forever to reach the other side of the pool. Not only was it bigger than it had first seemed, but there was also a ring of mysterious menhirs surrounding the pool like guardians. There were twelve of them, fashioned out of some smooth tapering stone, each set with a glistening rune. They radiated power no less than the water and he took care to give them a wide berth. Yet eventually he came to the foot of a svelte staircase, which led up to a dais nestled into the corner of the cavern. On the dais was a sculpture of an eagle, whose outspread wings bore a great shining orb. Far more luminous than the Tear of Mírianna in the lower cavern, it was impossible to look directly at. All the rest of the cavern slumbered in the pale gleam of the pool, but this area was lit up like moonlight enhanced a hundredfold. So dazzled was he by the orb that he could not see the further parts of the dais. Thus, it was only when Kulothiel stood up from his chair and moved in front of the great orb that Curillian could see him.

The king of the armists gasped. The figure standing before him was bent and aged, haggard and horribly scarred. The king's mind flashed back to the figure he had seen in the entrance chamber of the Mountain, when Kulothiel had revealed himself to the contestants, and the person before him could scarce have been more different. The proud and dignified mage-lord of unguessable power bore no resemblance to this shrunken apparition. He was equally unlike the mysterious stranger who had accosted him and Lancoir outside the Mountain, and different again from the benevolent old visage which had accompanied the invite to the Tournament. Kulothiel, it seemed, had many faces – but which was his true form?

The old man hobbled down the steps and came to stand before Curillian. He was so bent, and so utterly dependent on the staff he grasped, that it was impossible to tell what his real height had once been, but now his face was level with the king's shoulder. Reeling from shock and distaste, Curillian looked awkwardly down at him.

'Pity and contempt are in your eyes, O Curillian.' All power and authority was stripped from the voice. Up close, and without guise, it was thin, cracked and wheezy. 'Would you prefer it if I looked thus?' As he spoke, he changed before the king's eyes into the wise old grandfather from the invite. 'Or like this?' He changed again, becoming the tall, stern wizard-lord from the entrance chamber. Both forms faded, leaving the pitiable bent old man again. 'I am not as you expected, am I, king of the armists?' Curillian could find no response, but Kulothiel didn't need one. 'I am Kulothiel, and this is how I truly am now. Yes, Kulothiel, Head of the League of Wizardry and Keeper of the Mountain.' He trailed off into something like laughter which turned into a coughing fit. 'Alas, Curillian, we can none of us retain our vigour indefinitely. I yet possess the power to mask my decay, but all mortals must expire sooner or later, even I. But would you be so good as to climb the steps? Stand by me, I need to sit...'

With that he turned and climbed the steps with torturous difficulty. Following him beyond the immediate glare of the orb's brilliance, Curillian watched as he lowered himself slowly into an ornate carven chair with worn velvet upholstery. Beyond him was a dark window that seemed to have been cut into the very side of the Mountain. It looked out onto a black night, but he could imagine what a spectacular view it must command out over Kalimar. And for the first time since entering the Mountain, he could guess at the time of day – between dusk and dawn. How long had they been inside?

'Two whole days now,' announced Kulothiel, answering his unuttered question. 'That is what you were wondering, is it not? How long you've been here? Yes, the moon is already setting on the second night since you entered, and little do you guess it, but in that time you have climbed right up from the feet of the Mountain to its summit. Were you not dazzled by the orb, you would see the valleys and plains of Kalimar stretching away eastward. There is another window on the opposite side of the chamber which looks west.'

'How can I have climbed so high in just two days?' asked Curillian incredulously. 'It has taken me longer than that to scale peaks in the Carthaki Mountains, which are surely much smaller than this Mountain, and even on them I felt lightheaded from the altitude – why not here?'

'Little do you guess, O King, of the ways of this Mountain. Your own adrenaline in the heat of the Tournament brought you further and higher than you may have deemed, but you had only climbed a little more than half way up before you reached my levitator.' Curillian thought of the disc which had shot him up that impossibly high chimney to deposit him at the threshold of this topmost chamber. 'That brought you up more than ten thousand feet in just a few moments. Did you think it was just weariness that made you feel woozy when you stepped off? Believe me, but for the power of the pool you would collapse in minutes from the thinness of the air at this height, and even if you survived that, the cold would claim you shortly afterwards. You are on the roof of Astrom, Curillian, a place where life and death are separated only by Prélan's grace.'

A rush of tiredness swamped the king and he nearly fell. He steadied himself on the chair, but still his mind swam. This was a place of extremes that his mind could not even begin to comprehend.

'Do not feel ashamed, O King, for this is a place that has overawed many a first-time visitor. Many wizards came here only once in their whole career, and every one was affected just as you are now. Indeed, few of us ever dwelt here for long, for the very force of life in this atmosphere merely quickens the passing of normal existence.

Nowadays I only rarely come here, but it was meet that you should come here, the winner of the Tournament.'

'Why?' asked Curillian. 'What does it mean, to have won?' Kulothiel looked at him long and hard, as if weighing his ability to cope with what he had to say. If the rest of the Keeper's face was half in the grave, the eyes remained spirited and piercing. At last he spoke again, gesturing as he did so at the pool with a weary arm.

'Curillian, what you see here is the source of all good magic in the world. It is the place where Prélan's fingertip rests permanently on Astrom and the highest measure of His provision to us. You are breathing more rarefied air than is anywhere else in the world to be found. Alas, it is not as unique and singular as we all would have hoped. In the land of Urunmar there lies another such pool, high-crowned amidst ice and fire. Whether once it was it was as pure and holy as this pool we can never know, but it became a dread place, a channel of evil into the world. Just as this pool was the source of the wizards' power, so the other pool gave strength to the great enemy of the world.'

'Kurundar,' breathed Curillian.

'Verily, Kurundar. My nemesis. My opposite. My brother.' So, there was truth in the legend that the evil sorcerer was Kulothiel's twin. In a split second's vivid realisation, Curillian saw that the world's fate had, in large part, been governed by two men, both workers of magic, both deriving unnatural long-life from these pools, but where one was good the other was evil. Between them lay a contested world that had been fought over and menaced for three thousand years.

'Curillian,' Kulothiel went on, 'your spies and diplomats have sent back rumours that the north is troubled once more. I can tell you now that not only are they right, but that the situation is far worse than they suspect. Dark powers are on the move once again, some new and some old. For a third time, Kurundar will try and subjugate the world you know. Hendar, bulwark of the north, will soon be beset, and the Free Peoples are all threatened. Yet, just as the Pool of Dark Magic in Urunmar is the source of your great peril, so in this Pool of High Magic lies your salvation. That is why I have brought you here. So that you may understand your peril, but also so that you may know where your help comes from.'

Curillian reeled under the force of Kulothiel's words and tried to regain his footing in the conversation.

'But we thought that magic had already passed from the world, that we had entered a new age. I thought Kurundar perished in his defeat in the last war, that Roujeark was the only wizard left, if even he is...'

Kulothiel's tone became scathing. 'Perished? Did you see his slain body or witness his soul brought before Prélan for judgement? No... Kurundar escaped. Again. Twice now the Free Peoples have tried and failed to destroy him, and for their failure they must endure a third war. He has returned, and new devilry has been added to his power of old. As for Roujeark, he is certainly not the last wizard, for several others, curse them, survive in Kurundar's service. Nay, myself aside, Roujeark is the last *Godly* wizard, and I am not long for this world. That is why he was summoned to this Mountain, why you had to bring him here, do you not understand?'

Curillian remembered the voice of Prélan speaking to him in the courtyard of his palace back in Mariston, telling him to protect an unknown person and take him to Oron Amular. He had rightly guessed that Roujeark was that person, but little had he known just how important he was.

'So why am I here, and not he?' he asked at length, still trying to gather his wits.

'You are here, Curillian, son of Mirkan, because you won the Tournament. You are the answer to my prayers, the champion I have been seeking.' He paused, deliberating. 'Have you heard of The Oracle?' That name was just a legend to Curillian, a story from out of the mists of time telling how Prélan spoke in a special way to the Keeper of the Mountain. Whether it truly existed or not he could not say, still less what form it took. 'The Oracle is a mouthpiece of Prélan in this world. Forty years ago, its embodied form rose out of the pool and revealed to me that doom was near, for myself, for the League, and for the world. I passed on to my few remaining mages what it foretold about the coming of Roujeark, the last wizard, but I did not tell them what I believed had been spoken to me alone. I was told that the tools of doom had been found, that an unlooked-for ally would bring them forth. All I needed was the hands to wield them, and so Prélan decreed that I should hold a tournament to discover the chosen people. *This* is that tournament, and *you* are its winner. A great prize I have for you, but a great mission also.'

Curillian swore he could feel every single part of him alive at that moment, alert and tingling. His neck hairs stood on end, his hands quivered, his heart thumped and his mind raced. The weariness and the fog in his head were passing, and a fearful excitement was igniting in his veins. With his mind clearer, he asked another question.

'Is the prize for me alone? I did not win this Tournament alone and could not claim as much. Roujeark, Theonar, Lancoir, there are many others down there who contributed just as much as I.'

'My dear Curillian, how much I regret that we have not met until now. What an alliance we would have made in the days of our vigour. Truly, it is a sign of your fitness to be standing here that you display such humility. Other champions would have grasped the prize for themselves with no regard for others, and that is why the Tournament was arranged as it was, to bring forth a victor not only of the greatest strength but also of the soundest virtue. You are the champion given me by Prélan, and I give thanks for that. *A prize awaits you, but not the only prize*. Rewards await many of those you have named, and more besides, and just as there is more than one prize so there is more than one mission. The great task that lies ahead is too big for any one pair of shoulders, and so many have been assembled, and a few have been chosen. But it falls to you, O King, to see the overall picture, to have the full revelation. You will have the responsibility to guide and sustain all the winners in their various roles in a great undertaking.

'Kurundar threatens the whole world, and he is mightier than any nation alone. So, all the Free Peoples must unite against him. New weapons must be wielded; and new quests must be fulfilled to bring about his final destruction. Your forebear King Firwan fought in the Great Alliance that overthrew Kurundar in the First War, and in your youth the Silver Empire staved off his second onslaught; now a new coalition is needed to fight a Third War. Hendar, Aranar, Ciricen, Ithrill, and especially Maristonia, are all needed, or all of them will fall one by one.'

Curillian swallowed hard, the prospect of another war making him feel suddenly old. The moment of elation had passed; dread was creeping over him like a living thing. The last war had been so terrible – how could there be another? So many long years of toil and tears. The broad fields of Hendar had been tilled with blood, Ciricen had been engulfed in flames, Aranar was laid waste and the enemy had even shaken the ancient towers of Kalimar. The land of Maristonia might have been spared, but its sons, late come to the slaughter, were cut down in their tens of thousands. A hundred old memories of strife and loss passed through his mind, chilling his bones and oppressing his mind. Slowly he became aware of Kulothiel speaking again.

'Would you know of your competitors? Soon you will meet them again, but come now and see how they fared.' The old mage-lord gestured to the orb. Shielding his eyes at first, Curillian watched it grow dim enough to look at, and then he saw that pictures were moving through it like a conjured vision, one scene rapidly succeeding the last. Some of it seemed oddly familiar. There were the men of Hendar, the splendour of their armour dulled by soot and dust, their faces grimed and weary. They had fallen from a collapsing bridge and passed through a waterfall into a subterranean tunnel where terrible beasts lurked. Some of them died there before the rest struggled through tight holes into an icy compartment. There they had shivered and frozen nearly solid before the bishop, Nurvo, had solved the puzzle which unlocked the exit. Other riddles he had had to solve to save their lives from deadly perils. Killer bats had assailed them, and clouds of noisome darkness had choked them; flames had scorched them, and a long hall of nothingness had afflicted them with madness, from which they barely escaped in time. Now, led by Adhanor, the soiled, battered survivors were climbing the steps towards the wizard-guarded forcefield before the Tear of Mírianna.

Earl Culdon and his fur-clad Ciriciens had scaled a mighty wall that seemed to go on forever, before losing several of their number to a hail of great ice chunks. They had been hunted by giant serpents in a horrible maze and become trapped in a spinning cylinder where they had been hurtled round and round, half to death. Dark assassins had stalked their steps and giant pulverising levers had nearly pummelled them as they issued across a high and windswept bridge of crumbling masonry. They were now climbing by a different route up to the habitable parts.

The men of Aranar had braved many dangers and overcome many problems before meeting the armists in the firepit where the skeletons had attacked. The rest of their journey he knew first-hand, but now he saw the grisly fate that overtook the villainous free-riders who had been led to the Mountain under duress by Elrinde and the elves of Ithrill. Raspald Kin-slayer, their leader, had been stabbed by Elrinde on a high precipice and cast into an abyss at the roots of the Mountain. Benek Thunder-Eye had lost his other eye and been condemned to wander lost, blind and alone in the bowels of the Mountain. Sampa the Smooth, Vampana, Sceant and Lucask Lightfoot, all had been slain in dreadful ways as Elrinde, Astacar and Linvion took advantage of the Tournament's imaginative opportunities – almost as if they knew of Kulothiel's secret traps and could spring them on others. Yet other free-riders of Aranar, knights errant and soldiers of fortune, had survived the wrath of the elves and somehow stayed alive through all of the Tournament's nightmarish dangers. In ones, twos and small groups they now groped towards the same destination as the men of Hendar and Ciricen.

Curillian kept watching and saw the dark-skinned Alanai swimming across a great subterranean lake before being washed over a tall waterfall and subjected to boiling rapids full of rocks. They had fashioned a raft and braved extremes of heat and cold, as well as the attacks of crocodiles and sightless cave monsters. Some had perished as the raft melted in waters turned acidic, but the rest had gotten away to walk down wearisomely long tunnels infested with rats. They, too, drew near.

The dwarves had walked through beguiling lights and sorcerous visions to do battle with fire-breathing salamanders. Withstanding the flames, they had toiled on only to be crushed beneath fallen rocks. A remnant had burrowed clear and laboured mightily to clear a blocked tunnel. Using long-honed skills and every last ounce of resolve, they had made a way for themselves, coming up to the Tear by yet another path.

'Even as you struggled up your own road,' Kulothiel commented, 'the others trod paths of their own, for this Tournament had many ways. The challenges were different, but the danger was the same. As you can see, you came further and faster than any of them, through a mixture of luck, skill and bravery. And a little pinch of the bloody-minded refusal to be defeated that has been the leaven in your ancestors' bread. That helped.'

Then, the visions sped up, and Curillian watched the different groups converge in the habitable parts, so fast that it happened in a few heartbeats. Exhausted and bloodied, they slumped down to rest. For the moment they were too weary to wonder what would happen next. He watched the rest of his own party join the other groups near the Map Chamber. Together they discovered tables of food and pitchers of wine in an anteroom. Curillian glanced at Kulothiel – evidently the Keeper had made provision for famished contestants whose own food had long since been consumed or lost. Suddenly his own stomach growled long and deep, as if stirred by the sight of food, and his own long-ignored hunger flared up. Looking again at his companion, Kulothiel did not meet his eye, but with a gentle gesture of his hand he pushed a laden plate towards the king.

Curillian fell eagerly upon the food, quite forgetful of his own dignity and his exalted surroundings. For a while the two of them watched the scene in silence. As they did so Curillian continued to eat, refusing nothing that was on offer. Within the orb, his friends and rivals alike were also refreshed, and some among them took advantage of the lull to bind up injured limbs and staunch bleeding wounds. As some of them ate and some of them rested, others returned to the long hall where the tapestries of history were hung. Curillian was vividly reminded of the newest section, still being added to, and his question came back to him.

'The tapestry of history...how...we saw some of these things... though they had only just have happened. How can that be...?'

'Verily, the story of Astrom is kept and recorded in Oron Amular,' Kulothiel answered.

'But we watched it growing before our eyes, as if it were alive,' Curillian persisted. 'Roujeark thought that there must be a magical pen somewhere, and that you were up here, dictating it all.' Kulothiel smiled.

'Yes, yes, the pen in the Keeper's Chamber writes in real time. No hand directs it but the hand of Prélan alone, for it is His story that it records. With it, magical threads are woven upon bare rock, continuing the story of this world that began in the dawn of time, starting with my original predecessor: Avatar, Eldest of all. No, the tapestries are no work of mine, though I study them often and learn much thereby. For things nearer at hand, I have other means of gathering news. I have eyes, O King, in every nook and hollow of this Mountain, and what they see is conveyed to this orb, another of the Keeper's heirlooms. Very useful, and with it I have followed each of you in your progress. I felt sure you would overcome the lake monster, but the spiked ceiling was nearly the end of you. But for Roujeark you would all have perished in the lava, where several unfortunate rogues of Aranese blood met their demise. And in the upper chambers you had some rather timely help, but we'll not speak of that. Here you are.'

While the old wizard was still speaking, Curillian glanced back at the orb in time to see elves ascend to the higher levels with much less trouble than the others. This was not Elrinde and his two Ithrillian companions, but the deputation from Kalimar, representing each of the three kindreds. Tall sombre elves all, from the city, the sea and the forest. He watched them ascend right to the Council Chamber with its eternal flame and hold counsel with Kulothiel. Looking back at the wizard, he glimpsed a faint look of irritation quickly smothered in the other's face.

'My neighbours, O King, the ambassadors of Paeyeir, Marindel and Therenmar. They are below us even now. They came not to compete, but to consult with me. Whether that which they heard was to their liking, who knows? Yet I think you will not have much help from King Lithan in the war that is coming, except perhaps once.'

Curillian watched as Kulothiel raised himself painfully from his throne.

'Walk with me, King of Mariston,' the wizard commanded. Curillian went slowly back alongside the pool, gently assisting his enigmatic host.

'Where are we going?'

'Unless you wish to stay here until the magic quite overcomes you, then we must finish our talk elsewhere. Come, I know just the place.'

In what seemed like an eternity they plodded back to the steps which had brought Curillian up to the pool. Just before they descended, he turned and look back, regret tugging on his heart. Never again would he behold such otherworldly beauty. Kulothiel plucked impatiently at his mailed sleeve.

'Come, Curillian, there is still greater beauty in the life that follows death. Do not linger overlong.'

With that he guided him back onto the strange platform in its blue-lit shaft, what Kulothiel called his Levitator. Kulothiel tottered on after Curillian and twisted a ringed finger in a curious looking panel that the king had not noticed before. Nothing happened. Curillian looked expectantly at the mage, who had closed his eyes as if sleeping where he stood. Suddenly he opened them again, smiled mischievously, and an instant later they were whisked off. They flew through the air with such velocity that Curillian's stomach rose right into his throat. His senses were scrambled, but he felt sure that they weren't going straight down the whole time, instead shifting directions through unseen passages of various orientations.

His suspicions were confirmed when they at last came to a halt and a hidden door rose, allowing them out into a chamber which was not the one Curillian had left. Somehow they had come to the map chamber, that great cavern filled with its wonderful living map. They had stumbled across it after walking down the corridor of tapestried history and before fighting past the giant guardians of the gatehouse chamber. Now Curillian beheld it again, awed anew. He had not noticed before the hidden portal through which they had stepped, so captivated had he been by the marvel at his feet. Kulothiel lingered on a platform above, letting the armist king go down alone. Curillian was lost in reverie when suddenly the lamps in the chamber were doused, leaving just one part of the map illuminated – a singularly lofty peak in Kalimar. Kulothiel spoke in a professorial voice which seemed to swirl around him.

'We are here, Oron Amular. And this is your home.' The Mountain went dark and another part of the map was lit up, showing distant Mariston. 'Maristonia, just one of the free realms. Here are the others: Aranar, Ithrill, Hendar and Ciricen.' As he spoke, each country in turn was lit up, then all together. 'The lands of the Free Peoples… all menaced by the north, by Urunmar.' The south of Astrom was cast in shadow whilst Urunmar took the limelight, only now the map seemed to come truly alive, as the sounds of gathering war thrummed in his ears and vivid, lifelike characters moved across the map. 'Kurundar has gathered yet another army. Orcs and trolls bred in the mountains of the north and their northern allies on the coasts of Urunmar. But this time, Kurundar has meddled with arts and powers darker still. He has opened a portal to the underworld and recruited the mercenaries of hell. The great Fire-demon is still trapped down there, where Avatar cast him, but lesser demons have escaped and come to swell Kurundar's strength; foes such as have never been seen since the Great Wars of ancient Kalimar, immortal and terrible.' As the vivid pictures crawled across the landscape, massing for an attack on the south, demonic faces reared up out of the map as if to attack the armist king.

'I do not know how much Kurundar controls them, but I suspect the Great Enemy is now using him as a puppet to prepare the way for him. One thing is certain. They are allied against us, both bent on our complete and utter destruction. Kurundar has come close to that goal twice before, but now he believes he finally has the power to achieve it. Verily, even now his forces are mustering, ready to invade south.' In the map, an innumerable host was accumulating in the narrow base of Urunmar, where that land of mountainous winter was joined to Astrom like an ugly head to a body. In between lay the neck-like isthmus of the Haunted Pass – the time-honoured corridor of invasion – a bleak rocky strip of land long made dreadful by the passage and abiding of evil. Through its centre, like a rotten gullet, ran a crooked canyon, so twisted and filth-ridden that none but the emissaries of evil would use it. Through this haunted highway the soldiery of Kurundar was poised to pour.

Now Urunmar faded again, and the light moved south to the northern part of Hendar, whose broad flanks tapered towards the neck of the isthmus. The Guard Hills of that border-country were festooned with fortresses which were now illuminated in turn by Kulothiel's unseen touch.

'Curillian, whether in a year, two years, or ten, Kurundar's demon-led hordes will come south, and the Guard Hill forts will be overrun.' Swathes of flame swamped the fair rolling uplands of Hendar. 'So too, Ciricen. This time you don't have the mighty legions of the

Silver Empire to slow their advance – you will hardly have time to react before Nalator, bastion of the north, is besieged.' Nalator was one of the five dukedoms that made up Hendar, and the city of the same name was the greatest fortified city in the north, a place to rival Mariston. Kulothiel continued to demonstrate the likely narrative of the coming war in visual form as he spoke, with coloured lines, warlike figurines and moving colours.

'Lancearon will march from Ithrill with what strength he has left, and you must come north with all the strength Maristonia can offer.'

'Just Lancearon and myself?' Curillian asked.

'No, the Hendarians will be in the midst of the fight, as ever, and you must persuade the clans of Aranar to leave off their bickering and ride north also. Other help you may have, some unlooked-for, but do not count on Ciricen or Kalimar, for they will be unable or unwilling to give it. You must get to Nalator as soon after the outbreak of war as you can. If Nalator falls, all will be lost. Kurundar will seek to drive a wedge between you, coming from the southeast, and Lancearon, coming from the southwest. If you cannot unite, you will be overwhelmed piecemeal. Only Nalator has the strength to hold out long enough for your forces to come together. Nalator will draw the enemy like flies to a corpse, for there will be something there that they seek.'

'What do they seek?'

'This.' Kulothiel's voice gained still more in power and fervour. All the lights dimmed now except one, which illuminated Kulothiel. He was standing at a stone font which Curillian had not noticed before, and something he could not see was in his hands.

'Power Unimaginable.'

Curillian strained his eyes forward, but he could not see in the gloom what Kulothiel held.

'Patience, Curillian, you will see in due time. Here, in my hands, lie the prizes of the Tournament. The three greatest are for you, one for each of you.' Curillian thought he had misheard.

'What three? I'm the only one here.' Even as his voice echoed around the dark chamber, his skin prickled to tell him it was not so. Slowly, from the shadows at the edge of the chamber, two figures stepped. Roujeark looked quite shaken, as if recovering from a shock. Theonar loomed over him like a well-groomed tree, serenity in his handsome face. Curillian gaped at them. He had left them in the amphitheatre chamber, far away, and yet here they were.

'How did you get here?' he asked. Theonar answered for them both.

'The Keeper summoned us here. While you were gone, he provided a road hidden from the others.'

'While I was gone? How long was I up there?' He looked for an answer in Kulothiel's face, but the old wizard was inscrutable. Suddenly though, his questions did not seem so important, as his eyes and mind were drawn back to the items held in the stone font. A deep solemnity was in the air as Kulothiel beckoned them all forwards.

'King Curillian, Sir Theonar, Roujeark, son of Dubarnik,' the Keeper addressed them. 'You have each contributed to your success here in my Tournament. Sir Theonar, you kept your comrades from Aranar alive until they joined the armists, you organised the escape from the lake of lava, you uncovered the password which opened the way into the Chamber of the Tear, you unlocked the gates guarded by the stone giants, and you helped get the stranded Maristonians across the chasm where your lord abandoned you.

'Roujeark, despite being the youngest and least experienced fighter here, you showed courage at every turn and displayed great resourcefulness under pressure. You outpaced the collapsing ceiling, you solved the rock-puzzle which doomed the great squid, you destroyed the undead attackers, you got behind the forcefield barrier, and you risked your life in going to Curillian's aid against the ten jet warriors.

'Curillian, you thought of the escape route when the spikes nearly crushed your party from above and below, you confronted the jet warriors alone when everyone else was rooted with fear; you led your small party with courage, you guided them through the treacherous course, and you overcame your very self in combat with the final guardian. You reached the finish line before all others and won the Tournament.

'You three have proved yourselves above all the others, and thus showed yourselves to be Prélan's anointed. I was told how I would know you, and now I see you revealed. Prélan calls you to save His people.' He paused. An eternity of silence seemed to press in on them. At last the Keeper spoke again. 'To each of you a task is given, and to each of you a tool is given. Behold your prizes.' With that he lifted his arms and a great light filled the chamber. When its radiance receded, they saw that he was holding a glowing object.

'Sir Theonar.' Kulothiel beckoned the tall Aranese knight forward first. 'To you is assigned the Amulet of Avatar.' Curillian gasped – had he heard aright? From over Theonar's outstretched arm he could see a golden device, shaped like a half-star and hanging from an ornate chain. The links were all tiny gilt oblongs with concave ends through which ran a shimmering wire. Ancient power seemed to ripple across the magnificent artefact and seep out of it into the air around them.

'This is the great treasure and weapon of Avatar, the Elder-King. As well you know, with it he cast down the Fire-demon in the Great Wars and spellbound him in the underworld, deferring doom for another day. When he retired to the Triumblen Isles, he bequeathed it to his son, Avarone, with the charge of watching over it, lest the Fire-demon stir again. Each elder son of the House of Avatar, the glorious princes and kings of Kalimar, has borne this amulet in turn, until Avalar was slain for it. Lithan's grandfather fell far from home and the amulet was broken in two pieces, both lost to the knowledge of the League for long ages.

'This half was recovered but recently from the hoard of the last dragon and came into my possession. I entrust it to you. Not only must you guard it, but you must also find the other half and take it to safety. On their own, each piece can do nothing but entrance the beholder; together they become the greatest power source the world has ever known. In it is all of Avatar's strength and power of old, all the virtue he derived from Prélan as His eldest child. That same power which threw down the Fire-demon and incarcerated him could also be used to set him free. As long as it is in the world, it is a menace to the Free Peoples. So, you must take it away, from under the very nose of the enemy, and deliver it to Avatar. The Elder-King now dwells on an enchanted isle removed from mortal sight, but the bearer of his amulet will be able to reach him. Yet only with this one half can you find the lost half, and so you must bear it into the greatest danger before you can redeem it.'

Theonar took hold of the amulet and drew it to his breast. He clasped it against his breast and hung his head in silent prayer. Then he looped it over his neck and hid it beneath his tunic and armour. He stepped down and to one side. Next, Kulothiel looked to Roujeark.

'Roujeark, wanderer from afar, you have been called from your humble home to do a deed beyond the power of anyone else. With the noble blood of long-lost ancestors in your veins, you must rise up and fulfil the great gift given to your family. Your father had but the dying embers of magic in his soul, but you have it a hundredfold, more so than any of your forebears. You will be the last wizard after me, and so you have been brought here to be trained. Prélan has called you forth because a great task awaits that is beyond my strength. The Pool of Dark Magic must be destroyed forever, never again to blight the unhappy world. While Sir Theonar undertakes his labour, the throbbing heart of Kurundar's stronghold must be laid bare and emptied, or else the rescue and removal of the amulet will count for nothing. With this Star-shard you will accomplish this deed.' He held forth a glittering rock in his hand and Roujeark stepped forward to take it. Although no larger than an arrowhead, it shone like a heavenly jewel, for its light and wondrous pattern was like no earthly rock. 'Take this shard to Oron Cavardul, cast it into the Pool of Dark Magic, and all its foul waters will be drained. The shard came from Prélan, and to Him it will return once it has removed a great evil from the world.'

Roujeark gazed down at the great jewel in awe, his face bathed in its light. Curillian was no less stunned. He felt the ground had been shaken beneath his feet as he heard his friends assigned such staggering quests. Kulothiel seemed to be a merchant of dreams, a trader in the impossible, and Curillian's already reeling mind blanched as it tried to contemplate what undertaking he himself would be called to. Half-expectant, half-afraid, he looked at Kulothiel, awaiting his turn.

'Curillian,' said the old wizard, 'no less a mission is set before you than the defence of the world. Your prizes are here, but you must wait a while longer for them. Others must be dealt with first.' Curillian's heart lurched, wondering what was coming next. He held the wizard's weary eye, looking full in his haggard face, and then had to turn away as a blinding flash of light seared in front of him.

V

Reluctant Pupils

WHEN He was able to open his eyes again, shielding them with his arm, he saw that Kulothiel had been transformed into the stern mage-lord once more, standing erect and grave of face. Before he had time to wonder why, he heard noises from behind him. Many people had come into the chamber. Turning, he saw contestants of every race approaching the map-floor. Man, elf and dwarf, they all looked stunned, bearing the same expression Roujeark had shown a few moments before. Where they had come from, none could say, but here they were, all the surviving contestants.

There were the battered and bloodied figures he had seen in Kulothiel's orb: Elrinde and his elven comrades and King Adhanor at the head of his Hendarians. There were his armist comrades: Andil, Caréysin, Lionenn, Findor, Antaya and Aleinus. With them came Southilar and his party, and beside them were the grim-faced Ciriciens. Steel-clad dwarves stalked into the chamber, and there also were the swarthy southerners and many a free-rider from Aranar. All were assembled again, as they had been at the start, just reduced in number. They all looked exhausted, but they were not too weary to greet each other with hostility and suspicion. Where had these others come from? Why did they look so much better off, when they themselves had gone through hell? Wild questions broke out and angry accusations were made. Yet few of them had actually encountered each other during the Tournament, so their rancour was overtaken by curiosity. They turned their eyes and their anger on the statuesque figure of Kulothiel on the raised platform.

'There he is, the wizard!'

'He's responsible for all this, it's on his head!'

'Come down, conjuror, and explain yourself!'

All the while Kulothiel had been waiting patiently, but now he stirred and lifted up his arms, staff held aloft.

'HEAR ME!' he cried, and every ear was seized, willing or no. A peel of thunder smote the chamber, silencing all the words which sprang to various lips, and bolts of light crackled over the wizard's head.

'Hear me!' Kulothiel cried again, though less insistently now that he had their attention. 'Elves, dwarves, armists and mortals, kings and knights and warriors, brave contestants all. Forget the trials behind you, lay aside your petty quarrels and hearken to me. The Tournament is over, and you, the survivors, have been summoned here for a purpose.' All were captivated by the sight of a mage-lord in his majesty, wielding magic before their waking eyes. Every doubting heart was convinced and every angry thought was forgotten. Wonder overcame all else. Kulothiel went on.

'Look about you, my lords.' At his bidding, they turned to look at each other. During the wizard's outburst, each company had subconsciously arrayed themselves in that part of the map which represented their home, and now they stood in their relative positions. 'All the great nations and principalities of the free world are here assembled. Never before has a company of such mixed creed and colour been convened, not even in the days of the Great Alliance. Those not here are of small significance in the coming struggle. Look at each other, you who are neighbours, who have been allies and adversaries by turns down the long centuries. Look at each other now and see friends, for so you are. You have a common bond of civilisation, a mutual belief in freedom, a shared revilement of true evil. Think no more of past grievances, but consider how much you share in common reverence.'

The various groups and parties studied each other reluctantly, weighing up the wizard's words with dubious expressions. At Curillian's bidding they had kept their peace in the camp outside the Mountain, and now the wizard seemed to be asking the same of them. They had been expecting to fight each other once inside, but they had barely crossed paths, and now they found they were too weary to cause trouble. Their leaders exchanged glances, but it was Earl Culdon of Ciricen who spoke out.

'All right wizard, we're listening. Speak your piece.' Kulothiel turned a stern face on him, but his eyes were glittering with amusement at the impudence.

'Then listen well, man of Ciricen, and all you others. Events in the world outside hurry on to great deeds, so let us conclude our business here with no delay. Friends, prizes I have for you, and words of counsel. Accept the one only if you are willing to receive the other.' He waited, holding the eye of each chieftain in turn, until they had all nodded their assent.

'In the Tournament just finished, many here have displayed extraordinary skill and courage. In token of this, I have many prizes to award. They are as varied as the acts of valour which earned them and each suited to the recipient's future needs. Step forward first, Anthab the Undubbed.'

It was a name none of them had expected, and indeed, which few of them even knew. The man who stepped forward was big and scarred, with livid branding marks on both cheeks. He was dressed in Aranese fashion, though he was ragged and wayworn.

Theonar, who stood by Roujeark, leaned down discreetly and murmured in his ear, 'An Undubbed is a knight stripped of rank and position for some great crime. They are lawless outcasts, shunned and despised.'

Kulothiel told them more. 'Anthab, you came here a hunted man, a soldier of fortune. You came here with nothing to lose, seeking redemption from the shame you bear. Instead of the death which you several times cheated, you live, and shall be exonerated for the gallantry you have shown, for the lives you have saved. Let your dishonour be cast off; take this ring as a symbol of your pardon.' Grateful and abashed, the big man lumbered forward and took the proffered ring. Churlishly, Southilar growled from out of the company.

'Such a one will never find employ in my Clan.' Kulothiel eyed the Jeantar coldly, but addressed the prize-winner.

'No longer are you a mercenary, but a man with a mission, and perhaps you will find some other lord with a readier heart.' Kulothiel did not explain what his mission was, so Anthab turned and walked away, confused but appreciative. Kulothiel moved on speedily.

'Next I call your compatriot, Jeannor, he who is called Hoofbeam. The speed you have shown throughout this Tournament is truly remarkable, fleetness of foot and of mind. Such a one will be of great service as a messenger when desperate haste is needed. In token of this, take these shoes for your horse, Rowardo. Never again will he need to be reshod, and never again will he tire. He shall run quicker than ever, outflying even the arrows of the enemy. Take them, and ride to good fortune.' Jeannor, a rough-clad but baby-faced man, stepped forward eagerly and received his prize. He did not share the limelight for long though, since Kulothiel swiftly called the next recipient forward.

'Lord Hoth, step forward.' All eyes turned to the leader of the dwarves, who trudged into the limelight. He was a burly figure, made even larger by the suit of heavy armour that he wore as if it were a thin cloak. The steel was scorched and fire-blackened, his face smeared with soot and his plaited beard singed, but he still stood proudly, using his great double-headed battle-axe like a walking stick. 'You represent Carthak, the realm of the dwarves, do you not?' Kulothiel asked him.

'Aye,' the dwarf affirmed. 'Hoth, son of Hoth, of the house of Kharad, I am. My lord, Arthond IV, King of Carthak, has bidden me be present and know what passes.' Roujeark stared in fascination. Like every other child of the Carthaki Mountains, he had heard the tales of the fabulous underground city for which the range was named. Yet neither he nor most armists had ever seen a live dwarf, for they surfaced seldom nowadays. Great indeed must the dwarf-king's curiosity have been for him to send a champion to this Tournament.

'And to get here,' Kulothiel told him, 'you passed through fire which would have destroyed any other competitor. Great is the hardihood of the sons of Carthak, and great is the skill of their smiths. But ahead of you lies fire hotter than any you have known. If you are to emerge unscathed, then you must suitably attired. My gift to you is new armour.' The wizard lifted up a suit of sleek metal, tailored to encase the whole body. It shimmered in the light, its close-woven links gleaming. Hoth took the prize and hefted it doubtfully. It looked ludicrously flimsy next to the heavy plates he already wore, but Kulothiel explained. 'Its mail is of star-steel, as light as feathers and as hard as dragonhide. The mail is woven onto a flameproof lining which turns heat and foils flame. In it, you will never burn.

See, here are hose, gloves and a masked helmet to match. Take an old man's advice…don't wait too long to put it on.'

Hoth took the armour back to his place, where his companions gathered round to examine it with interest. As they conversed in low, gruff whispers, Kulothiel called another forward to the font.

'Culdon, Earl of Centaur, it seems you too are in need of armour. You've come through many scrapes with as many wounds. If I don't equip you properly, you will never survive the skirmishes ahead of you. You will fight in tight places and rarely in the open. For you too I have prepared armour, star-steel mail which will cheat the darts of evil and the assassin's dagger. But be alert, and always on your guard.' Culdon muttered thanks, and looked ready to speak further, but Kulothiel ignored him.

'Next, I summon Adhanor, King of Hendar.' The young sovereign stepped forward, armour dented but pride redoubled. 'No weapon have I for you, but a limitless supply of what you need.' A look of disappointment passed over the handsome face when all that Kulothiel poured into his outstretched palm was a single gold coin. 'Lord King, if the coffers of the treasury which you have inherited are less full than you would like, then fear not. This is a coin that when spent departs not. It is given so that you shall have no lack, for you are to be the treasury of a great endeavour. If Hendar's full strength is to be nurtured, then armies must be recruited and strong places made fast. But beware, young monarch: if you are tempted to spend this coin on unworthy things, you will find that it does not stretch so far.' Bemused, Adhanor returned to his compatriots, clasping the coin close.

Southilar, hoping to catch the wizard's eye, was again disappointed when a most unusual name was uttered next.

'Where is Parthir?' Kulothiel asked. From the shadows at the cavern's far side, a dark figure stirred. From the southernmost extremity of Astrom, he strode into the light. If he was surprised to be called upon, then the others were more so. As he walked past them warily, they eyed him coldly and murmured disapprovingly.

'Savage...'

'Pirate scum...'

'No good can come from Lurallan...'

'A barbarian like this has no place here...'

Yet Roujeark noticed how the man held firm and kept on despite the abuse on either side. There was a nobility in his olivine features, a hawk-like hauteur. He was indeed dressed like a pirate and armed for brigandage, but Roujeark sensed a cultivation to him that softened his buccaneering apparel. Kulothiel, too, took no notice of the comments of the more northerly nations, but beckoned the Alanai chieftain to the font. From the gift-giving font, he produced a most curious item. A garnet-studded shoulder-belt, hung with half a dozen bulging skins.

'Parthir of Raduthon, I have a prize here fitting for a seaman such as yourself, an apt reward for the deft touch you have shown on the waters barring your way in this Mountain. Keep these skins well, for in them is a substance like no other. Simultaneously a propellant and a caulking agent, this matter will give a sheen to your vessel that even the spirits of the ocean will covet. Caulk your ship with this and no craft upon the waves will be able to vie with you. Yet like Jeannor on land, this gift is given for the good of others, so that the beleaguered may have reinforcements sped to them.' Raduthon bowed his head reverently and accepted the strange gift. As he stepped away, a voice of dissent was raised from among the crowd.

'Armour for the Ciriciens and pardons for the felons of Aranar I can accept, but are we to stand by and watch a marauding corsair rewarded?' It was Xavion, companion of Adhanor who spoke. Outrage and indignation were in his face, and several others voiced agreement. The corsairs of Lurallan, though mainly the ancestral enemies of Maristonia, were loathed by all. 'What has this sea-scum done to warrant such a gift?'

'More than you,' Elrinde the elf answered Xavion mildly, but with an edge of scorn in his voice. Xavion choked on his rage but could find no words. Although he was a man unused to swallowing his pride, the elven warlord's reputation and the look in his eye dissuaded the young Hendarian noble from pursuing the matter further. Ignoring the ongoing consternation, Curillian broke ranks and walked through the men of Aranar towards the font. He confronted Parthir.

'I have more cause to hate this man than any of you,' he announced loudly to the gathered contestants. 'The desert tribes and corsairs of Lurallan have done great injury to my realm and people down the centuries.' Parthir looked like he expected a fight, one he knew he would lose, but nevertheless he braced himself and stood defiant before the armist king. Yet Curillian moved no hand to his sword hilt. Still talking to the hall, half over his shoulder, he went on.

'And yet Raduthon is a nobler city-state than some in the south. Urundair and Caulrir are hives of villainy and frequented by all manner of wave-scum; Cavard is a half-starved desert outpost; Arthon and Mouraxar are inhabited by snake-charmers and devil-worshippers. By comparison the Raduthites are cultured men, a race of merchant-warriors. They are more like to us armists in taste and temperament than any of the others.' Curillian looked Parthir straight in the eye. He held out his hand. 'And I would welcome them into the fold of the Free Peoples, since there are greater enemies at hand.' The last he said loud enough for all to hear, but then he spoke softly just to Parthir.

'You can either cut off my sword-hand or make a better friend than you deserve. Choose.' Parthir looked at him a long moment, trying to discern a trick. Finding none, he clasped Curillian's paler hand. Wordlessly they walked back from the font together, and in the sudden silence everyone heard Caiasan's stage-whisper.

'Bloody hell. Armists and barbarians making friends. *Now* I know something strange is afoot.'

When Curillian and Parthir reached the men of Aranar, Southilar planted himself squarely in their way, arms folded. The Jeantar towered over both of them. He said no word, but disgust was stamped across his frowning face.

'Get out of the way, Southilar,' Curillian told him. Southilar stayed where he was, the truculence deepening on his face.

Curillian dropped his hand to his sword hilt. 'I won't ask again.'

Slowly, reluctantly, Southilar moved to one side. The unlikely friends resumed their places, and the silence was replaced by a ripple of murmurs that spread throughout the cavern. A new figure stood forward to raise his voice above them. It was Nurvo, the mysterious Hendarian bishop. He was rather less well-polished than before the Tournament, but he still had an air of confidence and charm. He appeared to relish the chance to speak directly to Kulothiel.

'Well, my Lord Keeper, we're all friends together it seems. Have you other prizes to give?'

Roujeark felt sure the suave prelate wouldn't have minded one himself, or, better yet, the chance to rummage around the old wizards' workshops for a few days, but the Mage-lord answered his question at face value.

'I have indeed. Lord Elrinde of Ithrill.' The elf looked up sharply, and Roujeark could not tell whether he seemed surprised by the call or not. 'A message I have for your master, Lancearon. Will you hear it?' The Hendarians stiffened at the mention of their erstwhile conqueror, but held their tongues. For his part, Elrinde looked half-eager, half-hesitant, a sudden dilemma breaking through his cool façade. At length he nodded, then he and his two compatriots left the chamber. How they knew where to go, Roujeark knew not, but they left behind them an atmosphere of awkward curiosity.

'There are four more prizes,' Kulothiel announced, 'all of them weapons, and all reserved for the valiant armists who reached the finish line before all others.' His eyes rested on the Maristonian contingent, and slowly all their neighbours turned to look at them, faces full of mingled jealously and admiration. 'Step forward, Lionenn the Konenaire; step forward, Caréysin the Archer; step forward, Lancoir of Thainen's Order; step forward Curillian, king of the armists.' Curillian led his small band forward, clear of the throng. Roujeark remained behind with Findor, Andil, Antaya and Aleinus. No one else would know that he too had been given a prize, nor Theonar, he felt quite sure. He watched as his comrades all took a knee, and as Kulothiel called them by name.

'Lionenn, the mace is the symbol of your ancient order, and with them your predecessors have fought since before even I walked the world. Do me the honour of laying aside your own mace, and taking this new one instead.' The wizard held forth a mighty mace, a great iron-bound club with vicious metal spikes all down its length. 'You will not find a better, for the blow struck with this mace has power to lay low trolls and demons. It is a demonbane. It has been dipped in my pool, so that you will strike with the power of ten armists.'

'Caréysin, your unerring accuracy with the bow is no small part of why your company managed to win through. Such skill deserves deadlier arrows with which to shoot, for the targets you will one day aim at shall not be stopped by mere steel. Thus, I have prepared for you star-steel arrows: their shafts are unbreakable and their tips will punch through any armour. They too are a demonbane, but I have only twelve to give, so use them wisely.'

'Lancoir the Stalwart, it is my pleasure to honour and arm a Knight of Thainen. For you I have prepared this demonbane dagger. It is of a kind with the mace and the arrowheads, forged of star-steel, and imbued with the power of the pool. Alone among all the arms of Astrom, these weapons can slay demons. Alike in fashion, they are to be used in concert, for the greater good. Let the bearer of this dagger never depart from his king, lest evil befall.' As Lancoir returned to his place, Kulothiel addressed them all.

'Armists, bear these weapons to good fortune, and may the blessings of Prélan Almighty go with you.' Dismissed, the armist prize-winners took their trophies back to the Maristonian part of the map.

Curillian alone was left. He had remained kneeling, head bowed, during the whole ceremony. Now Kulothiel called him last of all. Every eye was on him, as was a light, which fell suddenly around him, whilst all else was plunged into shadow.

'Last of all I summon Curillian, son of Mirkan, King of Maristonia, bravest of the brave. You are the winner of the Tournament. To you falls a double prize, and a great responsibility. Receive these mighty heirlooms, long set aside in waiting for this hour. Firstly, a demonbane dagger, the twin of Lancoir's, to be your weapon when evil presses close. And secondly, this amulet is a Soul-Shield. The wearer shall confound the mightiest servants of the enemy and bring new heart to those who flag. Let its virtue be ever about your neck, to put hope in your heart and fire in your belly.' Kulothiel spoke commandingly out of the darkness, addressing the assembled lords.

'My lords…' The wizard stepped into the spotlight so that all could see him hold Curillian's arm aloft. '…Behold your victor.' Curillian had always been respected, even feared, but in that moment, he was held in awe by his peers. They gaped at him, for the amulet flashed at his breast and he seemed to have grown suddenly taller. No one missed the significance of the display. Here was the wizard's champion, a warrior anointed for battle. But Kulothiel was not done. His final words he spoke in a ringing voice that roused them all to unprecedented fervour and unity.

'The Tournament is over, the prizes have been given. Power Unimaginable is now bestowed in your hands, but hear now the true purpose for which you have been assembled. Kurundar has arisen again in the north, his strength of old fully regrown and his hatred redoubled. What your forefathers faced has returned to plague your days, only now the sorcerer is in league with the demons of the underworld and fell abominations are in their train. One day soon, a storm such as you have never known will break upon you out of the north. All your collective strength will be needed to weather it, and only complete unity of resolve will spell survival. So I say to you, men, elves, armists and dwarves, put aside your enmity with one another, and take up arms as allies.

'Curillian will be your leader, the standard-bearer of this great endeavour. He is Prélan's chosen champion; to him has been revealed the means by which not just survival but victory will be achieved. Therefore, put your trust in him. Pledge yourselves to follow where he leads.

'Free Peoples! Unite, or fall. Stand together, or die. With you is the light of civilisation and all the heavenly heritage that Prélan has bestowed. Do not suffer it to be extinguished. I have fought all my life to keep the darkness at bay, but my strength is all but spent, so I bequeath the struggle to you. Prélan grant you the victory that has eluded me. Leave this Mountain, but forget not my words. Go forth now, your way out will be shorter than your way in. Farewell.'

A blinding light flashed, the walls shook. Roujeark heard the Keeper's voice speaking on in his head.

Roujeark, you will be my final apprentice. When all the others have left the Mountain, you must remain.

When the blinding flash subsided, the room was plunged into darkness. The wizard was gone. None of them saw where he went, nor indeed could they see each other, so sudden was the blackness. The stunned silence lasted only a moment, then it was shattered by shocked consternation. Scores of voices rose in alarm and protest, splitting the pitch darkness, but so flabbergasted were they at first that no sense could be made of them. For a while all was noise and anger. Each party turned in suspicion on their unseen neighbours and soon scuffling broke out, just as it had in the entrance chamber at the beginning of the Tournament.

Roujeark was just as shaken as any of them, but he was concerned more with the voice he had heard in his head than with the darkness. Suddenly his elbow was seized by a strong hand.

'Roujeark, fire.' No trace of panic was there in the king's voice, just a cool certainty of what to do. Roujeark tried to focus his mind, and heard the king speak to Lancoir also.

Above the din, Lancoir's stentorian voice rose like thunder.

'HOLD! HOLD FAST! NOBODY MOVE!'

His parade-ground lungs had the desired effect, bludgeoning all the others into obedience. In the silent eerie blackness that followed, a sudden flame flickered into life. Piercing the darkness, it moved swiftly into the centre of the map. It grew stronger, illuminating Roujeark and those around him. The fire sprang from his hand and hovered there. Spellbound, the jostling men and dwarves gathered round. Bewildered faces were drawn like moths. Curillian and Lancoir moved into the light and stood either side of Roujeark, the other armists behind them.

'So the Tournament ends as it began, in darkness and confusion,' Earl Culdon commented drily. His battle-hardened face flickered in the flamelight.

'A cursed waste of time it's been,' blurted out Reubun, one of Adhanor's attendant noblemen. Xavion, next to him, spoke in agreement.

'True. We've come all this way and for what? A few pretty lights and some trinkets.'

Caiasan the Aranese scribe stuck out his nose pugnaciously. 'Trinkets? Didn't you hear what they could do? They're powerful gifts. And we-mmpf...' he was cut off suddenly as Sir Hardos clamped a big hand over his mouth.

Southilar rumbled discontentedly in place of his scribe. 'Some of us have completely wasted our time. What's in it for those of us who got nothing?'

'Survival,' Lancoir answered him tersely.

'Survival?' Southilar scoffed. 'From what? The wizard's half-crazed, doesn't even know what century it is. Kurundar's dead and gone, there's naught but a frozen rabble left in Urunmar. Our Hendarian friends are quite capable of dealing with them.'

'Is that what you think, my lord Jeantar?' Bishop Nurvo spoke up for the Hendarians. 'Perhaps it has been some time since last you visited the haunted frontier, but evil is truly stirring there. You would do well not to ignore it.'

Hoth the dwarf elbowed his way into the firelight.

'The Keeper has done enough to convince me,' he growled. 'Magic is not forgotten in the halls of Carthak, even though the halls of Carthak may have been forgotten by all of you. In the past some of our own fought with the League of Wizardry, and what little we heard from them told us that we could trust Kulothiel.' He turned to Curillian. 'King Curillian, I will go back to my lord and report what I have seen and heard. I will urge him to ally himself to you. If I can convince him, you will have the axes of Carthak at your side when the time comes.' Curillian nodded in acknowledgement, but others had yet to say their piece.

'Nobly spoken, dwarf,' sneered Earl Onandur of Hendar, 'but how will we know when the time comes? For all we know, it could be years yet. The wizard spouted mighty fine rhetoric, but we can't plan an alliance nor a strategy of defence on this basis of this alone.'

Curillian stepped forward then, and seized the acrimonious debate by the scruff of the neck.

'My friends, there will be a time to speak of details. For now, it is enough that we have all been brought together. I do not believe that we have been deceived, nor brought together only to amuse the whims of a dying wizard. The League of Wizardry was ever a friend to the Free Peoples, bringing succour, counsel and military aid in times of trouble. Its last Head has spoken words of clear warning to us, and our children will condemn us if we fail to heed it. We're in a strange place, and have seen strange things, but let us nevertheless weigh carefully what we have heard. If any of us are to secure a future for the people we represent, then let us heed the words of Kulothiel, for I believe that he speaks with the authority of Prélan himself.' Several in the shadows around him murmured assent, but just as many faces were unconvinced. Curillian turned slowly, holding every eye in turn.

'There will be a role for all of us,' he told them.

'Easy for you to say,' spat Southilar. 'The wizard named you leader. Well, I won't follow your orders, nor will any of my people.' No sooner had he finished speaking than someone contradicted him.

'I will.' The voice spoke from the shadows, and both Southilar and Curillian knew it.

'Theonar, you'll do as I tell you and not forget your place,' Southilar told him. 'So long as I am Jeantar, I will have the final say for Aranar on all this madness.' Theonar paused, the silence suddenly thick again, before answering.

'You will not remain Jeantar for long.' Southilar's knights had to restrain him from finding the other man and lashing out at him, and commotion reigned again. Curillian spoke once more, raising his voice above the din.

'Aranar needs a Jeantar who'll look beyond Hamid to the good of us all.'

Southilar rounded on him. 'Did you not hear me, Curillian? I'll not follow you.'

Curillian stood his ground, keeping his voice level. 'If you can't follow then you've got no business leading.' The Jeantar looked as if he had been slapped. White-faced, he was unable to respond. Curillian again appealed to them.

'I'm not looking to rule any of you, nor is that what Kulothiel had in mind. But just let any man here say that I won't give my heart and soul for the free world. Let that man speak now, and back up his words with his sword.' No one spoke. 'No, I don't seek command. But whatever needs to be done, I'll do it. Whatever comes, I and my Maristonians will be in the thick of it. When Kurundar strikes, I'll fight alongside any one of you, and I pledge my sword to that now.' He drew the Sword of Maristonia and held it up by the blade, turning in a slow circle and showing it to all of them. None of them failed to be impressed by the legendary weapon. Ever since the time of Arimaya, Curillian's grandfather, it had been a mighty force for good in the world, and never more so than in the hands of Curillian. Sheathing it again, he said, 'No one need commit to anything now. I propose we assemble for a proper council in one year's time. Will you all agree to that?' The lords around him all nodded or muttered agreement. Southilar alone demurred, insisting that he would have no part of it.

'A sound proposal,' said Earl Culdon, speaking over the Jeantar's sullen whisper. 'Decisions will be easier made in the light of day than in this wizardly gloom. Nothing more need be said. Come, let us eat what little food we have left and then depart.' Weary as they were, everyone was only too glad to agree.

'But how do we get out?' asked Parthir. 'We have only this one small torch, and there's much danger out there.' Only then did he appear to notice that the flame was coming from Roujeark's living palm, and he did a double take.

Theonar spoke again, drawing their attention to a single illuminated doorway.

'See, Kulothiel has provided a route. Remember, he said the way out would be shorter than the way in. Follow the light.'

Slowly they started to depart, minds chewing on all that they had heard. Adhanor of Hendar came close to Curillian. In the flamelight, the young king looked at the elder statesman with a worried expression.

'Do you really believe Kurundar will attack again?'

'Yes,' said Curillian, 'I do.' Swallowing his anxiety, Adhanor nodded, and then moved on. Bishop Nurvo went with him, but not before he gave Roujeark a lingering look of unsettling interest.

Roujeark, Curillian and Theonar were the last to leave. The tall Aranese knight held them back and spoke quietly but forcefully in the small light.

'We three are keepers of a secret trust. Only we know of the missions that Kulothiel gave to Roujeark and I. Do not forget.' He held out his hand, and in it was the gleaming piece of amulet. The others held forth their own tokens too. The firelight rippling across the otherworldly objects was enough to send shivers down the spine. 'Curillian, you must forge an alliance out of that unlikely material; I must find Avatar's amulet and return it to him; Roujeark must take away Kurundar's power. Amulet, Soul-shield and Star-shard: all must succeed, or all will fail.' Theonar folded his other hand over the artefacts, clasping both their hands with his. 'Prélan give us strength,' he said feelingly.

'Prélan be with us,' Roujeark offered.

'And Prélan guide us,' Curillian rounded off the tripartite prayer. Then he looked at Roujeark with a weary smile. 'So, you will remain here?' Roujeark nodded, reluctant now that the hour had come. 'Come down to the gates with us at least,' Curillian said. 'Say a proper farewell?' Roujeark was glad to accept, even though he could already feel the Mountain calling. The king looked from the wizard to the knight. 'Friends, we part for now, but let us come together again, when the time comes. Whatever help we can give each other, let there be no hesitation. We'll do this together.' They looked at each other and in silent understanding pledged faith. Then Theonar broke away and strode from the chamber. The armists followed him, joining their compatriots who waited outside. The great hall outside was dimly lit, and the footfalls of the others were receding along it. Smiling wearily, they took their first steps on the road home.

✹

VI

The Uninvited

ONE By one Roujeark counted off the landmarks they had seen on their way in. Along the Hall of Tapestried History, past the wash of blue light about the Tear of Mírianna, beyond the twin statues of the guardian wizards – whose staves parted willingly enough from this side – and down the long staircase. When they at length reached its bottom, they found themselves in the atrium with the three doors. Ahead of them, like a blemish on the ornate wall, was the small iron-bound door through which they had forced an escape from the tunnel above the lava lake. To the left and right were two others which were four times the size and infinitely more decorative. Roujeark wasn't sure he would know which way to take, but when they came to it, they found the right-hand portal illuminated for them. The Keeper's directions prevailed.

Roujeark didn't even know if he should go through at all. Kulothiel had beckoned him to remain. Wasn't the whole point for him to get here and stay, not leave like everyone else? As everyone else trudged through the magnificent archway, he hung back, uncertain. Curillian noticed his reticence and paused by him.

'The Mountain is calling, isn't it?' Roujeark nodded wordlessly. Curillian squeezed his shoulder. 'Come down to the main gate with us at least?' the king suggested. Roujeark gratefully accepted the idea. It deferred the painful prospect of parting. Most of him couldn't wait to study and learn at the feet of Kulothiel, but a part of him dreaded losing the friends he had so lately won. So, they descended together, at the rear of the weary exodus.

They were now in a part of the Mountain they hadn't been in before. These were more civilised parts, the pathways by which honoured guests would enter, rather than the sewers and dungeons through which they had crawled. The décor was grand and imposing, but not so intricate or otherworldly as the upper chambers from which they had just descended. They passed along wide echoing corridors and through many-pillared halls which were lit as if for their convenience. They went carelessly, the different races conversing amiably enough as they went along together, and their voices echoed in the shadowy ceiling.

As they passed from one smaller chamber into a larger, Roujeark stopped, feeling a check in his spirit. This was not the reluctance to part from his friends he had felt before, but a tremor of remembrance. He shivered, feeling the inexplicable wariness he had felt on previous occasions. The other armists did not notice but walked on ahead of him. All the while he stood rooted to the spot, fingertips twitching. In his mind's eye, he saw himself in a great library somewhere inside the Mountain. A gust of chill air rushed over him, and the whole chamber around him seemed to bend and flex. Then a book fell from its place. He watched it fall in slow motion, wondering what it was. He felt the thud of it hitting the floor like a blow on his back. It landed spine-up, but he had to come closer to see its title. *The Wars Against the Harracks.* He straightened upright in a flash, feeling suddenly hot and sick despite the cool air. Unbidden into his mind came a succession of images from his horrific time in Faudunum, and he felt hot pulses running down his arms.

'Harracks,' he whispered to himself. Both visions faded, and he found himself back in the lower chamber. His comrades were some way ahead now, their footsteps echoing in the distance. 'Harracks,' he said again, louder, but still no one heard him. All of a sudden his feet were moving, alarm rising in him, and he said it a third time, panic amplifying his voice to a shrill cry.

This time the others heard him, for the echoes winged around the larger pillared hall. Running now, he caught up with them to find men, dwarves and armists all staring at him, confused and irritated. Even Curillian looked bemused.

'What did you say?' he asked. All was suddenly quiet, the clinking of mail and the squeaking of leather fading away to dead silence. Roujeark swallowed hard, much more afraid of his intuition than the others' annoyance.

'Harracks,' he repeated, somehow unable to say more. They all saw that his face was pale and beaded in sweat, and their expressions changed to ones of concern.

'What did he say?' Onandur asked, puzzled. Evidently the name meant nothing to him.

'Harracks,' Culdon said, adding nothing to the big man's understanding, but the grimness in his voice and the gripping of his sword hilt spoke volumes.

'Roujeark,' Curillian pressed him gently, 'what are you saying?'

'Harracks. Here. In this Mountain,' he managed to say, at last able to add more words. 'There are enemies out there.' Alarmed, many of them turned to look fearfully around at the partially lit hall, whose further parts were filled with great shadows.

'Are you sure?' Curillian asked. Roujeark nodded.

'Ah, what does he know?' demanded Sir Hardos. 'He's as crazed as the old man, or so exhausted he's delirious.'

'He's been right before,' Findor protested stoutly.

'What are harracks?' demanded Earl Onandur, adding to the fraught atmosphere. Suddenly many voices were speaking, and Curillian for once looked indecisive. Maybe it was weariness, maybe it was some other factor clouding his mind, but he just stared at Roujeark, not heeding the hubbub around him. It was Lancoir who acted. Seizing Roujeark's hands, he inspected the palms. To his horror, he saw a fierce red glow welling up in each like an evil boil. That was enough to convince him.

'Quiet,' shouted the Captain of the Guard. 'QUIET!' His ferocious tone cut across them all like a whiplash, and silence settled once more. Only this time, it was not quite silence. Small pitter-patter sounds came from the hall's shadows around them, like the falling of little stones. The silence thickened, pressing close like an unseasonal garment. More noises followed. Quiet, far-off, strange, but definitely there. It was as if a horde of insects were crawling about in the dark corners, like the shards of a nightmare pricking the edge of consciousness. Hands fell to weapons and feet shuffled nervously about.

A sharp whizzing cut through the thick air and sped towards them like a berserk hornet. An arrow ricocheted off a dwarf's shield, and behind it, somewhere in the darkness, came an evil snicker. The dwarf turned, indignant, but the assailant could not be seen. Theonar's sword came into his hands as more arrows came spitting and zipping towards them. The air was suddenly alive with them, vicious little black-barbed darts. Theonar deflected several of them with his sword, and many struck armour or clattered on the paving stones beneath them, but one found its mark. An Aranaese man-at-arms cried out, clutching his throat. An arrow seemed to grow out of his neck, and he slumped to the ground, gargling and bleeding copiously. Curillian seemed to come out of his trance and stooped by the fallen man. He inspected the weapon and came to a speedy conclusion.

'Never mind harracks, these are goblin arrows,' he cried. Even more than the arrows themselves, his words sparked panic. All around him the warriors leapt into action, unslinging shields and whipping out swords. The group fanned out, unsure what to do, but desperately peering into the gloom for sight of the enemy. Another man fell dead, this time one of Parthir's crew. The arrows weren't coming in a deadly rain, but well-directed pot-shots and accompanied now by blood-chilling howls. Curillian felt sure that this was but the vanguard of a great enemy presence. Every now and then they caught glimpses of little figures darting between columns or climbing up pillars like demonic monkeys. How many were out there Curillian couldn't guess, but then he heard the drumbeat. BOOM!

It was deep, so deep that it sounded like the heartbeat of some giant at the Mountain's core. Sinister and compelling, it brought fear into all their hearts. BOOM. Another drumbeat reverberated the floor under their feet. Not all of them there had ever seen a goblin, much less fought one, but Curillian had, and he knew that war-drums were not in their repertoire. But harracks used drums. Monstrous great things that could shake mountains. He had heard drums like this before, borne by harrack war-bands and used as weapons in themselves.

BOOM.

'Back!' he shouted. 'Back to the smaller cavern!' Suddenly he was thinking clearly again, and he knew that an enemy as agile as the goblins could quickly outflank and surround their little company. They must get back to a narrower place, somewhere they could hold. 'BACK!' Lancoir repeated Curillian's command, lifting it above the din of panic and drumbeats. BOOM. BOOM.

Men and dwarves were only too glad to follow his order, and as one they hurried back to the great chamber's entrance, pursued by mocking laughter. Between this chamber and the next was a short, broad corridor, and into this constricted space they piled.

'Is this some kind of sick joke by the wizard?' demanded Culdon.

'Curse him!' shouted Southilar. 'He's lured us here to our deaths. We are betrayed. Look at us – all the leaders of the Free Peoples caught together in one sorcerous trap.' Curillian didn't believe the Jeantar's wild assertion, but if that had been Kulothiel's plan, he could hardly have done a better job. They were trapped. Between them and freedom was an unseen enemy, and behind was only a haunt of wizards. BOOM. BOOM. The drumbeats were getting louder and nearer.

'But why would he do that?' wailed Caiasan.

'Someone had better find him,' suggested the bishop, who was armed with a wicked dagger, priest though he was. 'Now more than ever we could use his help.'

'This is not his fight,' said Theonar, though no one took any notice.

Curillian looked at the warriors around him. They had different weapons and equipment and different experience of fighting. His eyes lighted on the dwarves.

'Hoth!' he called. Men parted to reveal the dwarf squeezing into his new gift of armour. Angry eyes looked out from the leathery face. 'Hoth, I need your dwarves to form a shield-wall across the entrance,' Curillian told him. 'Your shields and armour will block the corridor better than any of us.' Hoth just nodded grimly and hefted his enormous battle-axe. 'The rest of you,' Curillian ordered, 'form ranks behind the dwarves. We hold this place.'

The shield-wall locked together, the dwarves' great iron-bound limewood shields clacking as they formed an overlapping barricade.

Hoth's fighters were well-versed in this kind of warfare – underground clashes in tight spaces where victory went to the strongest arms and the most disciplined formations. BOOM. BOOM. BOOM. The throbbing drumbeats came more insistently, their pounding noise filling the subterranean world. In between each beat they could hear the lesser drumming of many heavy feet. The enemy was coming for them.

'What is happening?' Curillian looked around to see Elrinde and the other two Ithrillians coming up from behind. Wherever they had been, they were here now, and Curillian couldn't have wished for a better ally.

'Harracks,' Curillian explained abruptly, 'and goblins. It's an ambush.' Elrinde nodded. It was not fear in his face, but some other emotion that he had to quickly suppress as he took in the news.

'I thought as much. The racket they make is like the Black Dwarves of the Goragath Mountains. I hope they don't fight like those bastards.'

'Come and find out.'

The pounding of feet was coming much closer now. Goblin cries rent the air and as they gathered around the radius of the opening, they started to concentrate their fire. Most of the missiles snapped harmlessly against the dwarves' shield-wall, but some went over their heads. One Ciricien warrior didn't duck quick enough and took an arrow in his upper arm. Soon they were all crouching behind the shield-wall, and Lancoir and Onandur between them marshalled them all into place as second, third and fourth ranks. Suddenly the arrows stopped and a furious rolling wave of drumbeats burst over them like an orchestral climax of thunder.

BOOM. BOOM. BOOM. BOOM!

'BRACE YOURSELVES!' Hoth bellowed above the din.

'BRACE!' echoed Lancoir. None of them save the dwarves saw the enemy coming, but the booted feet came at a run and the bass war-cries rang loud. Then a wave of enemies hit them like a storm surge, and the impact shuddered through all the ranks to the very back. The dwarves were smashed back a few paces, and the men and armists behind were powerless to stop the backward momentum. The sound of shields smashing shields was like a rockfall in the mountains, and maces and hammers beat loud upon wood and metal. Then the dwarves pushed back. Grunting and cursing, they heaved at their enemies, and won back one of the lost yards. Axes forgotten, they used short stabbing swords to jab between the gaps in the shields, and the harracks did likewise. For harracks they were. Allied again to their old partners in crime, they had somehow come to Oron Amular with the goblins. Late, and uninvited, yet they seemed determined to have the last word. But where the short, sinewy goblins were good skirmishers and archers, it fell to the sturdier harracks to hammer home the main assault.

Hoth's dwarves gritted their teeth and put all their weight into resisting, but they were being driven slowly back. Between the shields they could see tight-skinned savage faces that were parodies of their own. All leathery skin, squint eyes and wild bushy beards. Mouths full of rotten tooth stumps spat and cursed, growled and roared. No one knew how many of them there were, but the weight of their shield-wall kept growing. Like an unstoppable juggernaut, it ploughed forwards. Their blades were forgotten; they seemed intent only on pushing their enemy out of the bottleneck.

Curillian and Lancoir knew the danger, but they could do nothing. Side by side in the second rank, squeezed up against the dwarves by the row behind, all they could do was push and heave in vain. A dwarf craned his neck back to look at them, red-faced and full of strain, his veins nearly bursting out of his head. Their world had shrunk to a claustrophobic oblong of noise and sweat, grunting and heaving.

Theonar, though, was at the back with Roujeark, Bishop Nurvo and Caiasan, the lightest of the company. The tall knight seized the young armist's elbow and hissed in his ear.

'They can't last long now. When we break, be quick and follow me.' The vague notion had formed in Roujeark's mind that as soon as he had clear sight of the enemy he would let fly with his bolts of flame, as he had done in Faudunum, but Theonar sounded like he had a plan. He hoped so, because the situation looked bleak. They numbered a little more a hundred, by his best guess, but the harracks seemed to outnumber them many times over by themselves; with the goblins, they were a great horde. Their numbers mattered for little in the corridor, but as soon as they were out in the open again, they would be horribly vulnerable. Unless they could find another place of defence, they could be encircled or cut down by a rain of arrows.

BOOM. BOOM. BOOM. The drums in the larger cave beyond still throbbed, like a deep and insistent headache. Every drumbeat seemed to instill fresh encouragement in the harracks, and they heaved anew with each new beat. Roujeark and his immediate companions were forced out of the corridor now and into the dimly lit cavern behind, and still the men in front of them were being forced backwards. Roujeark searched around for some feature that might serve as a refuge, but there was nothing, nor could he hear himself think above the awful noise of the drums and the war-cries and the thunder of hammers. He noticed Theonar studying what looked like a small groove in the floor. It ran the width of the cavern. The knight then looked up, scanning around the cavern's walls. Whatever he saw, he looked more hopeful than Roujeark felt. His hands were hot with pent-up power and he shook uncontrollably, but in his mind, he was fending off the despair that threatened to swamp him. Refuge or no, unless they could overcome this enemy there was no getting out. No future, no hope for the Free Peoples.

'Ready?' Theonar asked. Parthir's crew in turn had been pushed out of the tunnel, and instead they took up positions on either side, fitting arrows to their short bows and hefting throwing knives. Elrinde and his two companions dropped back also, long slender elven swords at the ready. Back and back went Curillian's shield-wall and the harracks, scenting victory, gave an almighty push that sent men, dwarves and armists staggering.

'Now!' cried Theonar, and off he sped into the gloom. Roujeark half-turned to follow him but tarried a heartbeat to see what happened. One minute there was a shoving mass of bodies, the next a human explosion as warriors were thrust willy-nilly from the confines of the corridor. All order vanished, and everybody found himself alone and with no clear idea of what to do except flee. Roujeark broke into a run, following where Theonar had gone.

'Back!'

'Retreat!' The desperate orders were hardly necessary, nor even audible, for the scattered contestants were already in headlong flight, and the deep victory chants of the harracks drowned out all else. They came pouring into the second cavern like an avalanche of bodies and jeered at the routed enemy. Yet for all their impressive pushing power, they were not fleet of foot, and so their foes were out of reach for the moment. The harracks parted ranks to allow the goblins through, and they came like an evil tide through sluice-gates, all slimy skin and dull iron. With horrible speed they flooded the cavern, shooting off arrows with nimble fingers even as they ran. Several arrows found their mark in their fleeing targets, and the archers danced and screeched in exultation.

Curillian ran through the pandemonium, his armists by his side. He had no more idea of what to do than any of them, all he knew was to get to somewhere more defensible. They were fleeing blindly back the way they had come, urgently seeking somewhere to use to their advantage. They came to some stairs at the far end of the second cavern and surged up them. A doorway was in front of them, but Curillian couldn't remember what was through it. Instead, he turned about to see what was happening. What he saw made his heart sink. The cavern was in absolute chaos. His friends and allies were scattered all over the place, some fleeing, some turning to fight. They were being shot at from every angle and yelling mobs of goblins were closing fast to commence their butchery. A dozen or more men already lay dead with arrows protruding from them. Hoth's dwarves were hindmost, weighed down by their armour, and looking like being engulfed. Behind him, Lancoir was ushering some through the doorway, while anyone with a bow and arrows he deployed as a flimsy rearguard. Their shafts were like spitting into a hurricane.

Then suddenly the king's eyes and mind were filled with a wall of fire. The floor seemed to erupt in flames that seared all the way to the ceiling, filling the cavern with lurid light and appalling heat. A line of goblins was caught in the inferno and incinerated. The roaring of the flames and the hideous screams of those caught in them raised the cacophony of noise to a crescendo of horror. Curillian's first thought was of Roujeark, but he was nowhere to be seen. The flames receded as quickly as they had burst forth, dying into the thin trench whence they had come. Curillian vaguely remembered passing over a little gutter in the floor, but he had thought nothing of it. For a split second he hoped that the flames would remain as an impassable barricade, but that hope was cheated. It had won them precious moments though, and once the initial shock passed the dwarves were able to make good their escape, jogging towards the steps. Just ahead of them came the heavily armoured Hendarians, the last of the contestants.

Not quite last.

A

Roujeark had placed his hand where Theonar indicated, a small panel in the cavern wall. It had not been visible before, but Theonar had smashed the coloured glass that had covered it with his sword hilt. Pressing his hand against the panel, Roujeark felt a tremendous power throb up his arm like someone was pulling it off. Theonar waited not a second longer but pulled him away and they were running again. Seconds later a whooshing sound went up behind them and a wave of heat threw them on their faces. From his hands and knees, Roujeark looked back in awe at the wall of fire. He had done that. Horror filled his tear-blurred vision as he glimpsed flaming figures running around and heard the awful shrieks of the dying.

Theonar tugged him upright again and ushered him to another spot. Already the enemy were overcoming their terror and coming on again, passing over the trench that had proved so deadly to the front-runners. Again, Theonar smashed the glass, and shouted, 'Here!' Roujeark put his hand to the spot and felt the same heat and twinge of pain. This time, a deafening series of clangs announced the falling of many trapdoors. A chequered pattern of holes appeared in the floor. Some goblins who had been standing on them fell instantly to an unseen fate, and many more followed them who couldn't dodge or stop in time. Scores of them vanished, their forlorn cries drowned out by the alarm of the survivors. The goblins' forward momentum was brought up short, but again they weren't stopped for long.

Madder than ever, and howling for blood, they rushed forward once more, harracks lumbering up behind.

Roujeark had time to steal a quick glance to where Curillian was conducting the escape of their friends before Theonar hauled him away. Together they ran to a corner of the cavern. Theonar turned and yelled to attract the attention of the goblins. A large band of them broke away from their headlong dash towards the steps and came charging at them. Arrows whistled and clattered all around them.

'Find the next panel, Roujeark,' the knight called urgently. Roujeark searched the rock walls, and behind a brazier he found a protruding stone that seemed a little loose. Pushing it, he felt it give and retreat into a hidden recess. Then there came a rumbling noise and a whole section of the wall swung inwards. Not a moment too soon, he and Theonar ducked inside. In total darkness, they hid to one side as fifty or more goblins came hurtling in after them, screaming and hollering.

Once the goblins were inside, the section of wall swung back to its original place, sealing them inside. The noise of them was an assault on Roujeark's ears, but in all the bedlam he and Theonar remained undiscovered. The awful noise only subsided when a dazzling light materialised in the centre of the dark chamber. Roujeark watched in amazement as the light dimmed somewhat to reveal Kulothiel standing there, a Mage-Lord in all his glory. The goblins surrounding him cowered away in fear. Their dark green hides, grimy leather garments and patchy iron armour were thrown into sharp relief by the light. For the first time, Roujeark got a good glimpse of them. They were short, slight and sinewy, mis-begotten creatures of filth and malice. They did not have even the traces of civilisation that the harracks could claim, only those instruments of evil that they had found a use for: sharp-barbed arrows, wicked knives, whips and light javelins. They were the skirmishers of Kurundar, his light infantry, bred for ambush and harassment.

One seemed to be a leader of some sort. He stood taller and more upright than the others. Gold was at his neck and wrists, and his armour was more complete, though still roughly made and primitive. Roujeark could not see his face, for it was turned towards Kulothiel. They stood locked in silent struggle, each seeming to know the other. The Mage-Lord looked at him with cold fury.

'This far you shall come,' he told the goblin chieftain, 'and no further.' The goblin barked in defiance and raised his scimitar, but Kulothiel was quicker. Incanting fell words of power, he raised both arms, fingers splayed, then quickly drew both hands into his body as fists. Instantly the goblins looked stunned. They held their hands to their ears in seeming agony, as if assaulted by sounds that neither Roujeark nor Theonar could hear. The wretched creatures danced, cringed and writhed in distress, but Kulothiel was implacable. He kept his fists clenched and maintained his measured words of command. No longer afraid of being overheard, Theonar backed away.

'Turn away now, Roujeark.' He drew the young armist away, leading him up a hidden flight of stairs. Behind them the goblins' screams reached fever-pitch and then cut out suddenly as each and every one of them was crushed like an egg. Theonar led Roujeark up and away before pausing at a blank wall. Just then they heard someone behind them, and they turned to see a solitary surviving goblin. Roujeark gaped as it dashed up the stairs, seemingly oblivious to their presence. Both hands were still clamped over its ears, as if trying to keep out some awful noise, but the only noise they could hear was its own screaming, a dreadful keening cry, like a pain-maddened hawk. It closed the distance between them in a few prancing bounds and bulled into Roujeark. The armist was caught off-balance and knocked to the floor, where he fumbled desperately for his dagger. But the goblin had a weapon of its own and removed a hand from one ear to brandish a javelin that had been strapped to its back. Still screeching in pain, it prepared to strike, seemingly more enraged by the hindrance to its escape than by out-and-out enmity. Roujeark saw the javelin point come glinting towards him, aimed straight for his throat, but then there was a swoosh in the dark and it stopped. The goblin's severed head toppled onto him, and he twisted away in loathing. Glancing up, he saw Theonar sheath his long blade. Roujeark expected him to extend a helping hand, but the knight was looking down at him with something akin to annoyance.

'Roujeark, what are you doing?' he said, half-puzzled, half-angry. 'You're better than that.'

Embarrassed and angry, Roujeark booted the headless corpse back down the steps and struggled upright, rubbing an elbow that he had fallen awkwardly on. He looked reproachfully at Theonar, but the knight seemed not to notice. Instead, he clasped Roujeark by the back of the neck and pulled his face close.

'You're not some mongrel man-at-arms who has to scrap in the gutter or scrabble for a blade. You have faster and better weapons than any of us; use them! There are hardened warriors out there who will one day quake at your coming. You're worth a hundred others in this fight. Next time, don't hesitate.'

Theonar released him and turned back to the dead end at the top of the steps. Another hidden button opened a door, and out they sprang into the tunnel passage where only moments before the last of their friends had passed by.

They found them in yet another cavern, by far the smallest of the three. Men, elves, armists and dwarves were all arrayed there, fleeing no longer but determined to make a final stand. Their leaders, Curillian, Southilar, Adhanor, Culdon, Elrinde, Hoth and Parthir, stood out in front, grim and resolved. Roujeark made a hasty count. Ninety-two were there, stretching nearly from one end of the cavern to the other. Sixty men of various nations, twenty dwarves, nine armists and three elves. A pitifully small force, but well-armed and counting in their number warriors of great renown.

Curillian looked relieved to see the two of them and beckoned them into the ranks near him.

'Prélan be praised you're still alive! Was that you back there? Well, we need more of it. This fight's not done yet.'

'It's just getting started,' said Lancoir. He was flexing his muscular forearms and tightening the cords that held his vambraces in place. He nodded at Roujeark, and the wizard smiled wryly at the wordless compliment. Lancoir wasn't the only one getting ready. As the harrack war-drums thudded in the nearby caverns, the whole company readied themselves for battle. The armists were dressed alike, leather-padded mail-shirts under their travelling clothes, with hardened leather plates over key areas like forearms and chests. The flaming sword emblem of Maristonia was etched into the leather and embroidered on the cloaks, which were now cast aside. Their bows and arrows were laid out in readiness on the floor in front of them, and their two-handed swords were strapped across their shoulders, ready to be drawn at a moment's notice.

Next to them, the men of Ciricen on one side were also in mail but with the added protection of thick fur cloaks. Brandishing their formidable skuxes, which were half-axe and half-halberd, they waited silently for the next round. On the other side, standing uneasily next to their armist neighbours, was Parthir's ragged crew with their curved sabres and long pikes. Beyond the pale Ciriciens, in the centre of their line, were the Hendarians in plate armour and Hoth's dwarves more heavily armoured still. They held great battle-axes and mattocks at the ready, eager for another chance to get at their ancient foes. The men of Aranar sported the badges of their respective clans. Swords were in their hands and small shields were unslung from their backs. On the far-right were the three Ithrillian elves, but they followed Elrinde as he came to take counsel with Curillian. He twirled his elegant sword as he came, almost absent-mindedly, and his casual swordcraft earned him many admiring glances. They had been allowed a short time of respite as the enemy gathered for a fresh assault, so the leaders came together.

'You know these scum best, Curillian,' said Culdon. 'What's the quickest way to kill them?'

'There is no quick way,' Curillian told him. 'They are tough and thick-skinned. Their armour is not as good as some of ours here, but the leather and fur they wear is enough to stop all but the strongest thrusts...'

Hoth interrupted him. 'They're nought but clumsy savages. They try to fight like us, only they're weaker and less good-looking. Leave it to us, watch how we do it.' Curillian smiled.

'But for those of you who find yourself facing a harrack and there isn't a dwarf to hand, listen to Lancoir. Captain...' Curillian gave Lancoir centre stage, and the stalwart armist raised his deep voice so all could hear.

'Slashing's no good, it's like hacking at a rock. They'll carry a thousand scratches and keep coming. Thrust and stab. Hard. Put all your strength into your blow. Make it count. They're slow, but they won't give you many chances. Keep moving, don't stop. Wait till they've committed themselves to a swing of their hammer, then step inside for the killing blow before they can recover.'

'And get close to the goblins.' Elrinde added his wisdom to the battlefield tutorial. 'Don't give them room to shoot. Keep your eyes on them, because they're quick and their knives will find the weak spots in your armour. An...' Whatever else he might have said was drowned out by more furious drumming. BOOM. BOOM. BOOM. Curillian saw the nervousness in their faces and stepped out in front of them all.

'Do not be afraid. Prélan is with us. We fight as one, and we fight with His strength.' The sound of many feet in the tunnels outside rose to a thundering din and Curillian had to shout to make himself heard. 'I say again, do not fear. There will be a tomorrow, our stories do not end here. If you could see the living tapestry in the halls of this Mountain, telling the story of time, you would see that there are other battles to fight, other struggles. It does not end here. We do not end here.'

Then the harracks were spilling into the cavern, stamping and snarling out of the corridors that led in. Behind crudely painted shields, they fanned out into the chamber. Gone was the mad rush of their first assault; this time they came with measured caution. More and more kept coming, filling the far side of the chamber until barely fifty yards separated them from their enemies.

For the first time, the contestants got a good look at them, for some had never encountered harracks before. To the Hendarians they looked like something out of their folktales, which told of Black Dwarves who haunted the Goragath Mountains in centuries past. They had the same primitive clothing, the same brutal weapons, the same eerie appearance of rational beings long fallen from grace. The Hawk and Falcon knights saw old enemies who lurked at the edges of their frontiers and whose mountain fastnesses they had never been able to eradicate. The Ciriciens saw barbarians who seemed to resemble the wild hill-men of Dorzand, the windswept plateau south of their realm in which they had fought for time out of mind. The dwarves of Carthak saw beings who had once been like them, but who had never achieved the heights of their underground civilisation, and who had already begun their descent into ignorant savagery when Carthak was still rising to new levels of power and skill. Elrinde looked with disgust at this stunted and unlovely race, and bitterly he regretted the far bygone day when his ancestors had first awoken them.

Roujeark saw the same implacable lifeforms he had encountered in the cold city of Faudunum. With faces like stone and animal eyes, they looked and were armed like maniac blacksmiths. He tried to stop his legs from shaking as fear crawled all over him like a plague of insects. The cavern seemed hot and he felt sick. More than once his hand strayed to his dagger, and more than once he checked himself. Instead he looked down into his palms, which were glowing angrily and throbbing with pent-up energy. Clenching and unclenching his fists, he resolved to give a good account of himself. He repeated as many of Theonar's words to himself as he could remember, but he doubted that he could live up to them. Whatever he had within him, he would throw into the fight, for himself and for his friends. He did not want to die here, before he had even begun his apprenticeship. Not after coming so far and waiting so long. No, he would use his untrained abilities in every way he could to make sure that he could live out his destiny.

Remembering how Curillian would pray before every action, he turned his mind to Prélan and his eyes to the cavern's roof. *Help me,* he pleaded. *Be with us. We need you. We need you badly. If you don't come through for us, this is the end. Help me to control my fears. Help me to control whatever power I have. Give me strength.* Looking down again, he saw Curillian's head bowed and lips moving. He too was praying, as were many of them. Not all there were devout: some just stared balefully at the enemy, steeling themselves.

A sudden noise made Roujeark jump. It was a great war-shout and a clatter of arms. The dwarves had advanced into no man's land between the two armies and taken up a strange formation. Their deep voices boomed out in a ritual challenge, chanting words of hatred and power. Accompanying the words, they made a war-music of stamping feet, gesticulating arms and axe-heads clashed against armour. Far from random noise, the sounds they made were rhythmic, beautiful even, in a haunting sort of way. Their eyes were locked on the harracks as they put on their defiant display. The harracks started a chant of their own, and their front rank broke out into a thumping war-dance, similar but completely different.

Curillian at least had seen this before, or had heard of it in the tales from when his ancestors had fought the dwarves in the Second Chapter. He knew what was coming, so he raised his sword, turned, and yelled an encouragement to his followers. The other leaders did likewise, and the whole line shifted forward a pace, tense and alert. The dwarves bellowed out the last of their challenge, and the harracks finally lost patience. With an almighty shout, they came forward at a slow, lumbering run. There was no order to them, just a rage-fuelled charging mob. But the dwarves were ready for them. Before they met, they changed swiftly into a new formation. They pressed close together and presented their shields outward and above their heads. In the blink of an eye, they had become an armoured mass and the harracks crashed against it like a wave against a cliff. The din was ear-splitting as battle was joined. The harracks wrapped around the dwarf formation and beat at it with their hammers and clubs. They seemed to make no impression, but every few seconds a gap would appear in the shields and a short stabbing sword would flash out, hacking into the nearest assailant. Roujeark saw several harracks fall like this before he lost sight of the dwarves altogether.

But he didn't watch for long. He charged forward right behind Curillian and Lancoir. Beside them the whole line was moving, dashing up in support of the dwarves. Before any of his comrades could strike a blow, Roujeark let loose with a fireball from each hand. He didn't think, he just did it. A far cry from the raw and misdirected missiles he had discovered in the ambush at Broadsword Ridge, these fireballs were bigger and much more concentrated in power. They scorched into the harracks and exploded, filling with cavern with garish light. Harracks were blasted from their feet and a ragged hole opened in their ranks. Yet he didn't have time to fire again, because Curillian and Lancoir were into the gap like foxes after chickens. They laid about them with their swords in terrible blows. Moments later, the Royal Guards joined the action, and in a brief glimpse Roujeark saw the dreadful power of the demonbane mace given to Lionenn. The stocky warrior swung it against the nearest harrack, whose shield crumpled as if struck by a thunderbolt. That harrack was thrown backwards and the force of the blow took half a dozen others with him.

Then Roujeark himself was engulfed by the fight and he forgot all else. His world shrank to a few square feet of cavern floor, which he shared with Antaya and a trio of howling harracks. He had but a split second with which to duck the swinging hammer right in front of him. He evaded it so successfully that he found himself flat on the floor and his eyes had to adjust to the unusual angle as the battle lurched above him. The harrack passed over him only to have its head cloven by Antaya's two-handed sword. For a second Antaya looked exposed, but Findor appeared beside him and drove back the enemies menacing him. Roujeark's feet were trampled on and he launched a fireball at the offender, who disappeared upwards and backwards in a gout of smoke and sparks. Two of the dead harrack's comrades looked down and in their inexpressive faces Roujeark was certain he could see shock and fear. He didn't give them a chance to recover but blasted them as well. He rolled aside as a hammer came crashing down from the side, and he was scrambling upright as it smashed a chunk out of the floor. He kicked the hammer out of the harrack's grasp before he could retrieve it and then blasted him backwards. Yet the harracks pressed thickly about him, those behind quickly taking the place of the slain. He had to twist and drop to one knee to avoid the next blow, and from his kneeling position he swept his arm round in an arc of inspiration. A sheet of flame scythed round and ignited one harrack after another until all those near him were aflame.

He was suffused with exhilaration at the revelation of what he could do, but it was swamped in seconds by the realisation that he was confronted with flaming harracks who could not escape because of the press of the battle from behind. He backed away in alarm, lest his own fire engulf him too, but the harracks followed, mad with pain and seemingly determined to have revenge before the flames killed them. Out of the corner of his eye, he was vaguely aware that a new presence was ploughing in where Antaya and Findor had been before. The harrack to his right was flung aside as Lionenn's mace smashed into him. Roujeark winced at the tremendous violence as the guardsman waded into the melee. Again and again, Lionenn swung his mace, imbued with the magical power of Kulothiel's pool, until he had cleared a space in front of them. The harracks who had been there were either mangled on the floor or cast aside in a wide radius of carnage. Roujeark breathed a sigh of relief and leaned on his saviour's shoulder as he caught his breath.

A

All the along the line, the Free Peoples had crashed into the harracks and joined the battle. Ciriciens, Hendarians, Alanai, Aranese and Ithrillians, they were all soon embroiled in a desperate fight and hard-pressed. None of them could see any of the others except their immediate neighbours, their world full of noise and flailing weapons, and none of the leaders could gauge how the battle was going. If any of them had been able to get up high and look down, they would have seen the cavern filled with an ungovernable mass of embattled warriors. No order or formation was there, just a deadly fight at close quarters. In the confined space, few of them had room to swing and strike a proper blow, so they resorted to punching, grappling, shoving and stabbing with short, powerful blows.

The dwarf formation still held firm, but it was completely encircled now, and their allies could not even see it, much less reach it. Dead harracks were heaped in great piles around the impenetrable shields. Whenever they managed to beat down a dwarf, the formation closed up again and the shields locked, leaving their fallen comrade to add to the corpse wall which was proving a great obstacle to their foes.

It was the arrival of the goblins that proved the undoing of the dwarves. They came late to the fight as fresh reinforcements now that the harrack onslaught had been checked. Sifting between their bulky allies, or clambering over them like ghastly gymnasts, they came whooping and hollering into the fight. Dozens of them leapt on top of the dwarvish shield-wall and scrabbled over it like sadistic monkeys. With long wicked daggers and javelin points, they found the tiny gaps in the defences and jabbed down. Underneath the shields, the helmets and armour of the dwarves were a solid second line of defence, but the attack from above succeeded in breaking the tight cohesion of their formation. As they started to shift about in a bid to protect themselves from the blades above, more goblins attacked from all sides, jumping up and seizing shield-rims. Clinging on with all four limbs and careless of the hands and feet they lost, they used their weight to pull the shields out and expose the warriors behind. When the gaps appeared, the harracks hurled their weapons in to batter and stun.

Within minutes of the goblins' arrival, the dwarf formation had disintegrated and they were left to fight as individuals. Then their axes really went to work, splitting helms, cutting off limbs and disembowelling harracks and goblins alike. Yet more of their own number were falling now, perishing to face-crushing hammer-blows or bleeding to death from scores of little knife-wounds.

The Hendarians found themselves in a similar predicament, able to match their enemies man for man but being worn slowly down. Bishop Nurvo went down to a hammer-blow and was thrust unceremoniously from the fight, his attendant priests dragging him free from the melee while the knights fought on. The young King Adhanor was giving a good account of himself, with the towering Earl Onandur on one side warding off blows and a sturdy knight on the other. Count Xavion and Duke Reubun were nowhere to be seen.

Beside the Hendarians, the Aranese were no less beset. Goblin arrows whistled from overhead to bring death and injury from every angle, whilst all about them their enemies were swarming. Yet they employed the skills they had honed at many tournaments, fighting skilfully at close quarters and giving their enemies as few openings as possible. At the Hamid Tournament, their great men fought for the right to be called Jeantar, and at dozens of small tourneys their young warriors were blooded and showed off their prowess. Now they were not fighting for prizes or prestige, they were fighting for their very lives. Caiasan had a bloodied head but was still on his feet and giving as good as he got. Southilar was using his great strength to deal out ferocious sword-blows. He loomed over the harracks like a highland tree above dry stone walls, but nothing they could do seemed to hinder him. Several arrows already jutted out from his armour, having been cheated of any effect, and his Pegasus men defended him well.

By the cavern's far wall, Elrinde and his companions were fighting a very different battle, avoiding the tight-packed bludgeoning going on elsewhere by keeping their enemies at sword's length with agile skill. Every time a club or hammer swung at them, they were no longer there, but had danced away to lash out another lethal thrust from a new position. They seemed able to dodge the javelins flung at them and wriggle aside when charged. Elrinde thwarted every attempt to pen him up against the wall and deny him space by ceaselessly moving, weaving and feinting.

The Alanai were used to the cramped conditions of shipboard fighting and threw themselves into the fight with deadly effect. No rules or disciplines governed their approach, so they scrapped tooth and nail, kicking, wrestling, gouging and stamping. Their pikes were useless after the first charge, but they were deadly with their sabres and their knives, both throwing and slashing. Each of them seemed to have an inexhaustible supply of throwing knives stashed about their person, flinging them like a storm of waves crashing over a ship. Time and again a rush of harracks was reduced to a pile of gurgling bodies, but when they succeeded in getting close, the Alanai proved no less lethal at close quarters, stabbing and ripping.

But the enemy that the harracks most feared was the armist king. Curillian fought like a tornado, combining the speed and skill of Elrinde with the brute power of the big Hendarians. Whenever a weapon came close to him, the Sword of Maristonia shore clean through handles and hafts, and arrows were powerless against his cunning armour. Lancoir was close by his side, guarding his flank, killing with ruthless efficiency. The enemy shied away from them only to run smack into the whirling mace of Lionenn or the greatswords of the Royal Guards. Aleinus, though, had advanced too far and found himself cut off with the young Ciricien warrior Kaspain. They fought back-to-back, desperately trying to fend off the enemy. But a low-swung mattock smashed into the armist's knees and his legs crumpled under him. As he fell, a javelin passed clean through his neck, finding the exposed throat above his mail-coat. Blood bubbled out of his mouth as he slid to the floor, eyes glazing over. Moments later, a sickening thud knocked Kaspain down over him, blood matting his blonde hair.

Roujeark was gasping for breath and almost spent. He didn't see the death of Aleinus, but he was distracted by the cry of anguish that went up from his right, piercing above the battle-storm. He watched a tall Ciricien with the physique of a prize-fighter charge into a press of enemies where his comrade had fallen. He broke a goblin's neck with one punch and smashed the heads of two others together. He cast the bodies aside contemptuously and then lifted a harrack clean off the ground. Roujeark was amazed at the feat of strength, and watched, captivated, as the warrior, whose name was Rhyard, threw the squealing harrack into his gang of subordinates. With hardly a break in stride, the massive man plunged into the gap he had created, but death found him an eyeblink later. A dwarvish axe, taken from its trampled owner, came hurtling out of nowhere and struck Rhyard full in the face. Like a fallen oak, he crashed back in ruin, the axe still buried deep.

Roujeark turned away, sickened by the sight. Whatever Sir Theonar said, he was not cut out for this wholesale slaughter. No amount of magical power could galvanise his heart in the face of such butchery. Others in the cavern might be inured to the horror of battle, but he was not. The sight of Findor losing a leg to a goblin scimitar and falling was too much for him. He dropped back and sank to his knees, tears brimming in his eyes. Through the tears the cavern shimmered, and its ghastly clamour receded to just a dull echo in his ears. His comrades seemed to be falling thick and fast about him, and he lost sight of Lancoir and the king.

Theonar found him in that state. The tall knight knew something was wrong when the booming sound of the wizard-pupil's fireballs ceased, and he extricated himself from his position near Earl Culdon, who fought stoically despite grisly wounds. Theonar himself bore countless small hurts, and his sword was rinsed in blood, but he had great reserves of stamina. When he saw Roujeark whimpering in abject despair, he seized him by the scruff of his scorched and blood-soaked robes and dragged him along.

'Pull yourself together Roujeark, we need you!' he yelled in his ear. With one hand, he pulled him back into the thick of the battle and with the other he cut down any goblin who scampered near. He reached the spot he was aiming for and saw a case of desperate need dead ahead of him. He manhandled Roujeark upright and pointed out the dense press of harracks ahead of them.

'Now, Roujeark, fire!' But Roujeark's knees were buckling and his thoughts were scattered. He could no more summon a fireball than conjure a wolverine from thin air. Theonar saw there was nothing for it. Stooping, he scooped the young armist onto his shoulder and turned his back on the scene. Fearlessly he stood in harm's way and prayed, sword outstretched in supplication.

'Now Roujeark, DO IT! NOW! NOW!'

Held over the knight's shoulder, Roujeark could barely see or hear. He felt consciousness sliding from him when a gust of vitality swept in and through him. Borne on the wings of prayer, it invigorated him with a sharp rush of life, like a cascade of icy water over a groggy man. In a split second, his eyes focused. A few moments later, his arms stretched out rigidly, and twin fireballs shot out. The group of harracks in their path was devastated. One moment they had been mobbing a fallen enemy, the next they lay flung about in charred ruin. Roujeark's eyes widened still further when he saw a dwarf in the midst of the ruckus, beard alight and rippling with flame. Theonar was still murmuring a silent prayer of thanks when he felt Roujeark slide from his shoulder. He was too slow to catch him as he darted forward, heading for the blazing apparition. Lancoir saw him go, plunging recklessly into the flame-licked charnel-house, and went after him, leaving the king's side.

Roujeark reached the dwarf and stopped short, horror and wonder mingling in him. The warrior was still standing, but his beard was half-gone and his face was badly burned. A moment ago, the flames had been writhing all over him, but now they were gone, dispelled as if by magic. It was Hoth, the chieftain of the dwarves. Seeing his brothers dying around him, he had charged, maddened, into a knot of his foes, ploughing deep into them. He had been on the point of being overwhelmed when Roujeark's thunderbolts had struck the harracks near him. What followed was an inferno that consumed his axe-handle like tallow and part-melted the buckle on his belt. But his new armour had saved him, cheating the flames. He had put it on shortly before the fight began, taking Kulothiel at his word. Now, ignoring Roujeark completely, he tottered unsteadily away, leaving the battle. Roujeark gaped open-mouthed after him, astonished.

Yet the battle went on. Virtually everyone had paused when the great explosion rocked the cavern, and many a goblin had fled, but enough harracks loitered nearby to converge on Roujeark in a rush. He did not even heed his danger, so dumbstruck was he by the scene which he had just witnessed. Lancoir arrived just in time to intercept the enemies who came straight for him. They thought to put an end to this accursed wizard once and for all, but instead they found themselves face to face with the death-eyed Captain of the Guard. Lancoir cut down the first harrack and quickly recovered his blade to hack down another. He moved fast, knowing the ring of enemies was all around. He didn't have time to land a killing blow on each of them, so he abandoned his own advice and slashed just enough to drive each one back.

A ring of them closed about him and Roujeark, who was slowly coming back to his senses again. Lancoir buried his sword in a harrack's chest, but there it stuck fast, and when he tugged it would not come. A heavy fist clobbered his head and poleaxed him. Roujeark found himself seized by a harrack and squeezed in a deadly embrace, but he slapped at the hate-filled face with his hands. Grasping the angular temples in both palms, he felt steam rise and the harrack's grunts turn into gasps of pain. The tight-stretched skin seemed to start melting, and then it burst into flame. Roujeark cried out in pain as his own hands were burnt, but he felt the vicelike grip about his waist slacken. He dropped to the floor as the harrack fled howling, burning like a living torch.

Out of the corner of his eye he saw Lancoir struggling to his feet, shaking his head. Bereft of his sword, he looked helpless as a harrack swung at him with a crooked blade. But Lancoir ducked under the swing, which cut home instead into the harrack who had been coming up behind him. Suddenly there appeared in Lancoir's fist the demonbane dagger that was his prize. Forgotten until now, he buried it in his assailant's throat. In a split second the harrack completely disintegrated, falling like a pile of ash to the floor. The very next second Lancoir reversed the lethal weapon into the other harrack, finishing him off in the same way.

Roujeark saw a harrack looming over him with a club, and he swung upwards with the hammer he had found lying on the floor. His hands were throbbing with blistering pain, but he managed to catch the harrack a savage blow which crunched teeth and sent him reeling. Roujeark lurched upright in time to see a goblin arrow embed itself in the back of Lancoir's shoulders. It was foiled by his armour, but another one followed hard on its heels and struck his arm with strength-sapping force. It found a gap in between the lacings of the knight's vambrace and he dropped the dagger with a grunt of pain. Lancoir took a fist-blow to his kidneys from behind and staggered forwards. He stumbled over a harrack who was coming in low to tackle him to the ground. He seized up his dagger again with his good arm and the harrack vanished from underneath him. Heavy boots kicked Lancoir while he was on the floor, and he slashed about him furiously, trying to regain his feet.

Roujeark was sobbing with pain, but he did his best to fight off Lancoir's attackers. They seemed to be alone amongst their enemies. Where were the others? A jarring blow to his elbow made him drop the borrowed hammer. With his hands in agony, and now weaponless, Roujeark felt panic rising. Another blow hit him somewhere on his back, and he fell forward, stunned.

Lancoir killed another harrack, then another, and another, but they kept coming. He saw Roujeark under attack, saw him fall. He went in that direction, trying to reach him. He slew the harrack standing over him with a swing of the dagger that left him at full stretch and off balance. Another harrack appeared fast and seized the hand that held the dagger. From the opposite side, another seized his throat. Pinioned from both sides, Lancoir looked down at Roujeark, and Roujeark looked up at him. The jagged sword seemed to grow out of his middle. The blow, dealt by a hulking brute of a harrack, had enough force to puncture through the armist-mail, jerkin, body and right out the other side. Lancoir hung, impaled, eyes defiant to the last, but his face overtaken by the throes of death. Roujeark's cry of loss seemed to sear across the ghastly frozen tableau. A moment later the sword withdrew, the vicious hands let go, and Lancoir fell heavily on top of Roujeark. The wind was driven from the young armist, cutting off his strangled cry of anguish. Lancoir's dying eyes bored into his, and he watched close-up as death claimed him. With his last tortured breath, the Captain of the Guard uttered one word.

'Lancaro.'

VII

At The Sight Of The Flaming Sword

FINALLY The battle lulled. Whether it was the terror of the wizard's fire, or a desire to fall back and regroup, the harracks backed away and departed from the cavern. The goblins went with them, their screeches dying away into the rock with horrid echoes. A pitiful remnant of the Free Peoples were left behind, standing amid a carpet of corpses. It was a horrific scene, the survivors standing like the lonely sentinels of some long-felled forest. Acrid smoke drifted about, stinging eyes which were already raw with weeping. A smell of charred flesh and blood hung in the air. Dreadful wounds were staunched and tended as best as could be contrived, and the weary warriors gulped in air. Elrinde cleaned his sword and Southilar squatted amongst the bodies of his fallen comrades. The Hendarians gathered protectively around their ebullient king, who exhilarated after surviving his first bloodletting, whilst beside them the Ciriciens sat around, exhausted, bloodied and smoke-grimed. Parthir's Alanai scurried about retrieving arrows and thrown knives and Hoth's dwarves, now pitifully few in number, stood like statues, singing a dirge over their fallen kin.

Roujeark saw none of it, though. All he saw, close as a lover, was the dead face of Lancoir. The captain's sweat had coursed little channels through the grime on his skin. He could barely breathe, still less shift the captain's weight off him. Moments passed like hours, and then a new face appeared over Lancoir's shoulder. It was Theonar, stooping down from on high, full of concern. With him was Andil, fresh from slaying the harracks who had done the deed. Then came Caréysin as well. Together they heaved Lancoir's body aside and liberated the shell-shocked Roujeark. Theonar helped him sit up while the two armists knelt over Lancoir.

'My friend,' said Theonar breathlessly, 'I am so sorry. I couldn't get to you in time. A charge of harracks came between us. I am so sorry…I should have been here…' Andil and Caréysin were incredulous. They could not believe that their indestructible captain had actually fallen. They had seen it happen, as helpless as Theonar to intervene through the enemies in between, but they still didn't believe it. Andil picked up the demonbane dagger and retrieved Lancoir's sword from the harrack it had killed and become stuck in, and after he had cleaned it, he laid it at the captain's side. Caréysin was holding his lifeless hand and murmuring a prayer over him, tears pouring down his cheeks.

That was when Curillian saw them. The tides of the battle had swept them apart, though he still had Antaya and Lionenn with him. He had been stooping over the maimed Findor, but when he had straightened, eyes smarting in the foul air, he had sensed something amiss. Looking around for the cause of it, his eyes fell on the sorry scene of his comrades stooping over a fallen body. All the rest of the battlefield vanished from his sight. Andil. Caréysin. Roujeark. But he could not see who they crowded around. He had watched Aleinus die, Findor he had just come from, and Antaya and Lionenn were with him. His heart went cold as he ran out of names. The sound of his heartbeat became the only thing he could hear, diminished to the barest of background flutters. Time itself seemed to stand still. He could not feel his arms or legs, could not move. The grief-stricken eyes of his surviving comrades looked at him, helpless to make it untrue.

Roujeark had never known pain like it. He was battered and bruised, groggy, parched and exhausted. His hands were horribly burnt. The stricken field filled him with horror and the smell nauseated him. Far worse was the knowledge of what he had done. He had contributed to this slaughter, his own hands had brought forth the flames which had burned friends and foes alike and now wafted about, stinging the nostrils of the survivors. The smell of the flesh he had charred lingered like an unclean spirit refusing to depart. But he had also been the cause of this. He looked down at Lancoir, whose face was now at peace. He looked up at the king. Curillian was frozen with disbelief and horror. He just stared at them. Roujeark's skin crawled under that baleful glance, guilt gnawing at him like rodents in his clothes. Weeping freely, he leaned over Lancoir.

'Lancoir...I...I can't...'

The words would not come. The gratitude he felt was swamped with guilt and shame and fear, and from that tangle nothing articulate would come. He squeezed the brave captain's hand and looked into his sightless staring eyes. How could such a valiant fighter be dead? Wouldn't Prélan save such a one? Yet if his lips and tongue would not cooperate, his fingers knew what to do. He pulled off the ring. He felt its loss like a silent but loyal friend. The plain silver band was scuffed and worn and possessed almost no shine. *Where I come from, rings are given in token of a debt of honour. I give this to you. I will not forget until I have repaid.* The long-ago words of the captain filled his head, making him choke with emotion. Gripping the ring, Roujeark leant forward and kissed the fallen armist's forehead. He left the ring on his breast. *You have paid your debt, Lancoir, my friend. Far more than was owed.*

Then he looked up and Curillian was standing over them, his face a mask of sorrow. Roujeark backed away as the king slumped down beside the body. Slowly the tears came, and then all of a sudden there was a flood. All semblance of dignity was gone from the great monarch as he wept in great sobs that seemed wrenched from his depths. Curillian dug his fingers into his friend's hair and caressed his face. All his armists and Sir Theonar stood about, sharing in the grief of their sovereign. Curillian pulled Lancoir's head into his lap so that tears fell on the captain's battle-grimed features. Then his hands reached out, grasped Lancoir's sword and pressed it into the lifeless fingers. With both hands he held it against Lancoir's breast, holding it tight.

'He saved me,' Roujeark said, feeling desperately that he had to say something. 'He came after me. He fought them off…but there were too many. He saved my life.' Painfully long seconds stretched out as Curillian's eyes bored into his, trying to understand what he was saying. Then the wizard saw a fell light come into the eyes. Curillian lurched, and Roujeark fell back. The king rose, getting unsteadily to his feet, his eyes still fixed on Roujeark. There was open accusation in them now, and furious, blood-chilling anger. Theonar stepped between them and then Curillian was ushered away by his guards. Theonar draped an arm protectively about Roujeark's shoulders and together they watched the other armists depart. But Curillian pushed his companions away and staggered into the centre of the battlefield. Unaware of all else, he sank to his knees, staring into space.

The survivors of the other nations, scarcely forty in all now, gathered about him slowly. All but Elrinde gave him a wide berth. The elf crouched down and looked into his face. He raised the armist king back up again and held him by the shoulders. Curillian's head hung limp, shaking as if refusing to heed what Elrinde was whispering to him in elvish. Then he thrust Elrinde away as well, and the elf, grave-faced, stepped back away from him. Curillian was shaking violently now, as if some great force stirred within him that could scarce be contained. Then the cry came, a great shout torn from the caverns of his soul. It blasted across the battlefield, through the tunnels and reverberated around the caverns beyond, powered by sheer hatred and carrying the promise of vengeance. The barracks heard it and blanched. Kulothiel heard it in his high chamber and closed his eyes in sorrow. On and on it went, until Curillian slumped again, drained by the effort of it. None were able to look upon his face, which quivered and twitched with storms of emotion. He took a step forward, his great sword clenched in his hand.

'Curillian.' A voice called, that of Earl Onandur. He ignored it and took another step.

'Curillian!' another voice called, this time King Adhanor. Again, Curillian took no notice, but carried on forward.

'Curillian, now is not the time,' called Earl Culdon, gasping from his wounds. 'We need to regroup.' Curillian kept going.

Sir Hardos from Southilar's party strode after him, shouting angrily for him to stay. He caught him up and grasped him by the shoulder. In a flash Curillian turned and struck him to the floor with a great blow. Such was his force that he left the big man reeling and dazed on the floor, spitting blood. Fury reigned unassuaged in Curillian's face, and madness was in his eyes. Not even Lancoir, were he still alive to see it, could claim to have seen anything like it. Then Curillian turned and strode from the chamber.

The armists hurried after him, fearful for what he might do, Roujeark included. Andil bore the body of Lancoir over his shoulder, and Theonar went with them. The others were not far behind. Southilar had been enraged by the assault on his lieutenant, and he yelled at his remaining men to apprehend the armist king.

But Curillian was well ahead of them now, picking up his pace until he was running full pelt through the tunnel. He erupted from it like a cannonball and sped down the steps of the great cavern beyond, the one they had fled through after the shield-wall collapsed. The harracks and goblins had withdrawn there, and now waited in an uncertain mob. Should they attack again or slink off with the partial victory they had scored? Then a strange noise cut through their indecision. An echoing cry, quite unlike anything any of them had ever heard, drifted through the high cavern and came to their ears. Moments later they heard the rumour of his coming, and they trembled. A single warrior came charging out of the tunnel, alone and enraged. His sword was bright and his face was a herald of death. They looked around, took comfort from their numbers, and hefted their weapons ready to receive him.

Despite being weak and feeling sick Roujeark stumbled on, driven by a renewed sense of urgency. In the tunnel he pushed past the other armists and so was next to emerge into the cavern they had so lately evacuated. The sight that greeted him took his breath away. Curillian was charging across the floor, heading straight for the whole harrack army, which was still hundreds strong. With the goblin mobs there must have been several thousand foes still in the Mountain, and in a dark, torch-lit mass they waited for the lone warrior. The other armists came alongside, and they too checked in horror and awe. None of them had ever witnessed such reckless courage. This was the Curillian that legends spoke of, the destroyer of armies, the champion of the Silver Empire, Kurundar's nemesis.

Yet he was going to his death. The enemies waiting for him would surround him in seconds and he would be overwhelmed, driven by madness to his death. Not if Roujeark could help it. He went to one knee, ignoring the throbbing pain from his hands, and raised them up. His companions watched, spellbound, as he drew a thunderbolt from his living flesh. A sinewy coil of fire snaked out of his palm and fizzled in his hands as he shaped it into a sorcerous spear. Then, with a strength they didn't know he had, he threw it. With the speed of lightning striking, it hurtled across the cavern, lighting it up and ripping the air asunder. The very floor seemed to ripple under its blistering onset. From behind Curillian's shoulder it sped, zooming past him and smashing home into the harrack ranks. They had been rooted to the spot as it came, filled with fear yet unable to discern what it was. It exploded on their front rank and burst through, flinging bodies into the air and punching through rank after rank. It did not expend its energy until it had torn the harrack army almost in two, incinerating dozens and blasting dozens more to either side.

And Curillian leapt into the carnage, following the lightning with a different kind of flame, the Sword of Maristonia. As Roujeark sagged down, spent, and as the others recovered from their shock to continue the pursuit, Curillian tore into the harracks. Half of them had already turned to run, and those that stayed were cut down left, right and centre. The Sword of Maristonia was like a living thing among them, striking death like a serpent. Fuelled by rage, Curillian cut them down and set them all to flight. And he went after them, chasing them through the corridor where the shield-walls had clashed. Theonar led those that came after. He called over his shoulder as he ran.

'Everyone take a shield. The goblin archers are still out there.' Many took his advice, snatching up the crude shields of the harracks and then carried on running. Still they could not catch Curillian, who charged on as if no weariness could ever come over him. He chased the harracks through the pillared cavern where Roujeark had first sensed their presence, cutting them down as they ran. Goblins to either side took pot shots at him, but none managed to do any damage. Curillian ignored the monstrous drum and its crew and heeded not the pockets of foes which he bypassed. His bloodlust drove him recklessly on, filled with an intense desire to kill every last one of them.

Theonar and the frontrunners crossed the pillared cavern, and they too ignored the harrack drum. Hoth's dwarves, coming behind, smashed it to pieces, stopping its great beats from throbbing out. Andil, burdened with the body of Lancoir, fell way behind, but Parthir came unexpectedly to his aid and helped him on. The goblins were massing again now for another attack, and their arrows were building up ominously in volume. Theonar's advice showed its value as their shields cheated most of the arrows. Unable to do anything else, the long straggling line of the contestants struggled on, desperate to keep pace with each other. There were enough enemies left alive in this place to swamp them yet, Curillian or no Curillian.

At length they came to the grand entrance hall, the very threshold of Oron Amular and the greatest cavern yet. They had not come in this way, and no eyes did they have now for the wondrous architecture and statuary around them. That final cavern before the open world was reached from a great balcony from which broad flights of stairs led down. Curillian was already on the floor, striving towards the great gates where pale daylight showed cold and alien to their sight. Theonar despaired of reaching the berserk king, but before going further he deployed archers on the balcony to fire down and try and cover Curillian. Then he somersaulted down, scorning the steps. Others charged down the steps, whilst the Hendarians formed a rearguard, fighting off the harracks and goblins who came at them from behind now.

Curillian was in grave danger. His vast strength was flagging, and his onslaught had carried him deep into the mass of his enemy. He did not notice the great engines of war that were being set up by harracks who hadn't yet joined any of the fighting. He was slowed by several small wounds and a great weariness which seemed to be stealing over him. All the great exertion of the Tournament was at last catching up with him and swamping his adrenaline. Yet even the end of his strength was still incredibly strong, and he kept fighting doggedly. Whirling around, he struck again and again, the great Sword of Maristonia making light of the harrack armour. No longer pressing forward, he made a ring of slain about him. But the enemy kept coming. Recovering again from their panic at the magic levelled against them, they returned to the assault. Only too late did the Free Peoples realise quite how outnumbered they had been.

Now their great engines, ballistas and catapults cunningly assembled from portable parts were deployed, and great arrows half the height of a man and thick as spear-shafts came hurtling through the cavern. Theonar narrowly evaded one, and another turned a dwarf almost inside out. With them whooshed great chunks of masonry torn from the walls; the Mountain itself was being turned against them. A Ciricien went down, and a Hendarian, then another and another was slain. The pitifully small remnant was being gradually encircled and slain to a man. Unchecked slaughter raged, and still Curillian fought on.

Yet cold sense and realisation were beginning to get through to him, and the awful predicament he had led them into slowly dawned on him. The enemy was all around; death lapped at their feet. His limbs were leaden and his heart was heavy. Feeling old and tired, he looked despairingly towards the arched gateway. Out there, so close, was sunlight and fresh air. So close. They had come so close to escaping…and now they would all die.

As he looked, the light in the gateway seemed to dim. Something was cutting off the light. A great banner. He lifted his eyes, not daring to believe what he saw. Though the cavern was dark otherwise, lit only feebly by a few braziers, he could make out the silver stitching on the great rectangular flag. A sword. The image of his own, sewn in shimmering thread and fringed with fire on a royal blue field. Beneath it marched legionaries of Maristonia in disciplined ranks, and Royal Guards with them. Beyond all hope, his troops had somehow found them. Somewhere behind him he heard armist voices lifted in ragged cheers, and a shrill trumpet blared out defiantly, shaking the ancient walls.

Ready to collapse, he watched a moment longer. Suddenly the flaming sword was cast into shadow by the passing of a shining object, flying in through the gateway. A great falcon, shimmering with silver wings, soared in above the advancing battle-line. It cast radiance on the scene below. The eyes of the Free Peoples were lifted in hope, but the hearts of the goblins and harracks were chilled. The mysterious falcon sped down like an arrow, but as it neared the earth it suddenly morphed into a pegasus, its bright wings now flanking a sleek equine body. It came to land by Curillian, all graceful strength and shining white. With his last strength he slid onto its bare back and slumped there. At last Theonar caught up with Curillian, and he fought off the enemies who menaced the king and the newly come creature.

Yet the strange beast and the Maristonian troops were not the only newcomers. Bringing gusts of sudden cold air, lines of snow-elves rushed into the hall like a snowstorm. Seeming to glide over the cavern walls above the heads of the goblins, they made straight for the war-engines, which had now been turned on the reinforcements and were doing grievous damage. Leaving behind frosted trails of ice, they descended like hail in savage anger on the harrack artillerymen and slew them with cold daggers. The machines themselves they froze solid, never to be fired again.

The Maristonian troops fought their way forward until they met the survivors. Curillian's companions were delighted to see their old comrades among the newcomers, Surumo and those members of the Third Cohort that they had left behind at Tol Ankil, and several of the trackers and scouts as well. Yet they had no time to greet them, for escape was their pressing need. The legionaries closed protectively around them, a great outward-facing square. There were several hundred of them, a couple of cohorts' worth, still fewer than the enemy but enough to hold them at bay. All the remaining contestants reached safety within the square, and Andil wearily passed the body of Lancoir up to lie draped in front of Curillian on the horse. Curillian clung to his dead friend as the newly arrived armist officers shouted orders at their troops. Slowly, pace by pace, they conceded ground and marched back towards the gate. The snow-elves went as suddenly as they had come, leaving the square to bunch through the gateway and spill out into bright daylight.

The sun was hot and riding high. The light was searingly bright in their eyes after so much time spent in dark caverns, and they raised their hands to shelter their faces. Gusts of fresh wind smote their faces, wafting with it the scent of wildflowers. Gravel and loose stones crunching under their boots, the square slowly reformed as it emerged from the great gate and made its way slowly downhill.

From within the Mountain the harracks and goblins hurled themselves against the retreating formation, but they were held at bay. Nor did the soldiery of Maristonia panic. They had trained long and learned well. Slowly, and with great fortitude, they kept up the ordered retreat. When they had all emerged into the daylight, the rearmost side of the square faced the enemy defiantly. Hard on their heels, the harracks and goblins fanned out onto the grassy slopes of the Mountain's toes. The goblins did not like the sunshine, which they usually avoided, and were not eager to renew the combat in its glare. The harracks egged them on, clashing weapons and shouting gruff encouragement. Yet they let the enemy square make it to the far side of the trough and take up a defensive position on the facing slope.

Curillian was only dimly aware of what was going on. Once upon the pegasus, his mind had switched off, his one and only thought being to keep a tight hold on Lancoir's body. Clutching it to him and slumped over the horse, his squinting eyes registered the change from cool gloom to warm summer air, but little else. The horse's measured hoofbeats lulled him as they crossed over the trough, and the sounds of battle died away in his ears. Then weariness and sorrow overcame him. As the winged horse knelt, he slid from its back and lay inert upon the fragrant grass.

His guards stood vigil over him. Roujeark sat nearby, forlorn and forgotten by all but Theonar. The rest of the Free Peoples stood and awaited the next stage. The legionaries of Mariston and the Tournament's contestants were equally weary, for the rescuers had pushed themselves through many forced marches to arrive in the nick of time. Now they watched the enemy gather and steel themselves. The senior officer in the rescuing contingent was a colonel called Estalor. He took charge and had the square formation change to a long line. He had done the impossible, and reached his king in time, but now it all seemed futile. More and more of the enemy were piling out into the open air, and every time he thought there could be no more, another mob emerged. He felt the spirits of his armists sag as the full strength of the enemy became evident. They needed a full legion here, not just the crack cohorts who could be deployed in haste.

Despairing cries went up as new enemies were spied. 'Look, there are more! Coming around the flanks of the Mountain. Hundreds of them...thousands!'

Like a swarm of ants, more and more goblins were coming to the fray. It seemed that some had not even gone inside the Mountain but had taken up positions on its lower spurs. Fresh and unbloodied, they came eager to the last confrontation. Despite the strong sun, and despite the unlooked-for arrival of the legionaries under their accursed banner, they knew they were going to win. One more push, and then they would be free to pillage the Mountain.

Roujeark was weeping now. Hope died in him as death came rushing across the valley towards him. It had all been for nothing. The long-delayed journey, his long years of carefully nurtured hope, the labours of the armists, the gruelling Tournament, the horrible underground battle. Why had Kulothiel bothered giving out his prizes and his missions if this was where it would end, just hours later? Why had *he* not done something? Now Roujeark would be denied again, and all talk of the future was vain. The battle joined, the slaughter resumed, and he let out a bitter, blasphemous curse. The end had come.

✳

VIII
The Bloody Vale

BLOOD Ran down the green slopes in slick streams. The cries of wounded and dying warriors rent the air and weapons clashed in a relentless din. The goblins had reached the armist lines first and they paid dearly for their onslaught. A whole rank was cut down before the second rank sprang up and hauled down the Maristonian shields. Armist by armist, they carved their way into the last stand, aiming for the banner that they hated so much. The Free Peoples fended them off for as long as they could, but their strength was fading, their numbers dwindling.

Yet so absorbed were the goblins in their orgy of killing that they did not see it coming. Theonar was the first to notice. Standing tense and erect above Roujeark, his ears heard the faint sounds above the roar of battle. His face turned, eyes boring into the distance. The harracks felt it next. They felt the tremor in the ground, faint at first but building in strength. They were accustomed to the movements of the earth, but no cause could they find for this.

The trumpet did not sound until the first horse had emerged from behind a spur of the Mountain. Theonar's eyes fixed on it in a split second. It was a great grey stallion, a beautiful creature galloping in full flow. Silver-shoed and caparisoned in ivory barding, it was the tip of a blade-shaped cavalcade. As each new horse thundered into view, another trumpet sang out until the whole vale was full of a brazen music. Louder and louder blew the stirring notes until the heights on all side were ringing. All the while, the ground shook as if the Mountain were flexing buried limbs. The elven cavalry swept across the flat bottom of the trough like a ship in full sail. For cavalry they were, mounted warriors in their war-glory. Dressed in flowing silk and mail so bright it hurt to look at, here were the noblest riders in Kalimar. They wore tall helms and above their heads a thousand pennons rippled in the breeze. A forest of spears glittered in the sun and golden hair streamed out behind beasts and riders alike.

The fighting had faltered at the first trumpet blast, then the goblins had fallen back altogether as each rolling note smote them. Mortals, dwarves and armists watched in awe as the elven charge gathered speed and came hurtling to the attack. Spears were lowered and warhorses snorted. The goblins broke in panic, but their retreat from the armist line only put them straight in the riders' path. The leading horses smashed the goblins over like wattle hurdles and then ploughed straight on through. Steel-shoes smashed foreheads and leaf-bladed spearpoints gored torsos. The momentum of the charge carried it clean through the goblin host with appalling ease. Those not slaughtered in the first moments were knocked over and trampled by the following riders. A storm of hooves crushed and smeared goblins into the ground. No mercy was shown. Gems flashed and blood spurted bright. The onlookers' eyes were drawn irresistibly from left to right as the charge swept by. In its wake it left a flattened horde. Where once hundreds of goblins had been swarming to victory, now a riot of bodies lay in red ruin. The pitifully few survivors were hunted down and put to the sword.

Nor did the harracks escape. They might have fallen behind the faster goblins in the last assault, but they had nowhere to hide. The elves employed slightly different tactics with them, knowing that they were heavy enough to disrupt a charge that tried to simply overrun them, so they rode either side of them instead and lashed out with long blades. Many fell in the first pass, but then the leading riders wheeled about in a fluid display of horsemanship and returned the way they had come. Down swung the swords again, and the harracks were too slow to either flee or dodge. By the end of the third pass none were left alive, and not so much as a single elf had fallen. Imperiously they rode on and clear. Passing under the eyes of the awestruck defenders, they looked like angels of death, proud and terrible.

The first trumpet call had awoken Curillian. Standing shakily, he watched the elven charge smash home and pulverise the enemy. Gasping in disbelief at this second unexpected rescue, his eyes shone with unshed tears. Then he noticed someone standing beside him. This person too was watching the massacre, eyes bright and shining, jaw set firm and cheekbones standing proud and shapely. Rich dark hair tumbled out of a mail coif and over a sleek mailshirt. She was tall and slim, standing like a queen dressed for war. She gleamed in the sun, looking more beautiful than any person had a right to. Curillian studied her from the side for a few moments before she turned her golden eyes on him.

'Carea,' he breathed. She smiled, but there was sadness in the smile. 'Was it you?' he asked unnecessarily. 'The falcon, the pegasus...' His mind struggled to catch up with his flapping tongue. 'The reinforcements...'

'It was all me,' she said. 'Don't look so surprised, Curillian. I told you before. I told you I would prepare the help you needed, and I did. I knew you would run into trouble here, and so I found troops to rescue you. Your 5th legion is still encamped on the marches of the East-fold. Horuistan is a very unworthy general, but the young colonel, Estalor, was willing to come. Defying a threat of court-martial, he led his cohorts over the mountains under my guidance.

The rest of your cohort from Tol Ankil joined us also, desperate to rejoin their king. And so we came here on a road known to none but the Cuherai.'

'Estalor…I know the name. And the snow-elves, you brought them too?'

'They needed little persuading. As soon as I told them about the goblins, they were all aflame, and the thought of their evil presence in Oron Amular had them boiling over. They went ahead of us in time of storm, some to summon extra help, some to block the enemy's retreat, and some to clear our path. Your legionaries endured the cold and the speed of their march to fight beside them.'

Suddenly it was all too much, and Curillian collapsed back to the floor. Carea crouched by him, full of concern. He grasped her arm.

'Thank you,' he said feelingly. 'Thank you.'

'My debt to you is paid. Now we have rescued each other from the harracks. But you, Curillian, you look as if you have barely survived…' She saw the grief welling up afresh in the king's face, and she knew its cause, but she was dismayed to see the sudden age and fatigue in her friend's eyes. She squeezed his hands.

'I know of your loss. He is with Prélan.'

'But I want him here still.'

'Mourn him, noble king, but let him go.'

Further words were prevented by the approach of another person. Curillian watched the ranks of men and armists part and draw back in awe as an immensely tall rider with others in attendance strode up the slope to where he sat. Once again Curillian struggled to his feet, only to go to his knees along with everyone else. For it was Lithan, High King of the elves. His tall riding boots came level with the kneeling faces, and when they looked up, they saw his scarlet tunic and gleaming Zimmerill armour, his jewel-crusted sword-belt and flowing cloak of the most gorgeous fabric. A star was on his brow and at his throat.

'Rise, Curillian, rise,' he said as he came up. Curillian stood shakily, finding himself level with the rune-chased fabric of the elven-king's surcoat. He looked up into the ever-young face, where a fell light was shining. This was only the second time he had ever seen Lithan, but whereas the first time he had been graciously serene, now he was angry. Anger too was in the eyes of his companions, all grave elven warriors.

'Your Grace,' Curillian began with an effort, 'thank you. We are all indebted to you and your cavalry.'

'I wish I could say you are welcome, but it is not so. I came because I had to.' Curillian had nothing to say. 'This is a bitter end to a foolish undertaking,' Lithan went on, 'and I grieve that I have been forced to intervene.' The High King swept his gaze over the survivors, none of whom could meet his eye. His eyes lingered long on Theonar, who alone of those present was prepared to return his gaze. The High King's lip curled in distaste. 'Look at this,' he said, seemingly to no one in particular. 'Every race under the sun gathered in a holy place, all lusting for glory and understanding nothing. Rogues and wanderers and stripling kings of men. And goblins – *goblins in Oron Amular.* Kulothiel has brought things to a sorry pass.'

He looked up at the Mountain as he said this, as if casting his eyes towards the Keeper. The assembled chieftains and lords all heard his words, and some bridled, but none could bring themselves to challenge this lofty sovereign. Lithan was older and greater than any of them. Lithan visibly struggled to control himself, gripping his sword hilt and sighing deeply. He looked at the leaders of the contestants.

'You all have my leave to depart. You shall not be molested, so long as you go in peace. First you will help us clear away the stricken from the field, but then you must leave. However you go, by land or by stream, go quickly. The land of Kalimar is not open for you to linger or ever return.' Then he turned to Curillian. 'Come, Curillian, walk with me.'

Curillian turned and walked stiffly with him. With them went Carea and one elf warrior, who seemed to be a close companion of the High King. Roujeark watched them go and noticed how Theonar also followed them with his eyes. He also heard the unhappy mutterings of those around him and felt the hostility of the dismounted elves as they set about their gruesome task.

Lithan led Curillian a way up the slope and then stopped, far beyond earshot of the others. 'Was it worth it?' he asked suddenly. Curillian's tired mind did not at first understand. 'Are you happy with your prize?' the High King asked. Curillian glanced at Carea, whose expression wordlessly conveyed that he should not be surprised that Lithan knew.

'It is…not…not what I expected.' He felt rather than heard Lithan judging what he might have expected. 'Kulothiel has laid a heavy burden on me.'

'On *us*, you mean,' Lithan corrected him. 'I know what prizes were given, and to whom.' Curillian could not guess how Lithan knew, but such things were quite beyond him. So, he listened. 'And what will you do with them?' The High King pressed him harshly. 'Do you have any idea what you are getting involved with? What you're up against?' He sighed again. 'Curillian, forgive my anger, but none of this is as it should have been.'

What do you mean? Curillian wondered, but did not voice the question.

'Though all mortals have short memories,' Lithan said, 'you at least of those here can remember the last war. You remember how close we came to utter ruin. This time, it will be worse. Curillian, I admire you more than any mortal, but I cannot approve of what Kulothiel has done.' At last, Curillian found his tongue.

'He said he was acting under the guidance of the Oracle.' Lithan looked at him long and sadly.

'So he says.' He turned away, looking once more towards the Mountain. 'But to me it seems that he is staking all his hopes on a very thin thread, trading the vestiges of his heritage for an alliance that will never come to be.' He turned back to the armist and spoke very slowly and gravely. 'Curillian, you cannot win this war.'

'Then fight with us, Your Grace...' Lithan cut him off.

'No, the elves of Kalimar will not fight. We have fought enough in this world, and we will not do so again.' Curillian glanced out of the corner of his eye at Carea, and he saw neither agreement nor rebellion in her face. Lithan came close and laid a gloved hand on Curillian's shoulder. 'Lancearon may fight with you, but I cannot. You know not what you ask. You have my blessing, though. I pray that Prélan helps you achieve the impossible, but my heart doubts.' He paused. 'But I am glad to have at least kept you alive to try. And you can thank *her* for that. Farewell.'

Curillian turned and suddenly noticed another elf close at hand. Different to the others, she was clad in pale furs and her eyes were downcast. When she looked up, Curillian found himself staring into familiar ice-blue eyes. It was Aiiyosha, the mysterious snow-elf who had rescued them after they had left Tol Ankil. For a moment her face was fixed in cold composure, but then a smile spread across her face as swift and bright as sunrise in the mountains.

'Aiiyosha came to my aid when I brought your troops across the Mountain,' Carea explained. 'Her folk led them by secret paths, and Aiiyosha herself sent a message ahead to High King Lithan in Paeyeir. For that reason alone, he was able to come in time. It was a long ride from Avarianmar to this remote vale. Thank her well, Curillian, for it is little likely that you will ever see her folk again.'

Curillian thanked the smiling snow-elf chieftain repeatedly, feeling clumsy in his effusion. Understanding not a word of what the strange elf said in reply, he bowed low and then watched her vanish up the hillside. When Curillian turned back, Lithan had gone too, striding down the slope to where his horse waited. He and Carea watched as Elrinde intercepted him with Astacar and Linvion in tow, and they exchanged words. Then Lithan continued to his horse, while the Ithrillian elves came up to them.

'I expect the High King did not have cheerful words for you,' Elrinde observed.

'What did you say to him?'

'I told him what Kulothiel told me, so that he may know the tidings I take back to my lord, his kin.'

'Which is?'

Elrinde shook his head.

'Ugh,' said Curillian disgustedly. 'The secretive ways of elves never change.'

'Do not fall out with us, King Curillian,' Astacar spoke for the first time. 'Not when we are ready to fight with you. Even if Kalimar will not.'

Curillian smiled ruefully at him, and when he looked to Elrinde for confirmation, his old friend nodded grimly.

'When the war comes, our lord Lancearon will send word. Yet it is not us you need to worry about, O King,' Astacar went on, 'but them.' He gestured back down the slope to where the other leaders were gathered.

Then the Ithrillian elves took their leave too, leaving Curillian alone with Carea.

'Are you the next to leave?' he asked her. She looked long at him, but though he could not perceive her thoughts he knew she could read his.

'Yes,' she answered at length.

'Will I ever see you again?' his voice sounded plaintive, even to him. Another long pause.

'I do not know. It depends on many things. My own course is yet unclear to me and I must seek Prélan's will. I urge you to do the same.' She came close and took his face in her hands. She looked deep into his eyes. 'Go home now, *Ruthion Curillian*, go home to your wife and to your son.' An unshed tear glistened in her eye, and he almost broke down. Recovering himself, he backed away and started to trudge down the slope. Carea called after him.

'Curillian, the decisions you take now will reach far. Have a care.' When he turned back, she was gone, but he watched the falcon winging high into the sky until it was lost amid the western peaks.

'You! We have a score to settle.' Southilar confronted him ferociously as soon as he came back. The Jeantar came aggressively forward with the other leaders close at hand. Curillian blinked, struggling to adjust from a very different conversation. 'You did grievous harm to Sir Hardos and honour demands that you make amends.' King Adhanor, Earl Culdon, Theonar, Hoth, Parthir and Colonel Estalor were all there to witness the accusation, and they all waited for Curillian's response.

'A single punch seems small recompense for how you betrayed us in the tunnel,' the armist king said quietly and tonelessly. There was a faraway look in his eyes as he spoke. As if wrenching himself from some heavy dream, the armist king raised cold eyes to the Jeantar. 'Let us leave it at that.' Southilar had been spoiling for a fight, but he did not press the issue, and withdrew in bad grace. In truth, none of them could muster the energy for any more confrontation.

Curillian summoned the last of his wits and addressed them, speaking slowly. Yet the far-away look remained in his eyes.

'My lords, our time here is done. Home beckons each of us. There are hurts to be healed and losses to mourn. But before we go, let us agree on something.'

'What do you have in mind?' Earl Culdon was grievously wounded, but he still spoke lucidly from under a bandaged head.

'Let us meet, a year from now, at midsummer. What happened here should be discussed in the cold light of day, after careful reflection and with due deliberation. None of us now are in any state to decide anything, but Kulothiel's wishes should not be forgotten.'

They all assented, some more willingly than others.

'I nominate Hamid as a location for this council,' said Adhanor formally. 'It is the most central place for all of us, if the Lord Jeantar is willing.' They all looked to Southilar, who was nursing his anger still.

'So be it.'

When the lords dispersed, Roujeark hurried to meet Curillian. Anxiety gnawed at him and he longed for some reassurance that all as well. But Curillian turned his face away.

'Stay away,' he said. Roujeark was thunderstruck.

'Curillian, please...my lord...' But Curillian was walking quickly, and at a nod from him, Colonel Estalor stepped in front of Roujeark. He was a beefy armist and he barred the way. Roujeark looked past him and called out again, but Curillian kept walking. For a moment he was tempted to fight, knowing he could blast this soldier out of the way if he had a mind to, but somehow he could not summon the energy. Estalor, a tough, capable looking armist, had no reason to think him anything other than a scruffy vagabond, and so looked down with confident disdain. He only turned away to follow his king when someone laid a hand on Roujeark's shoulder.

The young wizard turned to see Theonar standing by him. Theonar looked to the king, but then he turned sad eyes down on Roujeark.

'His grief is raw. He...' Even the eloquent Theonar seemed not to know what to say. Instead, he held out something in his hand. Roujeark opened his palm and Theonar pressed Lancoir's ring into it. Roujeark's burned flesh throbbed, but he held the ring tight.

'I took it from his corpse. I thought he would want you to keep it.'

Theonar helped him bandage his hands, expressing with regret that he could do no more. Yet healing would soon be at hand, he foretold. With nothing else to do, they stood in companionable silence as the battlefield was set in order. The dead goblins and harracks were piled in a great heap, and fire was set to their mangled flesh. The fallen men and armists were gathered and tended by their comrades, to be taken away for proper burial. The elves of Kalimar shared in the labour, silent and efficient, but they mounted up as soon as the flames took hold and a noisome smoke billowed out. The High King surveyed the dismal scene, then turned away. His cavalry left as suddenly as they had come, the thunder of their hooves dying away as the crackling of the flames became the predominant sound.

The various companies of contestants prepared to leave as well. Conversing little with each other, they packed up and made ready to leave. Their camp had been destroyed whilst they had been inside the Mountain and all their horses were butchered by the marauding goblins, so they went on foot with little more than what they had on their backs. The High King offered them neither pack-animals nor provisions. Lithan's contempt left a feeling of shame and resentment with them, so they departed in low spirits, their prizes forgotten for the time being. Sudden clouds came up the valley, casting shade over the palls of smoke that fouled the once-bright summer's day.

Roujeark and Theonar watched all this happen, and the tall knight seemed in no hurry to rejoin his Aranese companions. They watched as Curillian greeted Surumo and Piron, who were among the reinforcements brought by Carea. Royal Guards and legionaries mingled, the Maristonians formed up in a column, ready to leave. They began to march past, weary and downcast. Lancoir was borne on a makeshift stretcher, carried by Caréysin, Lionenn and two legionaries. Roujeark watched his fallen friend go but was unable to reach him. His surviving friends drew level. One-legged Findor was being helped along by Antaya and Andil, his wound cauterised and bandaged. Together they broke ranks to come and stand by Roujeark.

'This is a bitter end,' said Findor, 'and I leave more than a leg behind. We all loved him, but we also knew that he would give his life for any of us. As it happened, he gave it for you. And I, for one, do not begrudge you that.'

'Nor do I,' said Antaya, squeezing the wizard's shoulder. 'I wish we did not have to part so. You got us here, and you kept us alive. You have my thanks, my friendship, and my prayers.'

'I, too, wish to part in friendship from you, Roujeark,' Andil joined in. 'We've come a long way since I taught you how to hold a bow – remember, when the corsairs attacked?' He chucked briefly. 'And now look at you. You have no need of arrows, that's for sure. But if this is the last we see of you, then I'm a dwarf. When you come to Mariston, look for me.'

Roujeark embraced them one by one, blinking away tears as they rejoined the column. He looked for the king, who was further back in the line. As he approached, he looked earnestly for some sign of a change of heart. Curillian had his face set hard and looking resolutely ahead. Estalor marched by his side. Roujeark's heart sank lower when it looked like the king would march straight past without another word. He went by without even a break in his step. Roujeark fought to hold back his tears, trembling and sorely hurt. He watched the king keep going. Then, suddenly, Curillian broke ranks. He kept facing ahead, but he was no longer moving, letting the column pass him by. Then he turned around and looked at Roujeark and Theonar. His face was a mask, frozen in grief and anger. He approached.

'He should be marching home with me,' he said coldly, looking at the Mountain with tears in his own eyes, which the wind blew across his cheeks. Then he turned to look savagely at Roujeark. 'But he's dead and *you* survived. No prize is worth that.' Roujeark quailed under his gaze, and he felt each of the king's next words as a separate hammer blow. 'If you had not come, he would not have fallen. I regret now that I offered you the hand of friendship. You will find no such friendship if ever you come again to my realm. Stay here and do what you must.'

'Curillian!' Theonar barked sharply, surprising the king. 'This is not right. It doesn't have to be this way.' Curillian turned his eyes on the knight.

'It is how it is, sir.'

'We have a mission, Curillian,' Theonar tried again. 'We are called to something greater than any of our lives, greater than yours, greater than mine, greater than Lancoir's. We should let nothing come between us, for we must work together in days to come.'

'Don't use his name to preach to me, sir!' Curillian snapped. 'With you at least I have no quarrel, so let us keep it that way. When the times comes, you will find me ready to do what I must, but ask nothing of me now. Our mission can wait until we meet again. Farewell.'

He turned and walked away. The column had passed, and he followed it. A cold wind blew harsh through the valley. Smoke from the great burning billowed across between them, obscuring the marching armists from view. It stung Roujeark's nostrils and made his eyes smart. Suddenly the smoke was so thick that it completely engulfed him, concealing all else.

'Farewell, my friend,' he heard Theonar say, 'the last recruit of Oron Amular. Farewell, until our next meeting.'

'And what do you do now, Theonar?' he asked. But there was no reply. He looked for him but did not see him. 'Theonar?'

Panicking at the thought of being left alone, he hurried about, trying to get clear of the smoke. He couldn't do so, stumbling blindly across the valley. Only when he ascended the far slope and rose above the smoke did he escape. Suddenly the wind changed, and the battlefield became visible again. The grass was stained red and blackened, and the fire still burned fiercely. But no living soul was there, neither good nor evil. Theonar was nowhere to be seen. He had vanished in the smoke, to follow his own road.

And me? What should I do now? He thought miserably. *Everyone else has left, and I am here all alone.* He turned, looking up at the Mountain. The great gates were open wide, empty and dark. Only a short while ago a battle had spilled out of them, but now all was eerily silent. The cold wind gusted again, smiting him as he stood exposed. He shivered, feeling the cold caress the tears on his face. Of all he had hoped and dreamed for, this was very different.

Yet the Mountain beckoned him. The empty doors radiated power. They drew him upwards. Winter was in his heart, his hands throbbed in pain and his mind was blank, but his feet at least knew what to do. They carried him up the slope, right to the threshold. As he had done on the night of the full moon when the Tournament began, he paused and gazed upwards. Oron Amular rose impossibly high above him. He felt very small. He took one last longing gaze down the valley, but they had all gone. So he went inside, and the Mountain swallowed him.

＊

IX

The Apprentice & The King

S O. *You have come. Welcome.* Roujeark heard the voice in his
head first, then the words echoed around the chamber. At
first, he couldn't recall how he had come here, but then he
remembered. His feet had wandered through the dark passages of
the Mountain whilst he wallowed in grief and loneliness. He thought
perhaps that he might just find a dark corner and lie down and die,
but instead he had passed through a portal without realising it. Then
suddenly he was transported upwards, so fast it made his head spin.
And now here he was, somewhere in the roof of Oron Amular.

A spectral blue light was shimmering in front of him. Leaving the
smooth path he was on, he crossed over gnarled rock, and as he went
forward a ghostly lake came into view. It lay limpid in the middle of
the cavern, lapping a wave-smoothed shoreline of rock like polished
glass. Strange mists seem to hover above the water to thicken the air
and fill the cavern with fragrant warmth. Reflected patterns danced
around the ceiling above. He was bewitched by the sight. It was like
the time Prélan had spoken to him under the Aravell Bridge but
amplified a thousandfold. When he broke out of his reverie some
time later, he realised that he still had not seen the speaker, whose
words seemed able to penetrate both rock and bone. The mist-filled
air cheated his eyes when they roved about in search of him, so all
they reported was strange reflections and time-carved rock.

The voice spoke again, the words seeming to come from the mist itself.

Come to the pool.

Obediently he walked down towards the pool. He passed by tall menhirs of mottled stone that seemed to guard the perimeter and shivered in their shadow. Both the temperature and the mesmerising effect of the pool seemed to increase as he came closer. He was swaying and felt quite disorientated by the time he stopped at the point where the tiniest movement of water lapped the rock. His eyes were drawn forward until he was leaning over the water. He marvelled to see strange patterns and currents eddying in the deeps, though never a ripple disturbed the surface.

You are hurt. What magic has scarred, let magic heal. Take off your bandages and put your hands in the water.

Roujeark felt unsure about this command, but he was too tired and too dispirited to resist. He sank to his knees and felt that he would faint. If he were not careful, all of him would fall in, not just his hands, so he made a great effort to control his body. Gingerly he removed the bandages that Theonar had applied. The scorched skin underneath was a suppurating mass of flesh and blackened weals of skin. Suddenly it hurt more than at any point previously. Tentatively he leaned down and lowered his hands towards the surface. His whole body tensed, and he winced as if expecting great pain, but when his fingertips brushed the water the sensation was like nothing he had ever experienced. It did not feel like water, somehow thicker and smoother. It was burning hot and searing cold at the same time, rough and smooth, yielding yet crackling with an unearthly energy. Shocked, he jerked his fingers away almost as soon as they had had touched the water. The tips were tingling but unharmed.

He lowered his hands a second time, and this time plunged them in up to the wrists. He cried aloud in shock and gasped as his skin was subjected to extraordinary ministrations. At once it felt soothing, like the hot baths in the palace at Welton, and also so painful that it made him hiss and grit his teeth. The pain built to a vicious crescendo and plumes of steam rose off the surface. It felt as if his skin was being sloughed off like boiled meat from a bone, but just as he was about to withdraw his hands, the pain passed. What replaced it was a delightful, comforting heat that seemed to seep inside him and spread a warm glow right through him. It felt like gentle fingers were smearing warmed oil across his skin, massaging and soothing. He relished the sensation, feeling it drive away the hurts and the cares of the last few days and weeks. Then curiosity overcame him and he reluctantly lifted his hands out again, fearful at what he might see.

What he saw when he inspected his palms made him gasp again and jerk upright to his feet. Gone was the festering, oozing flesh and the burn marks, gone was the livid skin and blackened scabs. What was there instead was brand new flesh, soft as a baby's and completely unmarked. Were these even his old hands? He flexed the fingers and brushed the palms, making sure his eyes weren't deceiving him. For a split second, as the front of his mind marvelled, he was seized by an impulse to strip naked and cast himself in, but just then the voice spoke again, checking him.

Now we can begin again. Come here Rutharth. Follow my voice.
The soporific words seemed to lead him on, repeating on the still air in front of him to guide him. He traced a route around the pool and then back over the knotted rocky depression. He rejoined the path that he had left before and followed it beyond the pool's end to where a great luminescence now shone amid the pall of bluish steam. He had not noticed the great light before, raised dais, but by the time he reached the steps that led up to it his eyes could not look directly at it.

Covering them with his hand, he ascended the steps hesitantly. Not knowing what he might find, he went with infinite slowness, groping about with his feet before planting them each time. His other hand felt about in front of him too, and it touched a sculpted surface. The dazzling light seemed to be held aloft on a pedestal of some sort, and he stepped around it. The light was so bright that he could see nothing, but at a soft command from the voice, which now sounded very close by, it dimmed instantaneously. Suddenly he was looking at Kulothiel, Keeper of the Mountain.

A

The great wizard was a pitifully shrunken man, sitting in a great carven throne that looked designed to accommodate someone much bigger and less bent. His face was haggard, his eyes shrunken and his skin pallid. His hair and beard were thin and white as bone. Painfully thin hands gripped the arms of the throne with white knuckles. He did not look directly at Roujeark, so he seemed to be glancing sidelong, his gaze steady but lopsided. Roujeark felt like a newborn next to him and seemed to have an infant's capacity for rational thought and speech. The old man appeared to tire of his gawping, for annoyance flickered half-heartedly in his features and he sighed deeply, the breath coming slowly and uneven.

'An old man grows tired of being looked at thus.' The voice was real this time, spoken from frail lungs and through cracked lips. No more sonorous intonations that seemed to seep from the rock-walls and reverberate around his head. This was the real Kulothiel, and every syllable seemed an effort. Still Roujeark did not know what to say, but he made a great effort to change his expression.

'You are Kulothiel?'

The Keeper inched his head round a fraction and the deep-set eyes flashed. The countless lines etched in his face quivered with the effort as he spoke as forcefully as he could.

'Newly-arrived apprentices should address me as Lord Keeper.' His indignant outburst tailed off in muttering, from which Roujeark just about caught the word 'impudent'. Yet the effort seemed to have tired the old man out, for he said no more at first.

'I…I'm sorry,' stammered Roujeark. 'It's just…just that you've ch-changed so much since last I saw you.' His mind flashed back to their meeting on a narrow mountain-ledge on the path to Oron Amular. That had been on his first journey to the Mountain, a fruitless effort which led to forty years of waiting. He had almost forgotten the face of the wizard-lord he had met then, but now it came back suddenly, a much younger version of the ancient visage before him now. He would swear that more than forty years had been added to the face since then. He had been old yes, but still hale. He had leaned on a staff, but he had been mobile. This decrepit creature seemed chair-bound, more than nine-tenths dead already. There were livid scars across the hollow cheeks which hadn't been there before, and the cares of the world had redoubled around his eyes.

'Yes,' the old man spoke again, scarce above a whisper. 'I am Kulothiel. Head of the League of Wizardry, Keeper of the Mountain, and the last wizard…until now. You are Roujeark, my final apprentice. I say again: welcome.'

For some reason it was at that moment that the tears came. All his sadness, born of long years of loneliness, and rejection both fresh and forgotten, came bubbling over. He couldn't have felt less like the person he was supposed to be, or more pathetic in front of such an illustrious name. He felt like a snivelling schoolboy in front of an old master, and although he cuffed at his eyes and sniffed, the tears kept coming. Yet Kulothiel showed no impatience or embarrassment. No, there was compassion in his eyes, and his next words were kindly.

'Do not be ashamed of your tears. You have suffered much, and your grief has now caught up with you. The pool has had that effect before. Come, let us speak no more. There will be a time for all that must be said, and a time for lamentation. For now, let us go, I will take you to a place where you can rest.'

Roujeark had never watched anyone rise more slowly or with more discomfort, even with the aid of a stout staff. It was as if the skeleton of Kulothiel had long ago withered, and only fading enchantment was holding skin and bone together.

'Help me, young apprentice.' Roujeark came close and took his frail arm. 'The first service you shall render me is to get me to yonder portal.' With painful slowness they walked in that direction, Kulothiel clutching his arm fiercely the whole way, but explaining as he went. 'I have no energy for magical assistance, and no power to spare if I am to train you properly. It is just as well that the first Keeper had the foresight to install these *celagien*, otherwise this would be quite impossible. The name means 'from far', a network of convenience for the privileged, the lazy and those in dire haste. Or, in my case, for the infirm.' For an old man whose voice seemed ready to pack up at any minute, Kulothiel was proving quite the talker, but Roujeark had no idea what he was talking about until they reached the portal. Then, he understood. It looked just like that which had whisked him from the lower levels to this height just a short while before, and similar to that door he had passed through when summoned to the prize-giving ceremony. The fine-wrought spirals of shimmering steel, the luminescent stone set at the centre, the halo of runes about the frame, it was all the same. Now, as before, a gesture of the hand caused the stone to vanish and the spirals to unwind, allowing admittance to a confined space beyond, a claustrophobic cylinder bathed in a blue glow.

Once they were inside, Kulothiel gestured again and the portal closed behind them.

'Do keep hold, young one,' he beseeched the armist at his side. 'As you have already discovered, they move quite fast.' No sooner had he finished speaking than they set off, the flawless platform beneath their feet dropping away into the space below. They fell like a stone, whizzing through one of the Mountain's secret arteries, and Roujeark's stomach lurched into his mouth. He remembered the sensation from last time, though this was longer and faster than before, and there also seemed to be stretches of lateral movement as well, though so smooth was the motion that he couldn't be sure. Still, he clutched Kulothiel as firmly as the old man was clutching him and didn't let go till the platform hissed to a serene halt. Looking across, he felt sure Kulothiel was markedly less perturbed than himself, but doubtless the old mage had long ago mastered the art of this ride.

'Marvellous things, don't you know,' the Keeper commented, patting Roujeark's arm. 'Some time ago I found myself using them more and more, and now, if it weren't for them, I wouldn't have left the Chamber of the Pool for years.' Then the portal opened again, and they stepped out, after waiting for the metal spirals to retreat far enough.

'What are they?' Roujeark asked, his voice as shaky as his legs.

'Magical shafts. They criss-cross the Mountain, connecting all the important parts. Avatar made them. You are fortunate to get to use them so soon; in the old days, novices had to wait until they had graduated to the Second Circle before they were permitted to use them. There are less elegant means of getting about, but you will discover that for yourself in due course.' As he was speaking, he guided Roujeark up a dimly lit corridor. 'But for now, as I said, you need your rest. This will be your chamber.' Roujeark saw they had halted outside a door, one of many in the corridor. At first glance it looked quite ordinary, but around the edge were traces of gold paint and faded carvings. No lock was there, but a single glowing rune instead. Kulothiel touched a thumb to the rune, it pulsed, and the door gave silently inwards.

'It belonged to a former apprentice of mine and has housed many a Mage-Lord in its time. I hope you find it comfortable – everything you need should be inside. Rest now, and tomorrow we shall speak further.'

With that, the old wizard shuffled off down the corridor. Roujeark lingered outside, watching him dematerialise into the gloom. He fancied he saw him turn and vanish into another chamber further along, but he couldn't be sure. He went into his own chamber. It was black. Totally pitch black. He stumbled about, looking for some means of illumination, but all he managed to do was clatter into a table and smash a vial of some sort. He was too tired to do anything other than discover the bed by touch and cast himself in. His mind went blank as soon as he hit the pillow.

A

The journey was long and dispiriting. While they should have been admiring the luscious Kalimari countryside, they trudged on with heads hung low. Instead of the normally benign summer of the region, cast-iron clouds dogged them the whole way, and the ever-present escort of baleful riders was oppressive. If every other party was being treated the same as the footsore Maristonians, then High King Lithan was clearly serious about making sure that every single contestant left his kingdom fully accounted for. Few songs were sung, and conversations were short and whispered from armist to armist. Every now and then a jovial soul like Andil would lift up his voice in a barrack-room chant, but it soon died away under the disapproving stare of the elven riders.

They were steered away from all the wondrous sights that the oldest kingdom in Astrom had to offer, barred from even seeing the beautiful cities and waterfalls. When they came to the great forest of Therenmar, they were guarded even more jealously, as if their guards expected them at any moment to break into the trees and contaminate them. They were not permitted to cut wood for fires, nor to stray from their designated path to hunt, so their meals were hard-tack and their nights chilly. Sheer exhaustion weighed them down. The Tournament seemed to have sucked the life out of the contestants, while Estalor's cohort had been marching hard for weeks, right over the Black Mountains and now all through Kalimar. Findor had to be helped every step of the way, and the king's mood was black.

None of them had travelled with Curillian before, and so could not be expected to know how out of character he was, but his glowering brows and obstinate silence was quite at odds with the easy-going reputation they all held dear. He spoke to no one at all for the first few days, then only to a few, and even then, curt orders were all they got. He did not bother to protest about the elves' lack of kindness, but just trudged on with his soldiers, shoulders weighed down but still more tireless than the youngsters around him. Every night he stood silent vigil over the body of Lancoir, which lay in its shroud upon the makeshift stretcher. Everyone else kept well clear, unnerved by the intensity of the attachment.

Not even when the weather improved did Curillian emerge out of his grim withdrawal. When the late summer sun rode hot overhead, he turned neither right to see shapely tree-clad hills nor left to drink in the broad green vistas of vale and meadow. The great traveller-king had no appetite for anything around him, which was in keeping with the meagre portions he dolorously spooned down at mealtimes.

Yet when at last they reached the border, Curillian sprang into action. Trudging down the Armist Road with the smell of the nearby sea in their nostrils, they were abandoned at the frontier, which was marked by a line of white menhirs. No words were spoken except a grave warning not to return from the leader of their escort. On the other side they were met by a party of riders, armists from the 5th Legion. When Carea brought Estalor and Surumo's cohorts over the mountains, she had at least persuaded the truculent General Horuistan to decamp to the south, for he could expect his sovereign to return that way before long. And the legion's scouts had received word from elvish outriders, so they knew the hour of their king's coming. They had brought spare horses, which Curillian and Estalor mounted. With no delay, Curillian sent the other riders back to the nearest settlement, bidding them return swiftly with supplies and a waggon to bear the dead and wounded. The last spare horse he gave to Caréysin, with whom he held a hasty private conversation. With a smart salute the skilled archer had mounted and galloped away, and only later did the rest learn that he had been sent post-haste to Mariston with special instructions.

All through the long miles of the East-fold the Armist Road was lined with posting stations where fresh horses were kept for royal couriers, who could cover astonishing distances by regularly changing mounts. Caréysin would set the system in motion at Baldan before continuing on himself. While he rode fast with a personal message, the important state tidings would far outstrip him and reach the capital in under a week.

Baldan itself was the nearest town to the Kalimari border, but it was still many miles away. Long before they reached it, they met supplies coming the other way, which the legion's riders had procured for them. Lancoir's body was reverently laid in a large waggon, whilst the other corpses were interred in a nearby army cemetery. Not even pausing to eat, Curillian rode straightaway in the waggon with his fallen friend. With him he took only Findor, Antaya, Andil and Lionenn, although a cohort of the 5th Legion's cavalry rode too as an escort. The rest of Estalor's men were left in Baldan to recuperate and seek healing – they would return to their unit later. The king remembered to send a message to Horuistan via one of his subordinates that Estalor and his men were not to suffer for disobeying orders – they had rescued their king and were all in line to receive royal honours. But with that, Curillian forgot the legion and all other matters. He set off west, absorbed in his grief.

⋏

When Roujeark awoke it was still pitch black. So dark was it that at first, he wasn't sure whether he had really woken, or whether this was actually just another avenue of his dreams. But his fingers clutched the soft sheets and his nose inhaled the faintly musty odour of the chamber. He sat up, put his feet to the floor and rubbed his face. It was neither warm nor cold. No breath of air nor any chink of light. He could see nothing. He began to get uneasy, wondering what he had let himself in for.

'So, you are awake at last?' The voice of Kulothiel startled him, coming from somewhere close by in the chamber.

'Kulothiel?' He cursed inwardly. 'I mean, Lord Keeper.'

'You may call me Master for the time being. You are now an apprentice of the League of Wizardry, so you shall be treated like one.'

'But how did you get in here, why did I not hear you?'

There came something like a faint chuckle. 'My dear boy, you were so fast asleep you wouldn't have heard if a troll had come in. You have been asleep for a day and a half.'

'A day and a half!' exclaimed Roujeark.

'You were very weary, both in body and in spirit. Best you rested before we begin.'

'Begin what?'

'Your training.' That statement hung in the sightless air for a while.

'Why can we not have light?' Roujeark asked.

'You have no need of light for now. Just listen and speak. All apprentices begin their noviciate in darkness, to attune other senses and to refocus their minds. So shall you, but…first I imagine you have some questions…'

So many questions, thought Roujeark, *but where to begin?* His mind went blank, but out blurted the thing most preoccupying his heart.

'Why did Lancoir have to die?' Kulothiel did not answer at first, Roujeark just heard the sound of his breathing, so he carried on. 'He was my friend, and he died.' His voice caught in this throat. 'He died to save me, but the king would rather that I died, and Lancoir lived.' More tears flowed down his cheeks. Soon his gentle sobbing turned into huge wracks of grief that filled the chamber with hoarse, tortured sounds. Above it he was dimly aware of Kulothiel speaking soothingly.

'Yes, let it come. Let it come. Let all the tears out. Hold nothing back within yourself. Let nothing remain to distract you.' Then his words changed to a low, strange chanting that he couldn't make out.

Some time later the storm subsided, and his convulsions calmed down to gentle sobbing again. He became aware of Kulothiel praying, and in the midst of the darkness he felt a warm glow of peace touch him. Slowly, ever so slowly, it spread throughout him, quieting his inner turmoil.

'They just left.' He spoke aloud to the darkness, recalling how Curillian and his guards had all abandoned him that day. He had experienced rejection many times, being turned away from villages and denounced by rural clergy, but never like this. Never had he felt so abandoned. The memory was still raw, but he felt much better for having expressed his distress.

'This world is full of trouble, Roujeark,' Kulothiel said, 'and those with Prélan's calling upon them receive more than their fair share. Yes, mourn, but do not hold on to what is past. It was Lancoir's time to die, but for you also your old life is over. Another lies before you, and that is what you must look to. Yes, Curillian was unjust in his treatment of you, and if he clings to his anger it will hurt him sorely, more so even than the loss of his friend. Even for one who has confronted death many times, losing a friend never gets any easier, and Lancoir was dearer to Curillian than any other comrade. But do not carry the same hurt yourself. Leave it here in the darkness, leave it with Prélan. Unforgiveness will kill you, and thwart your mission before ever you come to it.'

Silence fell as Roujeark considered those words. It hurt, and what Kulothiel was telling him was hard, but he would try and do it. Kulothiel was content to let his young apprentice ruminate in silence for a long time. Then, slowly, other questions came.

'What was it all really about? The Tournament I mean.'

'Were you not there when I spoke to all the contestants?' Kulothiel responded. 'I needed to bring the Free Peoples together. They must learn to unite before it is too late.'

'But couldn't you have done that anyway? Why a tournament?' Kulothiel nodded, as if accepting that further explanation was required.

'The Oracle ordained it.'

'The Oracle?'

'Yes, the Oracle. The mouthpiece of Prélan, the principal means by which He reveals His will to us. It is beyond our control, and what it is we still do not know, but ever and anon it arises from the Pool of High Magic and speaks to us, to me. Sometimes it is silent for centuries, and at other times it speaks often and at great length. Its meaning is rarely clear to the undiscerning, but to those who have been given the gift of interpretation, and who respond with faith and prayer, it provides wisdom and direction from Prélan Most High.'

Kulothiel spoke in reverent tones before lapsing into silence. After a time, he spoken again, enlarging his answer.

'I'm not sure they would have come otherwise. There had to be some compelling reason for the representatives of so many different nations and races to come so far. Something to break through their preoccupations, command attention, rouse them to action and overcome their suspicion of old Kalimar, and of each other.

'In truth, the simplest answer is that Prélan commanded it. All I have done is merely to obey His bidding. Many years ago, the Oracle appeared to me and spoke a revelation from Prélan. It confirmed my fears about the return of evil to the north and warned of coming war. It foretold your coming, the last wizard. Your coming would coincide with the onset of a great struggle, and the world must be ready. Prélan had chosen champions to lead the Free Peoples, but it was my task to find them and to arm them. The Oracle decreed that a tournament in this Mountain would bring them forth and reveal who they were.

I had the prizes prepared in advance, but it was the performance of each contestant that showed which reward they merited.

'Understand that I could not simply give the prizes, they had to be earned. The Tournament was the perfect vehicle for revealing each one's true nature. When pushed to the limit, you see who a person really is, and what they are capable of. You of all people should know that, after all that you have been through.

'At first, I was as perplexed as you are now, and the High King thought it was foolishness when I told him of my plans. He still does. But I have given it much thought and have had many years to consider why things had to be as they were. The more I meditate on the will of Prélan, the more I understand it. Some things cannot simply be told to a person. They must be shown. The Free Peoples had to see for themselves that there is no longer a League of Wizardry to protect them. Only here could they see the greater matters which transcend their petty priorities, both the great danger they all face and the common bond they share.

'Some of this I told to Curillian after his victory, enough to guide him. It will fall to you, though, after I am gone, to ensure that this knowledge is imparted to those who need to hear it.'

Roujeark thought about all that he had heard, sitting there in the perfect darkness. So much of it seemed far above him, too lofty for him to attain. The thought that his own destiny had been foretold was staggering to him. With an effort he pushed the thought aside, lest he drown in it, and asked his next question.

'Did you know that Curillian would win?'

'Know? I would not say so,' said the wizard lord, 'but I suspected. Hoped, even. There are few in Astrom like Curillian Harolin. Yet I wondered if perhaps his time had passed, for a new generation is rising and others there are who might have triumphed instead.

The winners, if you could call them that, have a hard road ahead of them, the Harolins not least. Their worth has been proved, but it will be tested again and again in the years to come. I can only put my faith in Prélan that He will empower them and work through their weaknesses to bring about deliverance. No, I believe things have transpired as Prélan intended, though my heart tells me that there may be more yet that I do not understand.'

Again Roujeark pondered the words, and a certain phrase seemed to hover in the darkness, sparking in his mind.

'As Prélan intended,' he mused, half to himself. 'Did Prélan intend all this?'

'What do you mean?'

'The Tournament, the prizes, the winners...'

'Yes, even as I have said.'

'And the battle afterwards? Was that too as Prélan intended? How could He wish so many slain?'

Kulothiel made a strange noise, almost like a little laugh, as of one hearing something anticipated and being delighted that it has come.

'A fine question, young armist. And I will answer as best I may. "Intended", I think, is the wrong word. I do not believe that Prélan desired the battle or brought it about. Rather He worked *through* it. Not all that happens in this world is from Prélan, but evil chances, selfish decisions and the misguided desires of created beings can all be made to redound to His glory, abhorrent though they may be in the first seeming. We none of us see the whole story, how every thread and theme fit together, so no one is qualified to judge the true significance of every event. Even in tragedy and loss, there may lie great purpose that we cannot see. If nothing else, bonds of brotherhood have been reforged between erstwhile enemies, and they will be dearly needed in the times to come.'

'I'm not sure I understand,' Roujeark said, frustrated. 'But where did the harracks come from? How did they invade Oron Amular? I thought this Mountain was so strong, that no evil could ever come here.'

'Alas,' said Kulothiel feelingly, 'would that it were so. Verily, though it lies on the edge of tranquil Kalimar, Oron Amular has been beset by enemies for millennia. Goblins have prowled the Black Mountains for time immemorial, and harracks hold sway over their hidden vales. Long have they desired to come here and despoil the Mountain. It stands for everything they hate, and they are goaded on by the Great Enemy.'

'Kurundar?'

'Yes, Kurundar.' Kulothiel's voice was heavy. 'He is the mover of all that is evil in this world. He is not content with Oron Cavardul, his own sinister abode, but wishes to have Oron Amular as well. For millennia the League was always too strong, and our enemies were kept at bay. Yet over time our strength waned, while evil prospered. We spent what little power we had left forty years ago in a futile venture, and ever since then this Mountain has been exposed. No battalions of warrior-wizards to fight our foes, no Mage-Lords to bar our gates. Only one frail old master. Yet even so, the goblins and harracks could never have come here without help. We were betrayed. An old friend, who long ago turned to evil, gave them help, and revealed the ways here.'

A

As Curillian trudged home, and as Roujeark learned at the feet of Kulothiel, the goblins climbed the mountain. Slogging through the snows and driving wind, they came to a fist of rock standing proud of the high pass. This was their rendezvous, here on the saddle between Ustanzor and Hundereth, two mighty peaks of the Black Mountains, and *he* was waiting. A dark figure stood atop the fist. He was motionless, but his black robes blew wildly in the wind and snow frittered about. The goblins came as close as they dared, careful not to look at the masked face. The dark figure waited impassively for them to report.

'Master,' the goblin chieftain began, having to shout above the gale. 'We were defeated. They had reinforcements. Immortals came out of nowhere, riding their cursed horses, and we were routed.'

'Why did you not complete your task inside?' Somehow the words cut through the wind, and though softly spoken there was no mistaking the impatient malice behind them. The goblin chieftain cringed.

'The foreign lords fought harder than expected. They had magic on their side.' Keenly interested eyes bored holes in the goblin as he spoke, though they could not be seen through the rune-chased mask.

'Did you get what you went for?' The goblin hesitated a long moment, then shook his head fearfully. He heard the heavy exhalation of displeasure and braced himself for the inevitable blast. The dark figure looked away and was silent a long time, as if deliberating how to dispense death. Instead he spoke again, quiet and menacing.

'So…the old man made one final effort?'

'Him…and another.' The dark figure snapped his gaze down on the cringing figure, his intensity redoubled.

'Another?' Suddenly the goblin felt himself lifted up through the air and held close under the mask. He dangled, held by an invisible force.

'What other?' The goblin didn't know and couldn't speak either. Holding his victim in limbo, the dark figure stared out beyond the pass to where Oron Amular stood wreathed in storm-clouds driven up out of the eastern ocean.

Who are you? Lightning crackled and struck the flanks of the mountain, flaking away great shards of ice. The figure gazed at the Mountain as if trying to penetrate both rock and snow to discover who lay within. *It matters not. I will discover soon enough.* There would be time aplenty to deal with whatever final mischief the Keeper was brewing. His master would know what was to be done. Soon he would take back his tidings of the battle and the unexpected resistance, but with the elf-king and his woodwitch holding vigil in the guarded valleys, he could uncover no more.

Turning his attention back to the goblin, he found that the wretched creature had suffocated whilst he had been lost in thought. The ugly face had turned a fascinating shade of blue, making it still more repulsive. Disgustedly he tossed the corpse aside, where the snowdrifts would soon cover it. He looked down at the others, who cowered under his malice.

'Return to your maggot-holes. You may thank your petty gods that you will get a chance to redeem yourselves for this failure. Await my signal. It will begin soon.' Then he turned and strode north, putting the Mountain to his back.

A

'Who is this old friend?' asked Roujeark, feeling horribly out of his depth.

'That you shall know in due time. Some questions should not be answered yet.'

'But I have other questions…will you not answer those?' Roujeark heard the pleading tone in his voice and hoped that Kulothiel was looking kindly at him, for it was still pitch dark and he could not see the Mage-Lord's face.

'Ask your questions,' came the answer, neither kind nor harsh.

'You say that the harracks and goblins were led here, that we were betrayed, but did this traitor also open the Mountain for them? Or if not, how did they get inside? I had to use a Seal of the League of Wizardry to open the doors before the Tournament began.'

'The doors were not shut after the contestants entered. The Mountain remained open.'

'But why? Did you not know that enemies were approaching?'

'Yes, I knew.'

Roujeark was startled by the confession.

'Then why...'

Kulothiel cut him off impatiently, voice rising.

'Because an end needed to be made. I do not need to justify my decisions to you...' he snapped. Roujeark heard him sigh deeply before continuing. 'But I will explain, if it helps you find peace. Matters had built to a head and had to be dealt with. The threat had to be ended. When a hostile army that size is on your doorstep, you do not leave it to do as it pleases in a land of peace. Not when the inside of your home is much more dangerous than the outside. I did not know that High King Lithan knew of their coming – that was Carea's work – and so for all I knew, it fell to us to destroy the invaders.'

'But you gave us no warning,' protested Roujeark, thinking of how they had been trapped inside the mountain at unawares. 'Could you not have...' he trailed off, interrupted by another memory. The chill air rushing over him before the battle, the book about the harracks fallen from its place in the library. He saw himself leaning over it on the patterned floor, and sudden realisation dawned on him.

'...You did warn us.' A deep exhalation in the darkness was answer enough. Roujeark had more questions, though.

'But could you not have helped us? I know there were the traps that Sir Theonar showed me,' he went on, other memories flashing back through his mind, 'and I saw you destroy that group that followed us, but why did you not do more? Surely you could have?'

'Why are you so sure of that?' Kulothiel challenged him. 'You have no idea how much of my remaining strength I used to achieve even that much. You have seen awesome things, Roujeark, but I am not all-powerful. All the power of the Pool will not avail when the host is too frail to channel it. My strength and my energy are fading, and I must steward it with great care. Perhaps I could have shut the invaders out, or destroyed more of them, but then I would have had nothing left of myself with which to train you. I had hard choices to make, but make them I did. It grieved me sorely, not to be able to do more, not to save more lives, but I had to prioritise that which is of the utmost importance: you. I had to keep back what I needed to equip you. Do you understand?'

'Am I really worth so much?' Roujeark felt sick and overwhelmed. Struggling with his words, he said, 'given the choice, I would not have purchased my training with so much blood.'

'But the choice was not yours.' Kulothiel's voice was stern, but thick with emotion. 'You might not like it, but this is an investment that I have to make. If I could not train you, no one else could. If we were not here now, with the barest resource spared for your training, then all would be lost. You must look beyond the lives that were lost and think of the countless more that would have been lost had things gone otherwise.'

Roujeark was struggling to take it all in, mind churning with all that he had been told, so much of which he hated or could not understand and so many questions yet unanswered. He felt exhausted, so great was the inner turmoil, but he forced himself to ask one more question. *The question*. The question which had been long buried, but which burned close to his heart. Now at last he could ask it.

'Then tell me this: why now? Why turn me away before? Why have you kept me waiting *forty* years?' All Roujeark's frustration boiled up as he asked the question, but the anger and resentment in his words seemed to melt into the blackness, perturbing the voice which responded not at all.

'The reason is simply this: it was your ill fortune to arrive just when we could not welcome you.'

'What does that mean?

'You will speak respectfully.' The rebuke was softly given, but it shut Roujeark up instantly. He suddenly remembered that he was just a low-born foreigner, and that Kulothiel was a prince of wizards.

'It means just this, Roujeark: you came to us on the eve of war.' *War? What war?* Roujeark had not heard of any wars, but he managed to keep the questions in his head, sensing that Kulothiel would provide the answers anyway. 'A war that few participated in, and about which fewer still will ever hear, but a more grievous conflict there never was. The League of Wizardry marched out to fight its final campaign.' Roujeark suddenly remembered the strange lights he had seen the night Kulothiel turned him away. Now he realised they had been the illuminated staves of wizards issuing from the Mountain. 'We left Oron Amular and went north to confront the evil of Urunmar. Too long its power had grown unchallenged. Too many young wizards had been seduced to its allegiance. So, we fought...' There was a quiver in his voice as he spoke. 'Before it was too late.' As if oppressed by the memories, Kulothiel lapsed into silence, and a great weight came upon the air of the lightless chamber. At long last, the old mage spoke again.

'It *was* too late. The power of Oron Cavardul had outmeasured all our most fearful guesses, and I led our last wizards into a trap. There, amid the frozen wastes of Urunmar, and under the eerie lights of the northern sky, we contested with the forces of darkness. Bolts of magic scorched the freezing air and blasts of sorcery smote the snow to tremble the earth and throw up great pillars of steam. We were outnumbered, but we had the greater knowledge of the *Valiroen*. That much good I accomplished: we arrived before too many of the defectors were able to rise to their full potential. They went north to join the winning side, but instead they were cut down, their youthful promise as dead and frozen as their corpses. I wept as I fought, striking down one old pupil after another, using my strength in the worst possible way. Once I even dared to hope that we might prevail…would Prélan grant us victory on that day and stop the war before it even began? Alas, no. We, too, endured our losses. Friends died on either side of me, fellow workers over many lives of men.

'Reydoeir, Timell, Finarion, and dozens of young warriors. The old masters were slain alongside the flower of our last intake, and our enemies took heart. Orcs, trolls and fell beasts flocked to the battlefield so that we were surrounded. While we kept those hordes at bay, the dark wizards gained the upper hand. Baradon, valiant Baradon, was struck down by his own apprentice, and his eyes watched me as his spirit departed. Such grief I have never known. Our circle shrank as one by one we died. Iorcar slew the chimeras of the underworld, but died in the jaws of the last, burned and rent even as he struck his final deathblow. Elucar warded off one blast of sorcery after another, and might even at that hour have extricated himself, but he stood firm and met his maker on his own terms. Even as he contended at my side with Kurundar, he was cut down from behind by him whom I shall not yet name. Together, we might have overthrown Kurundar, and averted much evil, but I was left alone.

'My ancient foe, my brother, waged war from an outcrop of the volcano, and it burst into life even as he brandished his staff and sword. Fire and smoke filled the sky, cutting off the stars and raining ruin upon the field. Those who had no cloak of protection were smothered or incinerated. Thus, only a handful witnessed that final struggle. We had been at odds for three thousand years, the champions of good and evil, and this was our last confrontation. Neither of us could overmaster the other, and the very ground was riven by our contest. Yet at the last, I yielded. I could not fight him and yet also ward off his minions, both great and small. These wounds I bore on that day, a payment for my retreat, and I barely escaped with my life. I had expended the greater part of my power and sacrificed the lives of every wizard under my care. Every last one. The League failed. I failed.'

There was a long silence before he spoke again.

'And now we teeter on the very brink of doom. So, you see, my young apprentice, why you could not stay?'

Roujeark was weeping. Kulothiel's words had moved him to anguish, and the visions he had cast of death and fire and ice tormented his waking mind.

'Yes…I see. I understand now. And how I wish that I didn't.'

A

Every lord and dignitary in the East-fold heard the news of the king's return. Few had known of his going, but in his absence the rumours had multiplied and gained credence. They had all been wondering what he had been doing and when he would come back;

now they flocked to his column as it trundled along the Armist Road. Yet few of them were allowed near and the king paid little heed. Barons and magistrates of immense dignity and wealth were left by the wayside, and the grim procession continued unabated. Curillian eschewed creature comforts even more than normal and camped in the open country beside the road rather than in the towns and abbeys. That was, when he remembered to rest at all. His companions left him to his introspection, their unease growing with every day that passed.

At last they reached the Delarom Pass, that winding mountain corridor that climbed up out of the East-fold over the Carthaki Mountains. The last peaks of that mighty range, which curled around the Central Lands of the kingdom like a defensive hide, stood like great sentinels on either side of the narrow way. Ruined elven towers disfigured the rocky slopes like shattered teeth, but the modern fortifications were higher up, and stronger. At the height of the pass, where the mountain-bastions were barely more than a quarter mile apart, the armist kings had built a formidable rampart, sealing off the heart of their realm. Five other walls of increasing width guarded the lower slopes as they descended into the rich heartland of Maristonia. Together they made the fastness of Delarom, a statement of strength and a burden of inconvenience to the mercantile traffic that laboured unceasingly over the pass.

The crowds of merchants and peasants and travellers parted to let the royal riding go by unrestricted. Hats were removed and armists knelt, but no heed did the pale-faced king pay. He was greeted at the final and highest rampart by a deputation of officers and a fanfare of trumpets that set the ravines to ringing. Passing under the arch, Curillian walked on foot past the towers and across the pass which old labour had made smooth as a pavement. Through the midst of a parade-ground the flag-marked road ran west and downhill, and in the distance could be seen the fertile fields and forests of central Maristonia.

From the barracks on either side spilled a multitude of soldiers. They approached the cortege and surrounded the funeral-waggon of Lancoir. Curillian did not stop them but wept fresh tears as their honest faces crumpled in grief at the sight of their fallen captain. Helmets were removed, spears were dipped, and hundreds of blades were placed lovingly around the corpse. Lancoir had been Captain of the Guard in the palace of Mariston, but he had been of the legions' own, a soldiers' general. His reputation bestrode the realm, and not a one was willing at first to believe the grim news that he had been slain.

But slain he was, and now he embarked upon the last leg of his long journey home.

▲

'Is there any hope?' Roujeark asked plaintively of the darkness. They had been many days in the darkness, days of penitence and prayer and self-reflection. And from the darkness, Kulothiel responded without hesitation.

'Hope remains. Hope can never die, for an end to hope means that He in whom we hope has deserted us. That, He will never do. Prélan lives and reigns, and His power will make a way. His light shines in the darkness...'

A single flame appeared in the blackness, slender and frail, but dazzlingly bright after so long in darkness, and waxing stronger.

'...and the darkness cannot overcome it.' And behold, the flame danced between Kulothiel's gnarled hands, growing ever larger and larger until it illuminated the whole chamber, driving the shadows back into the farthest recesses. For the first time Roujeark was able to see the chamber in which he had spent so long. There was a bed raised on a small platform, a well-worn table and chair, and many niche-shelves filled with manuscripts and old artefacts. The privy which hitherto he had found and used by smell alone he now saw was a well-separated side-chamber, and the cold draught that kept it fresh came down from a fissure high above.

'So, you have learnt your first lesson, Roujeark,' Kulothiel told him. 'Learn it well. Never will you hear from me anything so vital. Prélan is the source of all hope, and in Him you will ever replenish your own, no matter how low it ebbs. No matter how dark it gets, no matter how close the storm clouds press, there is nothing that can overcome the light of Prélan. Come,' he said, standing. 'The rest of your lessons await. But first, I will show you the Mountain that is to be your home for a while.'

Roujeark followed Kulothiel and received sustenance to strengthen him on his tour of Oron Amular. It was vast and intricate beyond his wildest imaginings. True, the great mountain had seemed gigantic from the outside, but he had never guessed how much lay contained within. How many miles of tunnels, how many great caverns, how many armouries and smithies and pools and streams and chapels and holy places. There were kitchens, pantries, larders, refectories, dormitories, libraries, workshops and assembly rooms, none of which he had seen during the Tournament. Dimly, slowly, he began to perceive how they fitted around what he had seen: the Tear of Mírianna, the Hall of Tapestried History, the Map Chamber, the Amphitheatre where Curillian had vanquished the last guardian. Even with this vague knowledge he felt keenly his ignorance, for untold districts of the wizards' city lay unexplored and unknown to him.

'There were once thousands of wizards here,' Kulothiel told him. 'Prélan's own army, to match on Astrom below the hosts of angels in Eluvatar above. So many had to be housed and fed and entertained as well as trained. Thus, we acquired here the richest trappings of civilised life that has ever been seen. Not in storied Paeyeir or amongst the marvels of Avamar could such wealth and intricacy be found. Oron Amular was the mystery and wonder of the world, a place of unfathomable learning, of unshakable strength and of unending nobility. The elves of Kalimar barricaded their ancient arts from the outside world, but we, we taught the teachers, healed the healers, equipped the explorers, trained the warriors and schooled the loremasters. Here was the vision of Avatar, Prélan's great design for the succour and betterment of His world. The great plagues? We banished them. The mighty floods? We rolled them back. The suspicions of nations? We dispelled them. Peace we kept, knowledge we spread, virtue and honour of Prélan we upheld. All this we did… for six and a half thousand years.'

Slowly, by masterly told chapters, Roujeark heard the story of Astrom in its long history. Kulothiel took him to the Great Library, high in the uppermost levels, where marvellous books came alive and told their story with sounds and visions that sprang alive from the pages. In the Map Chamber, he watched the tale of nations unfold as the elves spread across Astrom in the dimmest recesses of antiquity. He watched the wars and great endeavours unfold, witnessed the fall of elvendom as great swathes of it forsook the faith of Prélan and beheld the dawn of mortality. From the ashes of the heathen altars mortal nations arose and contended with each other. Maristonia was born and Curillian's ancestors roamed its shores. The shadow of Kurundar darkened the north, and the south rose up in unison against it in the First War. But their victorious union broke apart, and from the ruins of shattered agreements dissension bred new wars and fresh tragedies. Lancearon's Silver Empire tried to forge a new peace and alliance against Kurundar, and Roujeark watched spellbound as it both failed and succeeded. Rapt until the end, he watched as history caught up with his own lifetime, where newly invigorated nations flexed their muscles as the Silver Empire retreated and evil grew once again.

He watched and learned until he felt his mind would burst, but after each spell of rest he came back thirsty for more. Something in him had awoken, a great yearning for knowledge. Kulothiel supplied his appetite from a limitless supply, teaching him theology, medicine, astronomy, rhetoric, mathematics, geography and weaponcraft. What Kulothiel himself could not do in his enfeebled state, he had magical denizens to do for him. Sentinels, like those they had fought during the Tournament, came awake again to drill and train him, and portals of knowledge poured forth in their respective disciplines while Kulothiel slumbered.

The Keeper put him through his paces, sending him on long runs and explorations of the Mountain, some of which had him away for weeks at a time. He learnt that the lowest levels of the Mountain were set aside for training areas, where novice wizards and apprentices were subjected to gruelling regimes of physical challenges. Some of these training areas had provided the backdrop for the Tournament, and Roujeark came across familiar spots. But there were many more they hadn't passed through, vast and labyrinthine. His sense of direction sharpened to a fine point and his muscles grew hard, but no matter how many miles he traversed, there was always more to discover.

⟁

Mariston was a changed city, for the king himself had changed. He rode beneath the gates in a mood as grey as the cloak that swathed him; as grey as the walls looming above him, as grey as the leaden skies and as grey as the cold seas buffeting the coast of Mariston Bay. A poor harvest had been followed by the onset of a winter as harsh and early as it was unusual. He had been many months upon the road, and he had not hurried. Now cold winds blew through the streets he loved so much, and crinkled leaves fluttered amongst the plane trees.

Joyful crowds had gathered to welcome him home, for news had gone ahead of his party that royal banners were approaching the city, but their cheers had swiftly tailed off when he did not stop or show any of his customary warmth. He and his escort had ridden on past, neither rushing nor pausing, and passed silently through the city. All who saw them pass knew something was wrong. No trumpets rang out, no armour glittered, no gifts were given, just a grey company winding its way into the heart of the city.

All had heard the rumour of Lancoir's fall, but they saw no body and heard no confirmation. Curillian had left the corpse in the care of a monastery on the slopes below Delarom Pass, reluctantly parting with it in order that his friend might be properly tended. The body had decayed on its long passage through Kalimar on foot, and it had only been crudely preserved on the East-fold leg. Now the monks would do what they could for the fallen knight and make him presentable while arrangements were made for his funeral. The other Knights of Thainen had all been recalled in haste from far-flung postings and missions, and all but a few reached Mariston before Curillian did, convening with the speed of devotion. Their sudden convergence on the capital was a rare event and a sure sign to the masses that something was afoot. Other preparations were set in train by Ophryior, the Lord High Chancellor, who met his sovereign at the gates of the Carimir Palace with Earl Cardanor the regent and a handful of other dignitaries.

The queen had not come to meet him. She had remained tearfully in her chamber, not wanting to believe what she had heard. The official post-riders had come first, bringing news of a distant victory and the king's return, and all had seemed well, but Carmen knew that something was amiss when orders were given for the recall of the Knights of Thainen. Then came Caréysin, and his news was less good. He brought the grievous tidings personally from her husband, and while he tried to remain cool and factual, he could not hide that some terrible change had come over the king. Since then, other rumours had reached her ears: his refusal to meet some of his most senior subjects along the way, uncharacteristic gloom and a seeming reluctance to speed his return.

Now she watched from her high balcony as he rode between the lines of Royal Guards who had formed up in perfect lines either side of the palace road. Her concerns grew when she watched his manner and bearing. His head, which normally gazed about in absolute command of all he saw, was bowed, and there was no spring in his step. When he dismounted, it was with barely a trace of his usual agility. Only a small, ragged party was with him, looking like armists who had endured great privations. They dispersed when Téthan, the king's son, had come hurtling from the gardens to greet his father. Carmen watched the two embrace, and then she held his gaze when he at last looked up at her balcony. Her breath caught in her throat. Even at this distance, the change was noticeable. His shoulders were slumped, his hair was long and unkempt; his whole demeanour was burdened. He had gone forth the greatest monarch in Astrom, evergreen and strong, and come back a weary traveller. He had left a colossus and returned a shadow.

'Why did you take so long?' She had not meant to accuse him like this, but the bitter words burst forth as soon as they were alone. With an effort, she had composed herself to receive him in sight of others down below, but now in their chambers, with all their servants gone, her anger flared. Yet it dissipated almost immediately when she watched him lingering uncertainly by the door. He was grey-faced and wayworn and looked ready to collapse. Where had her husband gone? A stranger stood before her, unassured and weary.

'Curillian?' She walked towards him, full of concern, and he too took a few unsteady steps.

'Curillian, my darling, what has happened?' She was shocked when she looked into his eyes. She knew those eyes, though she had never seen them so sad. Not since his return from exile and the tragic revelations of what had passed under the usurper had she seen a sorrow like to it, but then he had been in the summer of his strength and the grief had not clung to him as it did now. There was a look of defeat in those eyes and an air of utter dejection. Could Lancoir's death alone have wrought so terrible a change?

He spoke not a word, but when she folded him into her arms, wrinkling her nose against the smell, he began to weep. Trembling with shock, it was all she could do to stay strong for him. He had wept before, of course, but never had he seemed so helpless, so spent. She stroked the rough hairs of his beard and caressed the tears on his cheeks, all the while murmuring into his ear.

'Oh, my darling, my darling Curillian. It's all right, you're home now. You're home.'

ᛉ

E ver and anon Kulothiel would recall him to his one-on-one studies, and there at length the subject turned to the League itself. All until now had apparently been background knowledge and context, but now Kulothiel taught him about the League itself.

'The League has four circles and its members progress from one to the other.' He illustrated his point by indicating a diagram on the floor of the library. Underneath the tables and benches and between the colossal bookshelves, the entire floor was taken up with one great spherical design. There were four circles, one within the other, each coloured slightly differently. Kulothiel explained each circle as they stepped from one to the next.

'The Fourth and Outer Circle is the junior-most. This is where apprentices join the League and commence their training. Only once they have passed their tests and proved themselves do they become initiated as *Amthaen*, warrior-wizards. The warrior-wizards of the Third Circle were the backbone of the League, its foot-soldiers and primary agents. A warrior-wizard is assigned a master to give him more in-depth training, for the requirements of the next circle are much more demanding. Most wizards only ever attained to the third circle; it was only a gifted few who entered the Second Circle to become *Kenapayen*, or Overseers. The *Kenapayen* were powerful wizards with deep and wide-ranging powers. They conducted most of the day-to-day affairs of the Mountain, trained the outer circles and served as ambassadors in the courts of the world, where they spoke with the authority of the League. The final destination and aspiration of every wizard is the First Circle, the heart of the League. A wizard of the First Circle is an *Amulira*, a Master Mage. Rarely were there more than six at any one time, the elder statesmen of the League, its greatest minds and most exceptional workers of magic. From among them was chosen the Keeper, he who ruled the Mountain.'

When he had finished speaking, they were in the centre of the library, standing in the smallest circle of the design.

'You are in the Fourth Circle, my apprentice,' Kulothiel told him. 'Apprentices are able to discern the presence of magic and recognise it in others. We made it our business to identify mortals and elves the world over who showed a magical gifting, knowing that even the smallest spark could be trained into a great prowess. Before coming to the Mountain, they might perform small conjuring tricks or illusions, as you yourself have, but you are exceptional in being able to weaponise your skills without any instruction. You should not be able to do what you have done. Normally it would take an apprentice many months, if not years, of practice and schooling before he could fight with magic, and yet you have done so. In the past, magically gifted elves found it far easier to nurture and govern their talent, and indeed, many of the great among the elves have had wizard-like powers without having ever dabbled with magic, such is their innate ability. But with men and women it took longer, and progress was never quite so smooth. My brother and I were reckoned prodigies for being able to work magic before going to the Pool. You are one of only a few since our day to show such promise.'

Roujeark flushed with pride and felt much better about his early struggles with magic. They had left him feeling confused and afraid at the time, but now he was beginning to see that he had already progressed further and quicker than any observer would have expected. Yet he was also uneasy, not knowing what this meant. He asked the question of Kulothiel.

'Master, why have I been given such power? What does it signify?'

'Because you need it. Your coming was foretold: *the last wizard*. It was revealed to me that you were coming by the same Oracle which later instructed me to hold the Tournament. I was told that I would have no trouble in recognising you when you came, nor did I. When first we met on the mountain-path all those years ago, I knew at once that you were he. There was such an aura about you, though you yourself had no idea. It was with great sadness and trepidation that I sent you back, for the reason I have already told you.' Kulothiel looked away, a distant look in his eyes. 'You have been given ability equal to your need. All magic is a gift from Prélan, and always it should be used to serve Him. It is because He has such great purposes for you that you have been endowed as you have. And, I suspect, there is another reason.'

'What reason is that?' Roujeark prompted him. He waited for his tutor to look him in the eye again.

'You needed a head start, because I may not be able to complete your training.'

'Of course, you also needed a little bit of extra protection on your second journey here,' Kulothiel pontificated later that day. 'The perils confronting you were such that if your magic had not announced itself when it did, you might very well have died before ever you returned to me. Often it is thus, a situation of grave danger or extreme stress brings out the magical gift, which will otherwise lie dormant and undiscovered. With you, it happened to be somewhat more, err, incendiary.'

They had returned to the Chamber of the Pool and sat on chairs by the water's edge. It was only his second visit to the chamber, but Roujeark already felt more relaxed in the odd atmosphere, his brain and lungs adjusting to the potency of the air in the Mountain's upper levels.

'Most wizards naturally have an affinity with one or other of the elements. Some wizards have gifts that manifest themselves in control of water, some can shape the earth and others, much the rarest specimen, can manipulate the air. A fourth kind can, like yourself, master fire. But all have the same origin, given birth by the same Spirit of Prélan. It is time for you to learn the essence of magic. To know what it is you have already done, and how.

'Everything in this world, whether animal, vegetable or mineral, is made up of particles, units of matter so small the mind can scarcely conceive. And for every particle there is a *Valiron*, the magical counterpart of that which is ordinary. A *Valiron* is a spark of the divine, and together in their innumerable millions they make up the unseen fabric of magic which pervades this world. All things contain *Valiroen*, living or inanimate…these chairs, the walls around us, your very body. The vast majority of people in this world go through life have no inkling of the existence of *Valiroen*, still less any ability to control them.' Kulothiel cast out his hand over the water of the Pool, and his fingers seemed to summon a mysterious vapour. 'But for the wizard, for the servant of Prélan, they are the key to all things, an elemental source of power.' The vapour came upon silent command to Kulothiel's fingers, a fine mist that glowed with countless little pricks of light.

Roujeark watched, hypnotised, as Kulothiel gathered the mist like a barely visible net between his fingers. As if he were working a web of silken threads, he compressed it and shaped it into a glittering sphere.

'*Valiroen*, once trained, will obey your commands, and can be shaped into anything, for any purpose. Thus…' He moved his hands up and down, back and forth, and from side to side, and the magical ball mirrored his movements. Then suddenly it changed into a flower, and then a halo, which the old wizard raised above their heads. Setting it spinning, Kulothiel stretched it outwards and it expanded across the whole ceiling like a great net. He dropped his hands, and the whole thing slowly settled back into the Pool with a faint sigh.

'Master, are you saying that I have commanded *Valiroen* before without knowing it?' Kulothiel nodded. 'That when I cast missiles of fire, it was *Valiroen* at work?'

'Yes,' said his tutor. 'That is exactly what happened.'

'I remember seeing strange words form in my head, letters of an unknown language that screeched through my mind too fast for me to catch them.'

'Yes, yes,' said Kulothiel. 'Those were secret words of command, the only tongue which *Valiroen* respond to. It is based on elvish but devised by Avatar, with the guidance of Prélan's Spirit. It is known only to those who are taught here in Oron Amular, a language of creative power and boundless subtlety. An apprentice begins by learning just a few sounds and letters, with which he can affect small results, but he must utter them slowly and deliberately. A more advanced wizard can speak it fluently, while the greatest do not need to speak it at all, they merely think it, faster than any other kind of thought.

'I can only suppose that Prélan Himself spoke those words through you, for it is known intuitively to none; it must be taught. Now, having had experience with it, you must learn to speak it, then think it. I will teach you.'

Roujeark learned slowly, methodically, painfully at times. Kulothiel was patient, gradually teaching him the elusive and otherworldly sounds of *Amuyar*, the language of magic. As the weeks and months went by, he formed the sounds into syllables, then words. Next, he strung the words together into phrases of power and sentences of command. The earliest sounds could nudge a small object, ripple some water or conjure a fleeting spark, but with words he was able to create towering fountains of water, shift great boulders and move fire around in artistic whirls. Unlike before, it hurt him not at all, for he was able to channel it correctly. It no longer burst out of him like a wild arrow, but came and went at command. Soon he was speaking and even thinking nothing but *Amuyar*, and he gained steadily in fluency and confidence. Thus did Kulothiel open a world of wonders to him, and he forgot his loneliness in the amazement of it all.

Then, one day, Kulothiel sent him on a new kind of mission. For the first time, he was to go out of the Mountain. He was to find a tree and bring back a branch of suitable size and shape. He exited the Mountain by a hidden door and found himself on a high promontory. The cold smote him and the wind gusted around his robes. Clinging to the rock, he cringed against the elements. After so long indoors it took some getting used to it, but after a while he began to relish it. The sky was dramatic, half inky black and half bright sunshine. Shielding his eyes against the glare of the afternoon sun, he gazed northwards to where thick storms were brewing over the Black Mountains. He would have to be quick if he wanted to avoid getting caught in that. He scrambled down a steep path and came out on the plateau that separated the lower slopes of the Mountain from its higher flanks. On this plateau, a few hardy trees grew in wind-blasted copses, tough, bent and gnarled. Among these wizened old specimens, he searched for a long time before he found a straight enough branch. Unstrapping a hatchet from his back, he lopped it off and carried it away.

Reclimbing the dizzying steps to the door was challenging in the wind, and his heart was in his mouth the whole time, but he managed to regain the safety of the interior with his branch. It was only moments before the storm struck, with perilous winds whose howling could be heard for a long time as he walked back into the Mountain's passages. He took the branch to one of the Mountain's workshops, where a carpenter's bench and tools lay waiting. He stripped off the unwanted twigs and outer bark and then left it for several weeks to dry, returning every now and then to treat it with oil and ensure it was still straight. When things were ready, he bent over the cold fireplace and swiftly built up some wood and kindling from a nearby basket. Uttering a whispered phrase of *Amuyar*, he conjured fire and set the hearth blazing. Then he set to work. He hardened the stave in the fire and then applied more oil. He was instructed in the shaping of the wood, setting to work with an ancient plane, devotedly smoothing and sculpting the wood. He honed it to perfection and bound a breast-high indent with smooth leather binding for a grip. Into the top he carved a little hollow at Kulothiel's behest.

When it was ready, after many weeks of work, he took it to the Chamber of the Pool, where Kulothiel was waiting for him. He loved the feel of it in his hand as he walked and felt emboldened by the sense of dignity it gave him. His back even straightened as he walked. The old wizard inspected it and seemed content. He took his apprentice to a far recess of the cave where they had not yet been. They passed through what seemed to be a gossamer curtain and Roujeark gasped. They were in an alcove that was filled with glittering light. A thousand precious stones were embedded in the rock walls, catching and scattering the luminescence of the pool in a marvellous radiance. He stood entranced, seeing every kind of gem he had ever heard of, and many more besides.

'These stones have been here as long as the pool,' Kulothiel said, 'and none know whence they came. This is a privileged place, where a wizard comes just once, or twice if he returns with an apprentice.

To come here uninvited is forbidden, and a frightful death awaits the one who tries to take one of the stones without leave. They are sacred to Prélan and set aside for His service. Each wizard is given one, to last a lifetime. Now, choose yours.'

Roujeark walked about dazedly, drinking in the marvellous hues and textures. He was dazzled, but eventually his eye settled on one blood-red ruby the size of a large coin. Putting his hand to it, he felt a strange pulsing, as if it were the very heartbeat of the Mountain. Breathless with anticipation and nerves, he prised it loose, and it came willingly enough. It did not quite fill his palm, but it captivated his vision, glowing faintly and filled with wispy patterns. Kulothiel held out his hand, and, with a fierce reluctance, Roujeark gave it to him. Kulothiel weighed it in his palm, caressed it with his fingers, and held it up to his eye. He murmured to himself and eventually grunted affirmation.

'Verily, that is your stone. It is a jewel of pain, of toil, and of sacrifice. It signifies passion and labours which will require your whole heart. It is your stone.' He looked his apprentice in the eye. 'Do you want it?'

Roujeark looked at it in a new light. The ruby seemed to throb in the old wizard's hand, as if promising all the things Kulothiel had foretold. He hesitated. A feeling of great trepidation stole up on him. He reached out his fingers, then checked.

'Yes,' he said at last, and reached out further to take it back, but Kulothiel retained it.

'Good,' he said, turning on his heel and exiting the veiled space. 'Then follow me.'

Kulothiel led him back to the pool. Roujeark looked at him expectantly. He was commanded to strip to the waist, then to kneel. His master held both his staff and his stone above his head.

'Roujeark, do you accept the calling of Prélan upon your life?'

'I do.'

'And do you acknowledge both His authority and His love?'

'I do.'

'And do you swear to serve Him faithfully to the end of your days, wherever the road may lead, giving your utmost for His glory? Do you swear to use the gift of magic He has given you only for His ends, for what is good and true, forsaking all other allegiances?'

'I do.'

'And do you pledge yourself to The League of Wizardry, to obey the word of the Lord Keeper and to uphold the sacred mission and values handed down to us by King Avatar?'

'I do.'

'Then, with the authority given me as Keeper and as your master, I anoint you with the holy water of the Pool of High Magic.' As he spoke, Roujeark sensed something strange happening beside him. The pool, normally so placid, was bubbling and hissing. Obeying Kulothiel's command, a plume of shimmering liquid rose into the air and snaked across to the wizard's waiting hand. Kulothiel wetted his fingertips and then drew a circle upon Roujeark's forehead. It was hot to his touch, and his skin tingled. An aromatic vapour filled his nostrils. But Kulothiel did not let the water go. Instead, he wrapped it around the ruby, and then plunged the gemstone into the hollow atop the staff. There was a flash and a crack, and a temporarily blinded Roujeark feared his masterpiece had broken. But when his sight returned, he saw the staff was well and whole, but with the gemstone soundly lodged into its tip. Upending the staff, Kulothiel pressed the staff stone-first against Roujeark's breast, digging it in above his heart. He endured a moment of pain and then a thrilling pulse of power. Looking down, he saw a mark had been left, a circle bearing a strange rune.

He looked up expectantly at Kulothiel, but the old wizard was not done yet. He pressed the staff against several more parts of his body, each touch accompanied by a brief flash of pain.

'A touch of Prélan for your ear, for your hand, and for your foot, so that you might hear His voice, serve Him in your deeds, and walk faithfully in His ways.' He righted the staff again, and suddenly the faltering old man's voice regained some of its old power. 'Now, arise a wizard, a chosen champion of Prélan.' Roujeark rose to his feet, feeling stronger and bolder than ever before. He pulled his robes back over his shoulders. Slowly, reverently, Kulothiel laid the staff horizontally in his hands. His eyes fixed Roujeark's with unearthly intensity.

'This staff is your companion for life. Your guide, your support, your weapon. Never, ever, let it go.'

Roujeark gripped it fiercely, resolving to do no such thing.

'Now,' Kulothiel spoke again, 'dip it into the pool. Receive its power.'

Roujeark turned, and with infinite care he dipped the staff, stone-first, into the pool. He expected to feel a shock, like when he had put his hands in, but there was no resistance. Leaning over, he lowered the staff as far as the handgrip. At first nothing happened, then a glow lit up the stone. A red light suffused the water around the insertion and the staff started to throb. Roujeark watched the power surge visibly up it, the wood warping and flexing gently. At last an end point came, and the glow faded away. He lifted the staff out and brought it close. It carried a strange fragrance and was hot to his touch, but never a drip did it make, for every last bead of water soaked into it. He looked at the staff, his face aglow in the red ruby's light, and knew that he was a wizard at last.

⚔

A fter the emotional reunion with his wife, Curillian had slept for a week, barely stirring in all that time. When at last he rose, the queen ordered that he be taken care of. He was washed and shaved, massaged and dressed in soft garments. He was given what seemed to have been his first proper meal in weeks. Slowly he regained some of his former self, and slowly the tale of his adventures came out. Carmen had heard all his tales, but she was shocked by what he had been through this time. She began to understand the burden he had brought back from Oron Amular, a burden not just of grief and weariness and impending war, but of guilt and self-reproach. He no longer prayed like he used to, and he sat stony-faced in church. Gone was his perennial restlessness which used to take him all around the city and the surrounding country in pursuit of distraction and exertion. Now he kept to the palace, going no further abroad than the well-tended gardens.

A full season had passed, and only once did he leave the palace. They bade farewell to Lancoir in a packed city square surrounded by legions of mourners, mostly soldiers of many units but also city-dwellers and nobles and dignitaries from far and wide. Under cold dreary skies the funeral torches had burned fiercely, and the immaculate black procession had borne Lancoir in grave dignity. Curillian had led it with Lancoir's son, Lancaro, and all were able to see their grief. The rest of the royal family had watched from a balcony, black-veiled spectators all in a row. Sadly, they watched the scene unfold below with rigid posture and faces trembling with emotion. Curillian had roused himself to give an oration and a prayer worthy of the occasion, but the effort seemed to take a lot out of him. For many, it would be the last time they ever saw their king in public. With full military honours Lancoir had been buried in the sombre grove outside the city where a few privileged champions were permitted to rest alongside the kings and queens of Maristonia.

Once more the king departed the city, and stirred himself in a brief glimpse of the old Curillian, when the time came for a great council of the nations in Hamid, Aranar. With his knights and councillors he had ridden away, but this absence, although less mysterious, was more protracted. And it was futile. He came home more despondent than ever, laden with fresh worries after fruitless diplomacy.

Carmen had watched the pain of bereavement in Curillian turn from a fierce pain to a dull ache. She watched his faith crumble. She watched his energy and vitality seep away. She watched illnesses come and go and she watched old age set in at last. Always she watched, for she could not get through to him. His manners were impeccable, and kindness still flickered in him, but there was no passion, no intimacy. She wept for the romance of bygone days, recalling with tears what they had once enjoyed. Only Téthan now could make the old king come alive, and even he not for long. Carmen watched as the prince grew into a fine young armist, but with less input from his father than there should have been.

And so, age and sorrow had come upon the queen as well. She knew he must decline at some point, that age would catch up with him, but she was horrified by how suddenly it had happened, stealing up like a thief. She resented that his spirits had been so sapped that they could not enjoy their winter seasons together. She cursed the day that he had ridden off to Oron Amular. He did not speak of that quest anymore, but in all that he had told her, he had never uttered words of regret. With the last shreds of his faith, he believed that he had gone with Prélan's blessing and with a high purpose before him. He just no longer knew what that purpose was and doubted his strength to perform it even if he knew. Carmen prayed that the task would no longer need performing, that the rumours out of the north were worse than reality justified. If only they could live out their days in peace and leave Téthan a legacy of stability. Yet in her unhappy heart, the queen knew that prayer would not be answered.

⚔

'The stone is both the entry point for magic into the staff and its conduit for releasing the magic again. Without the stone, the wood would have just vapourised in the pool, just as would anything else unholy.' Another of Roujeark's endless questions came to his lips.

'But why have a staff at all, if control of the *Valiroen* is achieved by mastery of *Amuyar*?'

'A staff is to a wizard what a spear is to a warrior,' Kulothiel answered. 'The warrior's arm and fist might be animated by great strength and valour, but with the spear it can do vastly more damage. The staff is a means by which you may draw upon deeper magic. That power which lies in the pool is vastly more potent than the *Valiroen* of ordinary matter. Your staff is now charged with enormous power, extending and enhancing that ability which you already have. Some wizards never gain sufficient mastery in *Amuyar* to be independent of their staff, and so it is to them a lifeline. A wizard who is weary and at the end of his wits will find it easier to draw upon power through the staff than through his mind. It is a subtle art which you learn, but practical too. The staff will eventually lose its charge, of course, but the length of time will vary according to the stone and the purpose of the bearer. Young warrior-wizards are given only a little, sufficient for small errands, but as they grow wiser and more trusted, they are given longer doses. I have given you a surfeit, enough to last for many years, decades if used sparingly.'

Roujeark's lessons had taught him that the staff's power was drained by the performance of magic, and the drain would be greater for harder spells and greater feats. An irresponsible wizard could waste its power haphazardly and then be left vulnerable, but a wise custodian could nurse its strength for a long time of service.

'Master, why have you given me so much? I am still so junior, and untried in the field.'

'Roujeark, you are untried in the field because once you go out you will never come back. I have tried to train you as best as I am now able, but you will not undergo the full regime of tests and trials and expeditions. There is no time. *My* time is running out. It is needful that you be accelerated through the process. And Prélan be praised that He has given me so much to work with. Only a little time remains to us, my apprentice. Let us use it wisely.'

Roujeark continued to train both physically and mentally, not letting his body lose its fitness nor his mind its sharp edge. But his formal lessons grew fewer and further between. Kulothiel, increasingly frail and drawn, retired for ever longer periods to his bed. Many times Roujeark thought him dead, only for him to stir once more. Then came the day of his final lesson.

He went to Kulothiel in his chamber, a wondrous repository of many ancient and marvellous things. The Keeper had acquired many keepsakes and souvenirs on his journey through life, and their memories kept him company in the cold dark hours. Now he lay, ashen-faced and barely breathing, upon a bed beneath crimson covers.

'Roujeark,' the old man croaked. 'I have brought you to me for one last lesson. And to bestow upon you some final gifts that...may help you.' He motioned for Roujeark to sit in a chair beside the bed. In another part of the chamber a small fire burned, its light casting moving shadows upon the Keeper's death-postponed face. Every syllable seemed to take a whole minute for the old man to utter.

'Roujeark, you must face Kurundar.'

The young wizard grimaced, fear clutching at his heart. Those words hung upon the air a long while. All this time he had known this to be true, that it was the whole reason for him being here, but he had tried to forget. Tried to pretend that it was not so.

'My brother seized the second pool of magic, the twin of ours, and corrupted it. With it he has afflicted the world for long enough. Now, matters must be settled. A day of reckoning beckons. Your task, lest you forget, is to destroy the Pool of Dark Magic, as it has now become. Take the Star-shard, drop it in the pool, and that is all.'

Roujeark took out the Star-shard from the pouch tied securely within his robes. The arrowhead-shaped hunk of rock glimmered in the firelight as its many crystals caught the light. It looked so little, and yet so much. The rock was like no other, deep and cold and mottled, and yet he could not imagine what it could do. It would not keep him upon the road, nor grant him any extra powers. All he could do was bear it into grave danger.

'What will happen when I drop it in?'

'I do not know.'

Roujeark was shocked. 'What do you mean you don't know? How, then, do you know it will work?'

His master was now weary beyond rebuking him, so he just summoned the strength to answer.

'Because Prélan has said so. The Star-shard came from Him, from the heavenly star of Eluvatar. Back to Him the dark magic will go, for cleansing. How this is to be done precisely, I do not know. I only know what I have been told to pass on to you. What I do know is that Kurundar will guard his prize to the very last. It is long since he ventured abroad, and my foolhardy last venture achieved this much at least: he is no longer as agile as once he was. We have both lived far beyond the span of our years, and he has not weathered it to this point any better than I. While I relinquish my life willingly, my service done, He clings to life unnatural and is sustained only by dark powers. Great emissaries of evil have been welcomed to his dark throne, and they brought with them the life of the undead and power bereft of all joy or light.

'He will be there. He guards the pool jealously. His own minions he suspects, lest an able lieutenant usurp his place as Dark Lord and Tyrant of the World. He will send forth his armies, hurl his full strength against the world of mortals, but he will remain. So, you must go to him. You must confront him. Only by overcoming him can you get to the pool. Prélan preserve you, that you might get that far. And Prélan empower you to win that final combat.'

Roujeark felt his blood run cold. He had not volunteered for this. This had never been part of the bargain. Even when Kulothiel had first told him his mission at the Tournament's end, he had made no mention of such things. One on one combat with the greatest sorcerer who ever lived? It was absurd. Terrifying. His mind shrank from even contemplating it.

'You are afraid, Roujeark, I see it in your eyes. Do not let your heart falter. For mortal man it is impossible, but with Prélan all things are possible. He never ordains what He does not enable, nor demand what He does not supply. You have been called, therefore You have been made able. What you have within yourself you will never know until the time comes. If your heart will only remain steadfast, you will reach your goal at the journey's end.'

The old man lapsed into another long silence, eyes half-closed. Roujeark feared he was dead, and concern for his master temporarily superseded his own dread. But Kulothiel stirred, looking up as if surprised to see Roujeark still there. Then he recovered his wits and smiled feebly.

'Forgive an old man rambling on.' He motioned with his hand towards a stout wooden box beside the bed. 'Everything in the chest is for you. Things I have acquired over the years, which may prove useful to you...'

Roujeark got up from his chair and crouched by the chest. It was locked, but Kulothiel twitched his fingers and the clasps came away. Opening the lid, Roujeark looked inside. He frowned. The box seemed to be empty. Looking harder, he saw that there was a strange garment of some fine silver-black material. It was glossy and lightweight, like no fabric he had ever handled.

'That is a shadow-cloak,' said Kulothiel. 'Three times it will render you invisible, when danger presses too close, but only for a while. Wear it wisely, for after the third time has worn off it will be useless to you.'

Beneath the cloak lay other items which had been concealed. There was a dagger, a miniature manuscript, a pale coin and a blue crystal vial. Kulothiel explained each one.

'Let the dirk be your weapon, for I know you have none. It cannot compare with your staff, of course, but there may come times when you need something for close-quarters work. And it may come in useful in other ways. The blade is Mountain-forged, and spells of power lie upon it.'

'What spells?' Roujeark asked.

'Spells to make it unbreakable and sharp enough to cut any substance. In the dark it can be made to glow like a torch, and you can be sure it will never be turned against you.'

'How so?' For answer Kulothiel just muttered something, and the glowing runes on the grip seemed to extinguish.

'I have just released it from my service. Take it, it's yours. Now speak these words, and it will be bound to you. Any other hand that touches it shall be burned.' Roujeark gripped the hilt and repeated the phrase spoken by Kulothiel. Beneath his palm the runes flashed into life again, his own magical signature. Laying it reverently to one side, he turned his attention to the next item.

'What can I learn from so small a book?' he asked, handling the tiny codex. It was wallet-sized and fitted snugly in his hand.

'Everything,' Kulothiel answered. 'Almost…Open it.' Roujeark did so, and suddenly the manuscript grew in his hands till he was holding a vast tome. He nearly overbalanced from the weight of it, but he recovered himself and sat down with the volume. Wonderingly he turned page after page, seeing encyclopaedic entries on everything under the sun. There were histories, medical treatises, spells, maps, charts, letters and songs of lore. He shut the cover, thinking he would never be able to carry it with him, but he watched in amazement as it shrank back to its original size. Kulothiel chuckled, or as nearly as he could in his weakened state.

'A gift from a former librarian here. He was a wonderful one for books and tricks,' the old wizard said wistfully. 'Take it with you, and perhaps you will not feel my absence so keenly.'

Roujeark laid the manuscript aside and picked up the coin, turning it in his fingers. It was gold, heavy and traced with strange designs.

'The currency of the mountain?' he guessed, smiling in jest. But Kulothiel was serious.

'Verily. A most rare and precious coin. Few were ever made, and they were reserved for the most trustworthy of hands. For these coins can both pay and yet remain. When you give of it, you will not find yourself with less. Keep it well, for you have needs ahead of you that you do not guess.' Roujeark tucked it away, remembering that something similar had been awarded as Adhanor's prize during the Tournament. He could not imagine what use he would have for it, but perhaps it would prove useful.

Finally, Roujeark inspected the vial, which contained a clear fluid. He wondered what it was. He unstoppered it and sniffed. His nose wrinkled at the strong smell.

'What is it? Poison?'

'Nothing so base,' said Kulothiel. 'It is an elixir of great virtue, the recipe for which is now lost. How I miss its creator. It is designed to be of use in extreme situations: it will bring both warmth in deadly cold and refreshment in the direst heat. It also has a restorative power when all other sustenance fails. But, as with the cloak, use it sparingly. What you see there is all that remains of it; you will be the last to ever taste it.'

Roujeark placed the vial on the cloak alongside the codex and the dirk. Tears came to his eyes when he reflected on his master's generosity. These were gifts beyond price, treasures fit for a prince of mages. He knelt by the bed and clasped Kulothiel's hand. It was so cold.

'Master Kulothiel, I cannot thank you fitly for these gifts, nor indeed for any of your kindnesses.'

'Don't try.' The old man's words were so faint now that Roujeark could barely catch them. 'I'm just sorry I cannot do more.' Kulothiel's colourless lips still quivered, as if trying to frame more words the voice no longer had the power to utter. Roujeark leaned in closer, his tears wetting the coverlet on the bed.

'Master?' he called. Kulothiel squeezed his hand ever so slightly, and his eyes flickered one last time.

'*Prélan ditiios eres.*' Roujeark bowed his head to receive this last benediction, his tears streaming freely now. He felt the faint pressure on his hand relinquish and then disappear altogether. Looking up, he saw that the end had come. The old man had gone. Roujeark wailed at the ceiling and wept hoarsely, clinging onto the Keeper's arm as if to wrench him back. But he was gone. And Roujeark was alone.

X

Storm's Herald

The horsemen flew through the dark city streets in a storm of hooves. They splashed through puddles and rattled over the flagstones, cloaks swirling and nostrils steaming. Folk watched uneasily from upper windows as they passed, wondering what haste drove the small group on such a foul night. Round corners, under arches, through plazas and over bridges, the riders did not relent until they came to the guardpost. There they dismounted and made themselves known. Their mud-spattered cloaks dragged on the floor as they were ushered into shelter. They stood dripping and panting in the candlelit shelter while the officer of the watch was fetched. When he appeared, the officer stifled a yawn and eyed them darkly before listening to his subordinates, who showed him the damp parchment they had been given. After a moment he looked up with a worried expression.

Feet hurried up the empty corridor, echoing loudly in the alcoves of the deserted palace. Moonlight broke through the ragged storm clouds and cast pale luminance across the halls and window-lined passageways as he made his way to the Royal Apartments. The urgent message rang in his ears. *Go to the king. He must hear this straightaway.* Normally the Doorkeeper would have acted with more reserve, and even at this godless hour detained the visitors until the Royal Audience Chamber could be made ready, but not tonight. No, tonight he sent the messenger hot-foot straight to the king's own private residence, there to disturb him without delay. It mattered not if the king were sleeping. Of course, the Royal Guards at the door did not realise that, and they brought him up sharp. But he just thrust out his hand and showed them the token he carried. It was a seal from the Doorkeeper, the armist responsible for the comings and goings of the palace. He had a few such, and they bore the king's own authority. The bearer could pass any guard and go through any door. Anyone who hindered the bearer of a seal could expect to be dismissed, or worse. So he pushed past the astonished guards and burst into the antechamber.

Seated inside was Sir Cardeyn, the senior-most Knight of Thainen. Candlelight shimmered and reflected off his armour. He looked up in surprise but understood the situation at a glance. He was up out of his seat in a heartbeat, moving to intercept the breathless messenger. A Knight of Thainen ranked higher than any seal, save the king's own, and there was no way he would let this runner-boy get through the next set of doors into the inner sanctum.

'Give me the message, boy,' commanded the knight. The runner nervously divulged his message, and then beat a hasty retreat. Frowning, Sir Cardeyn thought for a moment, then knocked upon the inner doors. When there was no answer he slipped inside, bearing a small oil-lamp. On the inside he met a sleepy-looking young woman, one of the queen's handmaidens, coming the other way with a lamp of her own. She looked startled at the intrusion.

'Sir Cardeyn, what is it?'

'Wake Their Majesties please, an urgent message has come.'

In the combined light of their lamps he watched as she crossed the richly furnished room and slipped through another pair of gilt doors. A few moments elapsed before the queen emerged, hair tousled, in a rich velvet dressing-gown. A few moments later the king followed, massaging his face with his hands. Dressed in leggings and a loose shirt, the old king looked pale, thin and drawn. Blinking away his sleep, he looked wearily at his guardian knight. The sight of him made the knight hesitate.

'Well Cardeyn…what is it?' the king said impatiently.

Cardeyn recovered quickly. Clearing his throat, he said, 'Sire, King Adhanor of Hendar sends urgent word from the north; he thinks the war has started.'

For a long while the king just looked at him in silent shock. Once so imperturbable, now the monarch looked unsettled, scared even. So long did he pause that Cardeyn felt the need to prompt him.

'Sire, the messengers of Hendar are in your palace. They request an immediate audience. Will you go to them?' Still Curillian said nothing, but kept staring at the knight. Then he started, as if recovering himself. He half turned away.

'No, I will not.' He started walking towards another door. 'Have the Crown Prince speak to them.' He walked to the door, leaving Sir Cardeyn staring in consternation at his back.

'Sire?' the knight asked, unsure what else to say. The king did not turn.

'Do as I say.' Then he pushed through the doors and was gone. Queen Carmen mustered a slight smile of apology, then withdrew. Sir Cardeyn went at once to the prince's apartments.

꙰

Prince Téthan emerged much fresher than his elderly parents, in fact barely looking as if he had been asleep. He shrugged on a supple robe and smiled benevolently.

'Do foreign embassies often turf us out of our beds?' he asked ruefully. Yet he seemed not to mind, and went willingly enough. A manservant brought him a thick cloak and soft shoes, then they left the chamber. A squad of Royal Guards fell in with them as they left the prince's apartments and walked up the candlelit corridor. They found the emissaries waiting in a smaller audience chamber, still wet and mud-stained from their frantic journey. With them were more guards, for Commander Surumo took no chances, but others were in the room too. Lord High Chancellor Ophryior, who despite his advanced years never seemed to sleep, lurked in the shadows and watched from under heavy-lidded eyes. Standing by a giant candlestick was Commander Surumo, and seated discreetly off to one side was Eremiah, the prince's chaplain and private confessor. Someone had been efficient in waking the right people, and the cleric even sat ready with parchment and quill to take notes.

'My friends, I hope you've been offered refreshments?' the prince addressed the emissaries. They were all grim-faced men, weary but resolute and wearing the livery of the King of Hendar. Such men were rarely seen in Mariston, and never in living memory had they come with such urgency. Despite their evident fatigue, they all bowed, and then their leader responded, courteous but forceful.

'Lord Prince, I come with grim tidings. Ridgun of Belovern am I, personal envoy of His Majesty, Adhanor, son of Idunar. We have come straight from my sovereign and ridden hard for long weeks to deliver this message. When it is told, my companions and I shall gladly accept your hospitality.' His face was worn like a peasant's, but his voice was cultured, and he displayed great poise in his speech after a hard ride. The prince took a seat and accepted a goblet of wine from a newly appeared servant.

'Speak on,' he invited with a wave of his hand. The prince's manners were affable and assured, but he set his jaw firm and clasped his seat's arms in expectance of bad news. Ridgun said his piece.

'Lord Prince, war has come to Hendar again. The north is aflame. Kurundar's hordes are mounting ever larger incursions, bringing war and destruction out of the Haunted Pass. The signs have been mounting. The raids have been growing in intensity and black fumes now clog the northern sky permanently. After months of ominous build-up, Urunmar now looks set to play its hand.'

Crown Prince Téthan took the news calmly, but his clenched forearms betrayed the great effort it cost him. 'When was this?' he asked.

'A week before we set out, so two moons ago now. The war-beacons of the Guard Hills brought the news to Kalator, and a council of war was summoned.'

'There have been raids before,' the prince pointed out.

'This is no raid,' Ridgun said tersely.

'Large-scale raids,' the prince persisted.

'This is different.' The envoy was insistent, eyes set hard. 'Lord Prince, I was bidden to impress the gravity of the situation upon the King of the South and to seek his aid. In his stead, I beg you to hear my words. We are well-versed enough by now in the stratagems of the enemy to know how serious this is. What has been unleashed upon us is neither raid nor feint…but the beginning of the end.'

His last words hung on the air, and the candles guttered. The armists in the room exchanged worried glances, but Téthan stared straight ahead. Gazing fixedly at a carving on the wall, he thought for a few heartbeats. Then he sprang out of his chair. Striding closer to the envoy, he inclined his head.

'Thank you for bringing us this news, Ridgun of Belovern. I know how long the road is, and your heart must be heavy. Lay aside your cares for a while now. Eat, drink, rest. Rooms shall be made available for you and your men.' The prince nodded to Ophryior, who silently conveyed instructions to a waiting servant. The armists made to leave, led by their prince, but Ridgun stood his ground.

'Lord Prince, we have come for Maristonia's aid in time of great peril. What answer does she give?' Téthan turned and looked back at the man, whose resolute face showed the anguish of his cares.

'You shall have your answer...in due time. No pronouncement will I make in haste, until I have consulted with my father and his advisors. But Hendar can rest assured, Ridgun – Maristonia will do what must be done.'

◮

Curillian stumbled across his night-dark apartments, banging into furniture and knocking things askew. His mind whirled. His breath came in short, ragged gasps. He felt sick and unsteady on his feet. He tottered over to his nightstand, seeking a remedy. His questing fingers knocked over bottles and scattered parchments aside until they found the marble bust of his grandfather Arimaya. Feeling up the shoulders, he found what was hanging there. For months he had gotten out of the habit of wearing it, but now he had need of it. the fine metal links of the chain were cool under his fingertips, and he traced down to the charm suspended at the end. He pulled up the stone and held it before his eyes. Bending over it, he scrutinised it, fixing all his attention on the strange colours and wispy patterns. It shone faintly, and a roving blue light seemed to flit across the veins and whirlpools in the depths. It was a blue gem, not so brilliant as a sapphire, but altogether more captivating. It was like a small corner of some storm-tossed sky had been captured in a glass prison, the shapes inside as elusive and indescribable as roiling clouds. It was long and slender, shaped like an elven menhir, bulbous at the top and tapering down to a slender point.

As he lost himself in the shifting forms within, his breathing calmed and his mind cleared. More and more now it seemed to grow in power the more he needed it. Maybe that was why it had seemed dull and lifeless when first he received it, and why he had forgotten about it in some drawer for so long.

Now it gave him strength. Taking it from the bust, he put it around his own neck, letting it fall within his gaping nightshirt. It also reminded him to pray. In the wake of Lancoir's passing he had let lapse the habit of a lifetime, but now he started to turn his fears into prayers again. *Can I do this? Will You give me what it takes, one last time?* Prélan did not answer so that he could hear Him, but the king did feel the peace of God enter into his troubled heart. *I cannot do this*, he prayed on, *but You can. Make a way, where there is no way. If You will spare me, I will do what I have vowed; but if not, let not our hope stumble with me. Raise up another, someone who can do what must be done. Make a way...*

A cool night breeze flowed in and wafted around his bare legs. Slowly he turned and followed the direction of the air to come out onto his balcony. Pushing the thin curtains aside, he walked out, the tiles cold against his bare feet. He made it to the rail and leaned heavily upon it. He felt so old. Where had his strength gone? Each passing season seemed to have taken a decade's toll, and now every day was wearisome and every night disturbed. He pushed this latest intrusion to the back of his mind. Whatever Hendar had to say, he had no energy to deal with it. Let it wait. Let Téthan deal with it. The boy was on the cusp of manhood, yet already he handled matters of state so well.

The cool night air was less refreshing than the king had hoped. It turned cold and clutched at his sparse frame where the muscles had wasted away. His skin broke out in goosebumps, and he shivered. Yet he did not want to go back in, back to the nightmares. Instead he looked out over his city. The view from this most privileged vantage-point was breath-taking: all Mariston lay spread before him in its concentric zones, awash with lamps and murmuring with its soft night-time noises. But then a cloud swept over the moon, and the city was doused in a deeper shade. Curillian looked up and saw that the rainclouds were scudding by, torn and shredded by the wind. But this wind came not from the south, whence it usually came, bearing the salty tang of Mariston Bay, but from the north. It was cold, and harsh, filled with the icy spite of the mountains. It bore with it a new storm. A bigger storm. Vast, menacing cloudbanks filled the northern sky and they rolled down upon the plains like siege-engines. Curillian shivered again. He could not face the onset, but neither could he turn away. He just clutched the charm and kept staring into the raging tempest, where thunder boomed and sheet lightning flashed. The storm was coming.

Λ

He shouldn't have looked, shouldn't have read. Now he spun away and fled the library, wondering what madness had possessed him to open that book. Knowing your enemy was supposed to empower you, but by the time he had dropped the manuscript he had terrified himself half witless. Reading about Kurundar, the Arch-Mage and sorcerer, about his fearsome history and devastating powers, had been a mistake. How could he face such a foe? The thought appalled him, sliding like a hill in ruin and crushing his quavering hopes. Now he came away in a blind panic, snivelling and struggling to breathe. The Star-shard lay abandoned on the dreadful pages, and his staff was cast aside. *Roujeark.* He heard his name called faintly, as if echoing in his mind. But no one was here to call him. He stumbled on, knowing not where he went, just aware that he had to get away. He found himself in a narrow tunnel and, with arms outstretched to feel the rock, he tottered along. A sharp wind gusted down from an opening somewhere ahead to smite him, trying to drive him back. *Roujeark.*

'No,' he called aloud, denying whomever was trying to reach him. He drove onward, striving with the wind. He was alone. His mentor was dead. He had no friends, no support, no hope. So he thrust his responsibilities away also, resolving to have nothing. Perhaps he should find some high precipice and cast himself off? The last wizard of Oron Amular? He sneered despairingly at the notion. What could the last wizard do except end himself upon the empty Mountain?

The tunnel ended in a high balcony, and he came to a pulpit-sized projection on the mountainside. The wind was awesome in this high, lonely place, and the air was so thin that his breath came in thin gasps. Below him the icy flanks of the Mountain fell away into mist-shrouded obscurity, but out there the view was terrific, looking out right over Kalimar and to the sea beyond. An immense storm was brewing in the north, where lightning lit the horizon and illuminated swollen storm clouds in nightmarish colours. His hands gripped the thin rock wall of the balcony, which came only up to his waist. Looking down, he gulped. Would he feel the impact, or would he freeze to death before the rocks broke his body?

'Roujeark!' That was a voice, a living sound. Lurching back from the edge, he turned around and saw a dark shape filling the tunnel. The person came towards him, calling his name again.

'Roujeark?'

Sir Theonar joined him on the balcony, straightening up as he escaped the confines of the tunnel. The tall man filled the rest of the remaining space. He placed a hand on Roujeark's shoulder and looked down at him.

'Roujeark? What are you doing here?' The young wizard backed away, as much as was possible, until he felt the rock wall behind him. His stomach reeled when he thought how easily he could topple backwards. With an effort, he opened his eyes against the wind's ferocity and focused on the blurry shape before him. Slowly his friend the knight came into focus.

'What are you doing here?' he yelled, just as the wind suddenly dropped, so it came out in a shrill cry.

'Paying my respects,' the man said simply. 'Now come inside, Roujeark, this is no place to be with a storm rising. A lightning strike could bring an avalanche down on our heads or a sudden gust might pluck us both to oblivion.' Roujeark glanced up at the dizzying heights of the Mountain above, which were lost in frigid, ferocious clouds. Theonar ducked to re-enter the tunnel, but Roujeark cried again, still needlessly loud.

'No, I will not. Why should I? What's the point?' Theonar straightened again, keeping his eyes on the armist's.

'We still have a job to do, my friend.' Freezing cold tears were driven across Roujeark's face as he shook his head.

'No. I can't. It's not possible, what he asked of me.' Compassion was in Theonar's eyes as he regarded him.

'No one ever said it would be easy. But you're not alone, Roujeark. We're in this struggle together.'

'But I can't,' sobbed Roujeark. 'I can't do it. Such evil is beyond me.'

Theonar took him by both shoulders and looked deep into his eyes. Distant flashes made the handsome face flicker and almost glow with a strange intensity.

'Roujeark, listen to me. Prélan does not command what He does not enable. He does not call where He does not make a way. He does not send what He does not equip. His strength within you is more than you will ever need.' His next words he had to shout, as the wind rose again. 'You only have to let Him in. Lean on Him, and there will be nothing you cannot do.'

No sooner had he said it than Theonar was distracted, his eyes flicking urgently upwards. A great whooshing rumble descended on them from on high. Theonar shoved Roujeark back into the tunnel and dove in after him. Moments later, a mass of snow crashed upon the balcony. It was snapped off and swept clean away by a great cascade tumbling down the mountainside. The noise in the tunnel was deafening, even though Theonar's bulk was covering him and stifling his ears. As the rumbling faded, Theonar extricated himself and crawled on past Roujeark. Sitting with his back to the tunnel, he looked over at his friend. Roujeark was pale and wide-eyed, but when his heart stopped pounding, he managed a smile.

'That was not your path, my friend,' Theonar said. 'Your way takes you out of the doors of this Mountain and into the world. When the time comes, you'll know where to be.' Roujeark nodded. Though he felt shaken, he had drawn away from the brink. Glancing around his mind, he found that his fears had, for the moment, fled.

'What about you?' he asked. 'Don't you have to go back to Aranar?' Theonar smiled enigmatically.

'Yes, I will go back to Aranar in time, but I have business also in the south and in the north. Many tasks beckon me.' He got up to crouching. 'Prélan go with you, friend Roujeark…oh, and you'll be needing this…' he passed Roujeark's staff to him. The ruby-stone shone warmly as Roujeark passed his hands over it. '…and this.' Theonar pressed something hard into his hand, and then he was gone, slipping back up the tunnel.

Shakily Roujeark got to his feet, leaning heavily on his staff. He went as close as he dared to the tunnel-mouth, where now a void yawned. Looking out, he saw the same view again but through a fine shower of snow. He opened his palm and saw the Star-shard nestled there. Closing his fist protectively over the prize, he looked up again. In the north the storm was still raging, seeming to fill his vision. But in his heart, there was peace. Now he felt he could face it.

✳

The adventure will continue…

Subscribe at www.worldofastrom.com to get updates on the sequel.

Character List

Characters listed in alphabetical order, with a syllabic guide to pronunciation and short description for each entry.

ACIL, SIR (Ah-sill) – Man, Hawk Clan Knight from Aranar

ADHANOR (Ad-an-or) – Man, newly-succeeded King of Hendar

AIIYOSHA (Eye-yo-sha) – Elf, chieftain of the Cuherai, the snow-elves of the Black Mountains

ALEINUS (Ah-lee-nus) – Armist, member of Curillian's Royal Guards

ANDIL (An-dil) – Armist, Royal Guardsman; native to the Phirmar

ANRHUS (An-rous) – Man, Culdon's scout

ANTAYA (An-tie-ah) – Armist, member of Curillian's Royal Guards

ANTHAB (An-thab) – Man, free-rider of Aranar

ANTRUPHAN (An-truh-fan) – Armist, architect to King Curillian

ARAMIST (Ara-mist) – Armist, younger brother of Curillian, died young

ARDIR (Ar-deer) – Angelic messenger of Prélan, usually taking elven form

ARIMAYA (Ah-rih-my-ah) – Armist, late king of Maristonia; grandfather of Curillian

ARVAYA (Ar-vaya) – Elf, late king of Kalimar; great-grandfather of Lithan

ARTON/CARDANOR (Car-da-nor) – Armist, duke of Arton who acted as regent in Curillian's absence

ASTACAR (As-ta-kar) – Elf of Ithrill, companion of Elrinde

ATELLIA (A-tell-ee-ah) – Armist, servant-girl working as a masseuse in the duke of Welton's palace; a favourite of Lancoir's

ATHRICK (Ath-rick) – Man of Hendar, squire to Adhanor

AVALAR (A-va-lar) – Elf, late king of Kalimar; grandfather of Lithan

AVAR (Ah-var) – Elf, long-dead prince of the Avatar; a relation of Lithan

AVARONE (Ava-rone) – Elf, former High King of Kalimar and eldest son of Avatar

AVATAR (Ah-vah-tar) – Eldest elf and first High King of Kalimar

BARADON (Bara-don) – Man, erstwhile Master-Mage of Oron Amular

BENEK THUNDER-EYE (Ben-ek) – Man of Aranar, member of Raspald's band

CAIASAN (Kya-san) – Man, scribe and healer of the Pegasus Clan

CARDEYN (Kar-dane) – armist, Knight of Thainen

CAREA (Sah-ree-ah) – Elf, princess of the wood-elves

CARÉYSIN (Car-ay-sin) – Armist, army tracker and expert archer

CARION (Cah-ree-on) – Elf, noble wood-elf, father of Dácariel

CARMEN (Car-men) – Armist, queen of Maristonia and wife of Curillian

CELKENORÉ (Kel-ken-or-ray) – Man, former Jeantar of Aranar, of the Unicorn Clan

COMMANGEN (Coh-man-gen) – Armist, clerk in the Royal Library

CUHERL (Soo-hurl) – Elf, father of Aiiyosha

CULDON (Kul-don) – Man, Earl of Centaur, a fiefdom of Ciricen

CURILLIAN (Su-rill-ee-an) – Armist, king of Maristonia and husband of Carmen

CYRON (Ky-ron) – Armist, member of Curillian's Royal Guards

DÁCARIEL (Dah-sah-ree-ell) – Elf, queen of Tol Ankil, niece of Carea and mother of the triplets Sin-Solar, Sin-Tolor & Sin-Serin

DAULASTIR (Daw-luh-stee-ah) – Armist, Lord High Chancellor under King Mirkan. He murdered his master and usurped the throne of the young Curillian, before later being overthrown by the prince when he returned from exile

DEÀREG, SIR (Day-ah-regg) – Man, Falcon Clan Knight from Aranar

DENCARIL (Den-kar-ill) – Man of Hendar, Duke of Nalator and uncle of Adhanor

DUBARNIK (Do-bar-nick) – Armist, conjuror and father of Roujeark

EDRIST (Ed-wrist) – Armist, member of Curillian's Royal Guards

ELRINDE (El-rind) – Elf, a statesman representing King Lancearon of Ithrill

ELUCAR (El-oo-kar) – Elf, erstwhile Master-Mage of Oron Amular

EQUERRIN (Eh-queh-rin) – Man of Hendar, physician to Adhanor

ESTALOR (es-tah-lore) – Armist, cohort commander in the 5th Legion

FINARION (Fin-ah-ree-on) – Elf, erstwhile Master-Mage of Oron Amular

FINDOR (Fin-dor) – Armist, member of Curillian's Royal Guards

FIRWAN (fir-wan) – Armist, former King of Maristonia and ancestor of Curillian

GAEON (Guy-on) – Armist, tutor to Prince Téthan

GANNODIN (Gan-no-din) – Armist, general of the elite 1st Legion, garrisoned in Mariston

GARTHAN (Gar-than) – Man, master-of-arms to Earl Culdon

GERENDAYN (geh-ren-dane) – Wood-elf, antiquary and gatherer of news

HARDOS, SIR (Har-dos) – Man, Pegasus Clan Knight and close ally of Southilar

HAROTH (Hah-roth) – Armist, member of Curillian's Royal Guards

HORUISTAN (hor-uh-stan) – Armist, general of the 15th legion

HOTH (Hoth) – Dwarf-lord from the subterranean realm of Carthak

IDUNAR (Ee-doo-nar) – Man, late King of Hendar, father of Adhanor

ILLYIR (Ill-year) – Armist, duke of Welton; cousin to Curillian

IORCAR (yor-kar) – Dwarf, erstwhile Master-Mage of Oron Amular

JEANNOR (Jean-or) – Man, free-rider of Aranar. The first syllable is pronounced as in the French *Jean*, not the English Jean.

KASPAIN (Kas-pain) – Man, household warrior of Earl Culdon

KULOTHIEL (Koo-low-thee-ell) – Man, Head of the League of Wizardry and Keeper of Oron Amular

KURUNDAR (Kuh-run-dar) – Man, sorcerer from Urunmar, brother to Kulothiel

LANCEARON (Larn-sa-ron) – High-elf, king of Ithrill and former Silver Emperor

LANCOIR (Larn-swa) – Armist, Captain of the Royal Guards

LINDAL, SIR (Lin-dal) – Man, Unicorn Clan Knight from Aranar

LINVION (Lin-vee-on) – Elf-woman of Ithrill, diplomat and companion of Elrinde

LIONENN (Lee-oh-nen) – Armist, army tracker and expert archer

LIOTOR (Leo-tor) – Man, former King of Ciricen, father of Thónarion

LITHAN (Lee-than) – Elf, king of Kalimar

LOSATHEN THE LUCKLESS, SIR (Loss-ah-then) – Man of Aranar, a knight errant

LUCASK LIGHTFOOT (Loo-cas-k) – Man of Aranar, member of Raspald's band

MANRION (Man-ree-on) – Armist, member of Curillian's Royal Guards

MARINTOR (Ma-rin-tor) – Elf, king of the eponymous sea-elf kindred, ancestor of Aiiyosha

MELNOVA (Mel-no-va) – Armist, celebrated poet of Maristonia

MÍRIANNA (Mih-ree-ah-nah) – Elf, second oldest elf and first High Queen of Kalimar

MIRKAN (Mur-kan) – Armist, prior king of Maristonia; father and predecessor of Curillian

NADIHOAN (Nad-ee-ho-an) – Alias of Curillian during exile

NARHEYN (Nar-hayn) – Man, household warrior of Earl Culdon

NIMARION (Nim-ah-ree-on) – Elf of Kalimar

NORSCINDE (Nor-sind) – Armist, member of Curillian's Royal Guards

NURVO (Nur-vo) – Man of Hendar, Bishop of Losantum

ONANDUR (Oh-nan-durh) – Man, Earl of Oloyir in Hendar and Captain of Adhanor's bodyguards

OPHRYIOR (Off-ree-or) – Armist, Lord High Chancellor of Maristonia; Curillian's chief minister

OTAKEN (O-tah-ken) – Armist, general in the Maristonian army

PARTHIR (Par-thear) – Man of Raduthon, a barbarian principality in the south

PERETHOR (Peh-reh-thor) – Elf, resident of Faudunum

PIRON (Peer-on) – Armist, junior officer of the third cohort of The Royal Guards; second-in-command to Surumo

PRÉLAN (Pray-larn) – God, deity of the elves and all believing folk. Prélan is one and the same as the Triune God of Christianity. He reveals Himself differently to the inhabitants of Astrom than He has to us on Earth.

RANE (Rain) – Man of Aranar, knight of the Pegasus Clan

RASPALD THE KIN-SLAYER (Ras-pald) – Man of Aranar, bandit chieftain

REUBUN (Roo-bun) – Man of Hendar, Duke of Lalator and favourite of Adhanor

REYDOEIR (Ray-doe-ear) – Elf, erstwhile Master-Mage of Oron Amular

RHYARD (Ry-ard) – Man, household warrior of Earl Culdon

RIDGUN (rid-gun) – man, emissary of Hendar to Maristonia

ROMANTHONY, SIR (Row-man-tho-nee) – Man, Eagle Clan Knight from Aranar

ROTHGER (Roth-guh) – Man, a Hendarian sheriff and pathfinder

ROUJEARK (Roo-jark) – Armist, a gifted young magician; son of Dubarnik. The second syllable, 'jeark' is pronounced similarly to the South African forename 'Jacques', with an accented first vowel; not like the flat-vowelled English 'Jack' or 'Jake'.

RUFIN (Roo-fin) – Man, household warrior of Earl Culdon

RUMORIL (Roo-mor-ill) – Man of Hendar, Duke of Malator and uncle of Adhanor

RUTHARTH (Roo-tharth) – Correct pronunciation of the elvish form of Roujeark's name

RUTHION (RUE-THEE-ON) – Alias of Curillian during his service to the Silver Empire

SAMPA THE SMOOTH (Sam-pah) – Man of Aranar, member of Raspald's band

SCEANT (Skee-ant) – Man of Aranar, member of Raspald's band

SIN-SERIN (Sin-seh-rin) – Elf, princess of Tol Ankil, sister of the brothers Sin-Solar and Sin-Tolor

SIN-SOLAR (Sin-so-lar) – Elf, prince of Tol Ankil

SIN-TOLOR (Sin-toe-lore) – Elf, prince of Tol Ankil and brother of Sin-Solar

SOUTHILAR (Soo-thi-lar) – Man, Jeantar and lord of Aranar, of the Pegasus Clan

SURUMO (Suh-roo-mo) – Armist, commanding officer of the third cohort of The Royal Guards

TEKKA (Tech-ah) – Pony, erstwhile mount and companion of Roujeark in his youth

TÉTHAN (Tay-than) – Armist, prince of Maristonia; son and heir of Curillian

THEAMACE (Theam-ace) – Horse, favourite mount of Curillian

THEONAR, SIR (Theo-nar) – Man, Pegasus Clan Knight and rival of Southilar

THERENDIR (Theh-ren-deer) – Elf, king of the wood-elves, father of Carea

THÓNARION (Tho-nah-ree-on) – Man, King of Ciricen and liege-lord of Earl Culdon

TIMELL (Tim-ell) – Man, erstwhile Master-Mage of Oron Amular

TORLAS (Tor-las) – Elf, prince and swordsmith who forged the Sword of Maristonia for King Armista

UTARION (You-tah-ree-on) – Armist, member of Curillian's Royal Guards

VAMPANA (Vam-par-nah) – Woman of Aranar, member of Raspald's band

XAVION (Zay-vee-on) – Man of Hendar, Earl of Koros and favourite of Adhanor

The Races of Astrom

A short guide to introduce the main races of Astrom that we meet in *Oron Amular*. More information on the people and places of Astrom can be found in the online glossary at **www.worldofastrom.com**.

Armists

A hardy mountain race originally from the foothills of the Carthaki Mountains. They awoke at the dawn of the Second Chapter, the second of the Free Peoples, and shortly before the coming of the dwarves. Fostered and taught by the elves, they moved into the lowlands and slowly spread across Maristonia, which in the passing of time became their own kingdom. They are a species apart, sharing some features with their elven and mortal neighbours but being quite unlike them in others. As a rule, they are short and stockily-built, are adaptable and persevere well in difficult tasks. They have a reputation for valour and stubbornness.

Dwarves

Like the armists, the dwarves are children of the mountains and they awoke in the Carthaki Mountains at around the same time as the armists. But whereas the armists were befriended and tutored by the elves, becoming like them in their worldview and habits, the dwarves were long isolated in a remote part of Astrom. They had a different temperament, being more secretive, more industrious, and preferring to live underground in excavated halls and caverns. With time they also built an overground civilisation and dwelt side by side with the elven kingdom of Alanmar. In this time of peace, they sent forth colonists and delved halls in many of the far-flung mountains of Astrom, from which came many different breeds of their race, some noble and some less so. After the ruinous Carthaki Wars they shut themselves underground and forsook the outside world. For long centuries they were not heard from at all, but later they did venture forth to participate in the great events of the world. The dwarves are short, rarely exceeding five feet, but incredibly strong. They are excellent craftsmen and ingenious artisans, working wonders in stone, wood, metal and minerals of all kinds. They are fearless tunnelers, hardy mountaineers and formidable warriors. They do not share the elven view of Prélan but have their own conception of the divine and their own law-codes to govern their affairs.

Elves

The elves are the eldest children of Prélan, exalted and excellent among the Free Peoples. They were the first to awake in Astrom, having come to the world in star-capsules. They were known as *Avarian*, the People of the Stars, but they called themselves *Genesi*, the First. There are three main kindreds, the Avatar, the Firnai and the Marintors.

The *Avatar* are the eldest of all, named after their first king, Avatar. Also known as the High-elves, the Avatar are the most senior of the elven kindreds, and also the most populous and powerful. They are great scholars, warriors and craftsmen, preferring to live in cities or in the open country.

Firnai is the elvish name for the Wood-elves, named after their first king, Firnar. The wood-elves are the most secretive of the three main kindreds of the elves, rarely coming out of their woodland fastnesses to interact with the outside world. They are as varied as the trees they love, some loving oaks, some building high homes in giant beeches and some loving riverside willows and alders. They are wonderful weavers, passionate storytellers and great lovers of animals. Some of them even have the gift of shape-shifting into the forms of beasts. Most Firnai dwell deep within Kalimar, but one colony live in the forest of Tol Ankil, on the borders of Maristonia.

Marintors are Sea-elves, dwelling by the coasts and enamoured of all the sea. Dwelling in caves, grottoes and white-walled havens, they are the mariners, explorers and traders of the elves. Their realm once embraced all the coasts of Astrom, but whilst in latter days they may have relinquished much of it to armists and Mortals, they also have innumerable havens and colonies on the far-flung islands and continents of the planet. The Marintors are great singers and lovers of music, but they are also the most worldly of the elves, and the readiest to have dealings with Mortals.

The *Cuherai* (Snow-elves), who dwell amid the high snows and ice-fields, and the *Irynthai* (Deep-elves), whose mansions and workshops are underground, are amongst the many lesser kindreds of the elves, but the rest do not feature in this tale.

Harracks

A mysterious race who inhabit subterranean halls and caverns in the land of Stonad. Lying in the southern Black Mountains, this mountainous domain lies between Kalimar proper and the wood-elven realm of Tol Ankil. The harracks are little known to their neighbours except as a source of trouble and few among either armists or elves know the secrets of their origins. In fact, they are an ancient race of dwarves, descended from an outcast chieftain of Carthak who journeyed north in exile with a few followers. These were ignoble individuals who founded a nation which bore their own traits of harshness, injustice and ferocious insularity. Through long millennia of isolation the harracks degenerated into a fallen race of coarse, unlovely warriors and craftsmen, barely recognisable to their old dwarvish kin but not dis-similar from the Black Dwarves of the Goragath Mountains, another evil scion of old Carthak. The harracks are short, stocky and incredibly tough, strong and with thick skin that is difficult to harm. They are ruthless with outsiders and extremely secretive about their ways. However, they do have redeeming features, being quite capable of great feats of engineering, excavation and construction. They are frightful to look upon, for not only were they unlovely to begin with, but they have also added to their horrifying demeanour by affecting brutal customs like head-binding and eschewing all but the most rustic garments and decorations.

Mortals

The elves are the only immortal race among the Free Peoples, and though the armists and dwarves are also mortal, the name Mortals is reserved for those elves who forfeited their immortality for rebellion against Prélan. Though by the time of Oron Amular they may resemble human beings, they are in fact the descendants of elves who fell from grace. In the second half of the Second Chapter, large swathes of the population of Elvendom fell away from the true faith and embraced manifold heresies and false religions. In a cataclysmic event known as the Great Betrayal, those who forsook Prélan were cursed with mortality, losing their deathlessness and many of the virtues of mind and body that went with it. The faithful elves remained in Kalimar and Ithrill, but the Mortals were to be found across much of the rest of Ciroken, in Aranar, Hendar and Ciricen. In all these countries there arose mortal nations and kingdoms which lived uneasily alongside their immortal neighbours. They were still related by blood, but utterly estranged in mindset and values. Mortals were subject to sickness and deformity, as well as ageing, but they made up for their limited years with a great zest for life that expressed itself in invention, literature, art and zealous politics. As such, their realms were characterised by rapid change and frequent upheavals. Had they refrained from fighting each other and amongst themselves, mortal civilisation might have rivalled that of the elves, in accomplishment, if not in longevity. Opinion is divided among the loremasters of Astrom as to whether mortality was in fact a curse, denying Mortals the long bliss of the elves, or a blessing in disguise, speeding their way back to Prélan.

Follow Michael J Harvey
on social media:

Facebook.com/worldofastrom

Twitter: @worldofastrom

Instagram: @worldofastrom

Website: worldofastrom.com

Please review this book on goodreads.com
by scanning the QR code below with your smartphone:

Printed in Great Britain
by Amazon

13767614R00163